IF TWO ARE DEAD

Sally DeFreitas

PublishAmerica
Baltimore

Hardcover 978-1-4560-7945-1
Softcover 978-1-4560-7944-4
PUBLISHED BY PUBLISHAMERICA, LLLP
www.publishamerica.com
Baltimore

Printed in the United States of America

THREE CAN KEEP A SECRET
— IF TWO OF THEM ARE DEAD.
Benjamin Franklin
Poor Richard's Almanac

Sally DFreitas

CHAPTER ONE

An icy chill ran up my spine as I climbed out of my car. Looking back on the events of the day, I suppose one could call it a premonition. But at the time I didn't look for any explanation beyond the obvious. It was January in Michigan.

Already I was beginning to regret my promise. My destination, the frozen surface of Arrowhead Lake, was shrouded in heavy fog. The damp, near freezing air was creeping into the space between my gloves and the cuffs of my coat. I seriously considered getting back into my car and leaving Frank Kolowsky out there in his ice shanty without any lunch or hot coffee.

I wiped my nose on the back of my glove and tried to remember what had prompted the offer to bring lunch to my boyfriend. It must have been guilt. Or perhaps it was relief — relief that he had let me off the hook, so to speak, after I had first agreed to spend an entire day with him on the lake. Why had I imagined that I could tolerate sitting on the ice for even an hour, much less an entire day?

Maybe it had sounded a little romantic. Maybe because our relationship was only six months along and the initial glow was still there — although definitely beginning to fade. But more likely the reason was that I was living in Shagoni River, Michigan, population one thousand, a village that offered next to no diversion once the holidays were over and winter arrived in earnest.

Call it the Winter Blahs, call it Cabin Fever, or call it Seasonal Affective Disorder. By whatever name, winter in West Michigan affects the mental health of even the most stable of those who are unable to escape to sunnier climes.

This was my second winter in Michigan and it was certainly going better than my first. For one thing, I was learning to drive in the snow. But the other really nice development was that I had met Frank Kolowsky, a retired Detroit cop who was now a detective with the Cedar County Sheriff's Department.

So that's why I was standing on the shore of Arrowhead Lake, holding a bag of ham sandwiches and a Thermos of coffee, while I tried to figure out my trajectory. Until now, I had figured it would be no problem. Frank and I had been here on Wednesday — when there wasn't any fog — and walked together onto the ice to visit his green canvas fishing tent. But on Wednesday the sun had been shining and there were only three or four tents on the lake. Since then the population had multiplied exponentially.

I tried to remember the instructions Frank had given me that I had pretty much ignored, being so sure I wouldn't need them. I was to stand at the edge of the lake, next to the big oak tree, with Long Bridge on my left. That's where I was. From this point I was to walk straight ahead for five hundred paces. But did that mean paces of his size or my size? And what about all those structures sitting smack dab in my way?

What to do? Giving up was not an option. I should be able to figure this out. I was, after all, a reporter and asking questions was a big part of my job. So I wiped my nose again, clutched the brown bag to my chest and ventured out onto the frozen surface of Arrowhead Lake.

Thanks to a couple feet of snow, it was hard to tell where the lake actually began, but I started counting my paces. My steps weren't exactly paces, they were just shuffles through the knee deep snow. Soon I had to alter my course around a wooden ice shanty with a phone number painted on it in large sloppy strokes.

I detoured and kept walking. After four hundred and ninety paces, I started looking. There was a green canvas tent off to my right so I headed for it. I paused outside for a few seconds to gather my courage, then pushed aside the door flap. In the dim light I saw two men sitting on stools on either side of small camp stove. They were smoking cigars, playing cards, and paying scant attention to their lines which hung down through a hole in the ice.

The men turned to look at me. Neither of them was Frank. And neither one said a word.

"Hey," I said, trying to sound like this was something I did all the time. "I'm looking for Frank Kolowsky. Do you know where his tent is?"

The two guys looked at each other, then back at me.

Finally one of them spoke. "He the cop?" The guy had a scraggly beard and was missing a couple of teeth.

"Well, yes," I said. "He's with the sheriff's department."

Scraggly Beard shook his head. But his partner, a younger man who might have been his son, was more helpful. "I saw him this morning when I came out," he offered. "Said he caught a walleye yesterday. He's over that way." He raised his right arm.

"Okay," I said. "Thanks a lot." I backed out, my eyes tearing from the fumes and cigar smoke. I looked around and tried to remember what direction the guy had indicated when he raised that arm. I turned about ninety degrees and started walking again. It wasn't far to the next tent. This one had to be it. I located the door flap, bent down and pushed it open.

"Hi honey," I said. "Your lunch is here."

Nobody answered.

Uh oh, was I spouting endearments to the wrong guy? I couldn't see anybody and thought maybe I was talking to an empty tent. Then my eyes adjusted and I saw a figure in brown coveralls lying face down on the ice.

A tight knot formed in my throat.

Had Frank had a heart attack — out here with no one to help him? I stepped inside and moved closer to the form lying on the ice — but something stopped me. This guy was not big enough to be Frank — and the coveralls were the wrong color. So this man was not Frank.

But this man was not moving.

I backed out of the tent, my heard thudding in my ears.

Then I did something completely out of character for an independent female such as myself. I stood there on the ice and started screaming.

CHAPTER TWO

"FR-A-A-NK!" I yelled.

I never knew that word could have three syllables. I yelled again, "Frank, where are you?"

Within seconds, at least six heads were poking out of ice shanties, their owners curious to see who the madwoman might be. One of them was Frank. He walked over to me and placed both hands on my shoulders — like he was getting ready to restrain me if necessary.

"Calm down," he said. "What's happening?"

Someone else said, "She's gonna scare the fish."

"Frank, look in there, please." I pointed to the tent I had just backed away from.

Frank must have decided that I was not a danger to myself or anyone else since he let go of me and moved toward the offending tent. I stood there hugging the sack of lunch with a dozen eyes on me, while Frank opened the tent flap and stepped inside.

Things got real quiet. After about a minute, curiosity overcame terror and I stuck my head in through the flap. What I saw confirmed my worst fears.

Frank was kneeling beside the body. He had a grip on one shoulder and was trying to turn the guy over. The body turned up stiffly like a board and I had a glimpse of something blue that had once been a face. The glimpse was definitely more than I wanted.

Swallowing hard, I backed out, hoping that I wouldn't further embarrass myself by vomiting on the ice. I swallowed the bile rising in my throat and managed to keep it down. The watchers traded a few muttered comments but there was nothing I could understand.

Then Frank came out of the tent.

"The guy's dead," he said, looking around at the circle of gawkers. "Anybody know who it is?"

"I think his name is Vince," said one.

"Yeah, that's Vince — I mean that's his tent anyway."

"Should be him — I was in there yesterday. We talked for a few minutes."

Immediately Frank shifted into his professional mode. He pulled out his wallet and flashed his ID card. "I'm with the Cedar County Sheriff's Department. No one is to go inside this tent — and don't anyone leave here until someone gets a statement from you."

This announcement was greeted with total silence.

Frank pulled out his cell phone and punched in a number.

"We've got a code twenty-one here," he said. "Out on Arrowhead Lake. I need a deputy — right. Tell him to use the parking lot at the south end of the lake — the one by the bar. It's foggy so I'll send someone to meet him. — Okay. I'll need the medical examiner and I'll need the ambulance. No, no sirens on the ambulance. Probably been here all night."

Frank pocketed the cell phone and pulled a different wallet from his coat pocket.

He flipped the wallet open and read from it. "Okay, the ID here says Vince Crawley and gives an address of Apple Drive." He looked around. "Does that sound right to you guys?"

There were grunts of affirmation from members of the group who continued to stand, fishing forgotten, as they waited for the next act.

They didn't have long to wait. Within minutes, there was the sound of a vehicle arriving in the parking lot. It was too foggy to see anything, but Frank seemed satisfied that the new arrival was the deputy he had called for.

"We're over here," he yelled toward the shore — but got no response. He hesitated, then looked at me. "Could you go meet the deputy," he said, "or would you rather wait here while I go?"

The prospect of guarding a corpse did not appeal to me. "I'll go," I said.

"Tell him to bring yellow tape."

"Okay."

I started walking toward shore, glad for the chance to get my feet moving. Frank had earlier assured me that this was going to be a warm day — but such things are relative and my toes were already numb. I retraced my steps until I saw a figure emerge from the fog and begin to move in my direction. I waved and he waved back. As he drew closer I saw that he wore a brown uniform with the Cedar County Sheriff's Department insignia.

I was not exactly thrilled when I recognized Sergeant Curt Laman. The sergeant had recently made a traffic stop that found me in a compromising situation around three o'clock on a Sunday morning.

"Well, if it isn't Tracy Quinn," he said when we were within hailing distance. "Maybe we should deputize you."

"No thanks," I said, hoping he would have the decency not to mention our previous encounter. "Have you got the yellow tape?"

"Tape, the whole works." I turned around and we walked together out onto the lake. "What's he got?"

"Dead body in a fishing tent."

"Any sign of foul play?"

"I— ah— really don't know." Truth was, I hadn't thought that far ahead. A frozen body was creepy enough for me.

"Who found it?"

"I did. I was coming out to see Frank and I got into the wrong tent."

Laman made no further attempt at conversation as I led him to the spot where Frank was waiting. The two men exchanged a few words before they stepped inside the tent and left me standing in the cold. I thought about going back to my car. Or drinking the coffee in the thermos that I still had clutched to my chest.

My thoughts were interrupted by the sound of another vehicle. Frank came out of the tent, looked toward shore, and asked me to go meet whomever it might be this time. I set off again and soon spotted our undersheriff, Blake Walker. Walker was not in uniform. He wore a dark green coat sporting the letters MSU which identified him as a Michigan State fan.

I had met Walker a couple of times before, but I wasn't sure if he remembered me. "I'm Tracy Quinn," I said as he drew closer. "I'll take you out to the scene."

"You write for the *News*, don't you?"

"Yep, that's me."

"You got here pretty fast. I just got the call."

"Actually I was the one who found it — the body."

"How did that happen?"

"I was coming out to see Frank."

"Oh right — you and Kolowsky —."

I was saved from any further discussion of my relationship with Frank by the arrival of yet another vehicle, this one the Cedar County ambulance. Walker and I stopped and watched as two EMT's got out, one male and one female. The guy was short with a stocking cap and the woman had long blonde hair. Walker went back and exchanged a few words with them.

They opened the back of the ambulance and brought out a gurney. Walker and I led the little procession onto the lake.

"I see you're in street clothes," I said. "Did we interrupt the Sunday afternoon football game?"

"Yes, but I'm used to it. I'm a deputy medical examiner. There's two of us and we take turns with weekend call."

Walker and I and the two EMT's continued our trek. This time I had no problem finding the right tent. It was surrounded by yellow tape emblazoned with the words, POLICE DO NOT CROSS, words that repeated themselves in an endless loop.

"More company," I yelled as we approached.

The crowd was growing. Besides the onlookers, there were now four of us outside the tent and two inside — well, three if you counted the dead guy. Sergeant Laman emerged from the tent, looked at Walker and said, "Guess it's all yours in there."

Walker turned to the EMT's and said, "Just wait here a minute while I get some pictures."

Most of the fishermen were now gawking at the female EMT with the long hair. She ignored them. Laman looked around and then approached a guy wearing a plaid hat. I heard him say, "Like to ask you a few questions." The guy nodded and the two of them disappeared into his ice shanty.

I waited impatiently for Frank to emerge. When he finally appeared I said, "Do you think maybe I could get out of here?"

Frank looked me over. For a moment I was not his girlfriend but a witness. At last he said, "Sure, go ahead. But wait in the car until I get a statement from you."

So I finally got away. A wind had come up and the fog was starting to disperse. The wind made me even colder but at least I could see where I was going. I located my Honda Civic which had a new layer of ice on the windshield, opened the door and slid inside. I rummaged through my pockets for the key, slid it into the ignition and then cursed.

I cursed because nothing happened when I turned the key. Immediately I realized why. Met with heavy fog in the morning, I had turned my lights on and then, like an idiot, had forgotten to turn them off. My battery was dead.

I sat and shivered until I made a decision. I found a scrap of paper and a pencil stub and scribbled, *Frank Im in the boathouse.* I stuck the note on the dashboard and walked across the parking lot toward the red and green lights that marked the entrance to the Boathouse Bar and Grill.

CHAPTER THREE

"So — you figure he drank too much, passed out and froze to death?"

"This bottle that I found underneath him would suggest that."

Frank reached into his coat pocket and pulled out a flat brown bottle encased in a plastic bag. He laid the bottle on the table and pushed it toward Blake Walker, the deputy medical examiner. Walker turned the bottle over, revealing the Jim Beam label.

The three of us — Walker, Frank, and I — were at the Boathouse Bar having a late lunch after our adventure on the ice. Frank had chosen a corner table and we were keeping our voices low. Even so, our presence had piqued the curiosity of the boys at the bar. That group was now dividing its attention between the football game and the sotto voice conference going on at our table.

A blast of cold air diverted everyone's attention as the front door opened. Three of the fishermen walked in, some taking off their gloves and rubbing their hands together. They nodded in our direction but said nothing as they took a table on the opposite side of the room. Frank acknowledged the group with a stern look that was probably supposed to remind them not to start blabbing about the body that had just been hauled away in the ambulance.

The fishermen placed their orders and traded some banter with the waitress, but there was a strained quality to the exchange which suggested that something was amiss. Anybody with a bit of sense could figure out that something fishy had been happening out on Arrowhead Lake.

"I think we talked to everyone at the scene," said Walker, consulting a battered notebook. "And so far I haven't found any glaring inconsistencies."

"Me too," said Frank. "They all told pretty much the same story. Most of them knew Vince — or at least knew who he was. A couple of them had talked to him yesterday."

"Same here," said Walker. "One guy said he noticed Vince's truck was still in the lot when he left yesterday around dark. Said he didn't think anything of it. Figured the owner, whoever it was, came in here to have some supper."

"So you figure that Ford pickup is his?" Frank glanced out the window at the parking lot.

"Yes, the one with the snow plow. We ran the plates and it's registered to him." Walker took a bite of his sandwich. "Think we should have it towed in?"

Frank rubbed his chin and glanced outside again. "I guess we should. After all, this is a suspicious death."

I finally spoke up. "Do all the ice fishermen use this parking lot?"

"Pretty much," said Frank. "Burl, that's the owner, he says the ice fishermen are his bread and butter during the winter."

"That's right," said Walker. "You park there, you've pretty much got an obligation to come in for a meal or at least a drink."

"One of us should talk to Burl before we leave," said Frank.

"Right," said Walker, "but we also need to notify the family ASAP — before they hear it from somebody else. News like this travels fast."

Both men rolled their eyes in the direction of the fishermen's table.

"Apparently he's married," said Frank. "One of the guys mentioned a wife."

"And more than one," said Walker, "described her as, ah, good looking."

I smiled, guessing that the actual terminology had been cleaned up for my benefit. "You've lived here longer than I have," Frank said to Walker. "Do you know anything about the family?"

Walker shook his head.

"Then let's see what we've got here." Frank produced a black leather wallet, also encased in plastic, and laid it on the table. He maneuvered the wallet until it opened to the ID card. "Address is 2413 Apple Drive."

"That's a subdivision about a mile north of town," said Walker.

"And the *Person to Notify* is Fiona Crawley. So that must be the wife. We need to find her and give her the bad news."

The men looked at each other. "Want to flip a coin," said Walker, "see who gets the job?"

That's when I spoke up. "What's her name again?" I leaned against Frank to see the name on the card. "Oh my gosh, I think I know this woman."

"How do you know her?" said Frank. The two men, who had been more or less ignoring me, were now waiting for my answer.

"We're in the same book club. At least I think so. I never knew her last name, but I doubt if there are two women in the county with the name of Fiona."

"About how old is this woman in your book club?" said Frank

"Early forties," I'd guess. Then in response to their unspoken question, I added, "She is, um, attractive. Curly red hair, great smile."

"Would you consider coming with me to notify her?" said Frank. "It would help a lot to have a woman, that is, to have you — along."

I cast a sidelong glance at Frank, who seemed to be studying his coffee cup. This guy had never been very good at asking for help — and, when he got it, he was usually not very grateful.

"How about it?" said Walker. "It would help us a lot, you know." Walker had soft brown eyes that reminded me of a puppy dog.

I closed my eyes, thinking of Fiona with her apple cheeks and that mass of copper hair. Then I pictured her bursting into tears. "Okay," I said at last. "I'll go with you." It seemed the least I could do.

So it was decided. The men finished their sandwiches but I had lost my appetite.

Walker said he would talk to Burl, then file his report and make arrangements for an autopsy. Frank gave him the bottle and asked him to send it along to the lab. Then Frank seemed to remember that I was a reporter for the town's weekly paper. "Tracy," he said, "you are not to share anything you heard today with the *News*. We really don't know yet what happened out there."

I knew this was a touchy situation for Frank. He had explained to me more than once that folks in law enforcement are frequently at odds with the press. And now Frank was in the awkward position of sharing a bed with a journalist.

"Don't worry," I said. "I didn't hear a thing at this table. Besides police stuff isn't even my department. Our news editor will be on this Monday morning asking for police reports."

"Okay then," said Walker. "I guess we're done." He motioned to the waitress for our bill.

"But you know," I said as we rose to leave. "There's something I wondering about."

"What's that?"

"Why hasn't his wife reported him missing?"

"That," said Walker, "is a very good question."

Outside, the fog was gone, replaced by a light snowfall. Walker gave us directions to the Orchard Hills subdivision and we decided to leave my Honda behind to be rescued later. Frank opened the passenger door of his Blazer for me.

"Are you ready for this?" he said.

"No, I'm not," I said as I climbed inside. "But let's get it over with."

Fifteen minutes later, Frank and I were parked on Apple Drive, looking at a double-wide modular home where the driveway, yard and deck were all covered with unblemished snow.

"Doesn't look very promising," I said.

Frank checked the number on the mailbox. "This seems to be it. And we have to start somewhere."

We got out and shuffled through the knee deep snow. Fortunately I was wearing my tallest winter boots — a couple of winters in Michigan had taught me a thing or two about footwear. Frank pounded on the door. We waited but got no answer — looked around but saw no garage and no car in evidence. He tried the door but it was locked.

Frank shook his head. "There's no tracks anywhere. I'd say no one's been in or out for the past twenty four hours."

"All this snow makes detective work a breeze, doesn't it?"

"Yeah right. Let's try the back door."

In the back we found a similar situation — door locked, no response, untrammeled snow. And no lights inside.

"What now, Sherlock?"

"Let's try a neighbor."

We returned to the road and walked a few yards to the next house. This place looked more promising. Someone had shoveled a narrow path to the door, the steps were visible and light was peeking through a panel of lace curtains. Frank pushed the doorbell.

"I can't believe those things really work," I said.

"It's polite to try the bell first."

Apparently the bell did work. Almost immediately we were rewarded by the sound of a dog barking. The door was opened by a short, white haired woman wearing a bulky pink cardigan.

"Oh be quiet, Muffin." The woman bent over and picked up a small gray dog who was also wearing a pink sweater. "Don't mind him," she said. "He's bent on protecting me. She peered at us. "Do I know you folks? You're not from the church, are you?"

"No," said Frank. "I'm with the sheriff's department and — don't be alarmed — we just need some information."

"Well, come on in. No sense letting all the heat out. You should see my gas bill."

We stepped inside, closing the door behind us. "I'm Tracy Quinn," I said.

"The one who writes for the newspaper?"

"Yes, that's me."

"Well, this is the most excitement I've had all winter. I'm Thelma, Thelma Moore. What can I do for you folks?"

"We're trying to find your neighbor, Fiona Crawley," said Frank. "There's nobody home next door and we need to locate her. There's been, ah, a death in the family."

"Do you know where she might be?" I said.

"I think I probably do." Thelma Moore placed her little dog on the floor. "You be good now," she admonished.

"Come on in here," she said.

We followed the lady into a living room full of overstuffed furniture that was all but smothered by colorful afghans. An unfinished project was on the sofa, knitting needles in evidence.

"Excuse the mess," she said as she gathered magazines that were strewn across the sofa and coffee table. "I don't have company very often and my cleaning lady hasn't been here because she's pregnant and they put her on bed rest and I just can't find any one else that I trust. You know how —."

"Don't worry about that," I said. "Your place looks nice and homey. Now about Fiona."

Thelma Moore left off her housekeeping efforts and said, "I'm pretty sure that Fiona went to Manistee to see her mother. She goes there about once a month for shopping and to visit the casino. Fiona likes to get out and, well, that husband of hers, all he wants to do is hunt and fish. You know the type."

Actually I did know that type but decided not to go there. "It's important that we find her," I said.

"Do you know her mother's name," said Frank, "or telephone number — anything that would help us?"

"I think I have her mother's address but it might take me a few minutes to find it. Go ahead and sit down."

I sank into an overstuffed chair and Frank sat in a rocker. Thelma started sorting through the pile of magazines on her coffee table.

"I don't see a lot of Fiona," she said, "but she's a good neighbor. She always invites me to their Fourth of July party. I go, but I never stay long. Her husband and his friends get to drinking and, well, you know how that is."

"About her mother," said Frank.

"I'm working on that." She moved her search to a desk. "See, Fiona gives me these magazines from her mother. Now, I never met the lady but she takes magazines with all these patterns for knit and crochet."

"I see you do a lot of that," I said, eyeing the purple doodad on the arm of my chair.

"Oh yes, I do. I make mittens and scarves all year and give them to the church for Christmas baskets. Okay, here it is." She handed me a magazine with the cover showing people in striped sweaters. "Check the label on the back. My eyes aren't real good."

I turned the magazine over. "Mrs. Grace O'Malley," I said, "with an address in Manistee."

"That's her. That's the lady you're looking for."

Frank produced a pen and reached in his pocket for a notebook.

"Oh, just keep that magazine," she said. "I'm all through with it."

"You sure?"

"Of course. Just take it."

"Well, thank you," said Frank. "You've been a big help."

"Glad to have company. Would you like some tea?"

"That's very kind of you." He stood. "But we really need to get going. We need to find this woman as soon as possible."

"Oh yes — a death in the family. That's too bad. Must have been a car accident, I suppose?"

"Yes, it was an accident," said Frank. I had to admire his ability to obfuscate.

Muffin started barking again as we prepared to leave, but the dog fell silent when Thelma picked him up and scratched his ears. Out in the foyer, she grabbed my sleeve and said, "If you ever want to learn how to knit, just let me know."

"I'll remember that," I said as we made our exit. "And thanks again for your help."

Back in the Blazer, Frank handed me the magazine and said, "Feel like a trip to Manistee?"

20

No, I didn't feel like an eighty mile round trip. I had expected to be home by now, curled up with a good book. But we needed to find Fiona.

"Sure," I said. "Let's go."

CHAPTER FOUR

Frank and I shared the coffee in the thermos as we drove north toward Manistee.

Once there, we made a few wrong turns before we found the right street and house number. This house was brick with a large bay window facing the street. The building sat up on a hill so our approach involved a series of ice covered steps. I slipped once but Frank caught me and, after that, I made better use of the railing.

An icy wind came whistling around a corner of the house. Frank and I reached the shelter of the porch and he used the metal knocker. Seconds later the door was opened and a woman stood facing us.

If I had wanted to pick Fiona's mother out of a crowd, the woman in front of me would have been my first choice. She had the same mass of curly auburn hair, only hers was shot with gray. She was nearly my height, which is five foot ten. Her sweater was a green turtle neck and her pleated black slacks fit her nicely.

She stood in the doorway and looked us over. "You don't look like Mormons," she said. "Maybe Jehovah's Witnesses?"

"Neither," said Frank. "I'm with the Cedar County Sheriff's Department and I'm looking for Fiona Crawley."

"Oh her," she said with a laugh. "She's not in any trouble, is she?"

"No, nothing like that. But it is important that we find her. Can you help us?"

"Sure, come on in."

We stepped inside and introduced ourselves, talking over the sound of a large TV tuned to the shopping channel. Inside the living room was a large leather recliner facing the TV and flanked by two glass tables. One table held a stack of paperbacks and the other had an ash tray with a pack of cigarettes.

She muted the television and said, "I'm Grace O'Malley. Now can you tell me what this is all about?"

"We're trying to locate Fiona Crawley," said Frank. "She is your daughter, isn't she?"

"Oh yes, she's my daughter. What's she got herself into?"

"She hasn't done anything — but we need to give her some news. We understand she came up here for the weekend."

Grace O'Malley nodded. "Sure. Fiona came up yesterday and we went to the casino — saw a show, had some drinks and I lost a hundred dollars at blackjack. She won fifty so she bought dinner. She had the prime rib and I had —."

Frank looked around. "Where is she now? We need to talk with her."

"Here — now? Oh no. She left last night."

"What time?"

"About nine o'clock."

"And where was she going?"

"Why home, of course. Where else would she go?"

"That's what we're trying to find out. We just came from her place and she wasn't there."

"Oh." She looked puzzled. "Was Vince at home? Did he know anything?"

Frank was quiet for a moment, then glanced at me. Apparently he came to a decision. "No, her husband wasn't home, Mrs. O'Malley. That's the bad news. Her husband is dead."

"Vince? Dead?" The woman's hand flew to her mouth and she slumped into the leather chair.

"Let's put it this way, ma'am. We have a dead body and everything points to it being Vince Crawley. So tell me, where is your daughter?"

She looked up with a bewildered expression. "I'm sure she went home. She was probably just out for groceries when you went there."

"No. It looks pretty definite that she never came home."

"Well, I can't imagine —." She looked from Frank to me as though we should have some answer to this puzzle.

"So tell me," Frank said again. "Where did your daughter go when she left here last night?"

Grace O'Malley shook her head and began to cry softly. "I told her not to marry him. I told her that man was nothing but trouble."

"So what we have," said Frank, "is a dead man and a missing wife."

"I'm sure there is some explanation," I said.

We were on our way back to Shagoni River. Snowy pellets bounced off the windshield and the leaden sky was already darkening toward evening.

"Of course there's an explanation. But I'm just starting to wonder if there's more to this than meets the eye."

"Are you suggesting that his death wasn't an accident?"

"I try not to jump to conclusions. We'll know more after the autopsy. The body was frozen — but that doesn't mean that hypothermia was the cause of death."

"What are you thinking — double murder?" I shivered. "I can't imagine anyone wanting to kill Fiona."

"All kinds of people do get killed. And Grace O'Malley's comment did raise some questions about Vince."

"Like maybe he was involved in something illegal?"

"That's one scenario. But the Mafia isn't all that active in Cedar County. So maybe the wife did him in and ran off to the Caribbean."

"I'm not ready to condemn Fiona," I said.

"We're not condemning anybody. Let's check the house again when we get back to town."

And that is what we did.

This time when we reached Apple Drive, things had changed. A blue sedan was parked in the driveway and footprints in the snow led from the car to the house.

Once again Frank pounded on the door and this time we got a response. The door swung open and there she stood in all her glory — red haired Fiona from the book club.

"Hi Fiona," I said.

"Hello there, Tracy Quinn," she said with her usual smile. "What brings you out on a day like this? Come on in out of the cold." She led us into her kitchen.

"This is Frank Kolowsky," I said. "He's with the sheriff's department."

"Oh right. I heard you dated a cop." She reached out and shook Frank's hand. "Guess you already know who I am." She laughed softly, then her expression turned serious. "Is this about Vince? He's not here and it looks like he never came home last night."

Frank nodded. "Yes, it's about your husband."

"I was just getting ready to call and see if he's had another DUI." She shook her head. "I swear, sometimes that man is more than I can handle."

Frank cleared his throat. "No, it's not another DUI."

"Okay then, what's he done? Do I have to bail him out or what?" Her smile was fading. After a few seconds of strained silence, she said, "Is it something bad? Did he have an accident and kill somebody? That's what I've always been worried about."

"No," he said, "but it is bad news."

"Let's go sit down." I took Fiona's hand and led her into the living room. We sat together on the sofa and I put an arm around her shoulders.

"I'm sorry to tell you this," Frank said softly but clearly, "but your husband is dead."

There was no sound except the ticking of a clock as Fiona looked from me to Frank. Then she blurted, "No — please, not dead." She buried her face in her hands as though to ward off a blow.

"We found him today in his ice shanty," I said as gently as I could. I felt her body shake and then she began to sob. Frank found a box of tissues and handed them to me. I pulled out a bunch and stuffed them into her hand. So far, her shock and grief appeared nothing short of genuine.

After a few minutes, she raised her tear stained face. "Are you sure it was Vince?"

"Everything points to it being your husband," he said. "The wallet in his pocket, the other fishermen, his truck left at the edge of the lake. But, of course, someone needs to identify the body."

Fiona shook her head, covered her face again.

"Is there anybody else who could do it?" he said. "Is there a son or a daughter around?"

Her answer, when it came, was a bit garbled. "Not me, but yes, he does. What I mean is, Vince had children from a previous — you know. His son Chip lives out near Crystal Valley."

"So maybe we could get him to go take a look," said Frank. "Does he have a telephone?"

"Yes, he has a phone." She started sniffling again, blew her nose.

"When you're up to it," I said, "could you give us the boy's phone number?"

"Oh sure." Fiona took a deep breath. Then she stood, moved to a nearby table and wrote a number on a slip of paper. She handed it to Frank. "You'll probably have to leave a message on his machine — he generally doesn't answer unless he knows who's calling."

"Okay. So how about his address then too? We want to take care of this as soon as possible."

"Oh yes, of course." Fiona stifled a sob and said, "I'm sorry I'm such a mess."

"It's okay," I said. "We understand. Just take your time."

Fiona found a notepad and managed to write down an address. She started to hand it over and then said, "I'd better draw you a map if you're going out there. He's in a trailer about two miles north and another mile east of that bar out there."

"The Crystal Valley Tavern."

"Right."

26

She sketched some directions on the paper and said, "He's a little, um, paranoid. He'll probably freak out when he sees the law at his door." She coughed as she ripped off the sheet and handed it to Frank.

"Maybe it would help if you call him first and tell him what's going on."

"Okay," she said, "but let me get some water first."

Fiona disappeared into the kitchen and returned with a glass of water. She took a drink, then picked up a cordless phone and punched in some numbers. After a few seconds she spoke to a machine. "Chip, this is Fiona. Something happened to your dad. They think he's dead. Someone will be contacting you to identify —." She broke off, coughing, then continued. "That's what they'll be calling you about." She hung up and said. "Hope I didn't botch that too bad."

"Thanks for doing that," Frank said as he put the papers in his pocket. "Now maybe you'd like to sit down again. I need to ask you some questions."

"Questions?" She looked alarmed.

"It's all just routine," he said.

Fiona took another drink of water, put down the glass and sat on the sofa. "Okay," she said. "Ask away."

"When was the last time you saw your husband?"

"Yesterday morning. We had breakfast about eight, then he went off fishing and, about an hour later, I went to Manistee. Vince said he'd have a nice mess of fish when I got back."

"How long were you with your mother?"

"I just got home a couple of hours ago."

Was that a flicker of discomfort in her eyes?

Frank fixed his gaze on her. "Mrs. Crawley, we just talked to your mother."

"Oh, did you?" Her tone shifted slightly, taking on a note of defiance. "And what did my mother say?"

"She said you left there yesterday evening."

"Really? Is that what she said?"

"So I have to ask you ma'am. Where have you been?"

"I've been with my mother. You see, she's got it all mixed up. You'd never know it, but she has Alzheimer's. She gets things confused all the time, the poor dear."

CHAPTER FIVE

It was after dark when we got back to town. We were at my house, just sitting down to supper when Frank's cell phone rang.

"Guess I'd better take this." He glanced at me apologetically, then retrieved the little black gadget from his pocket. "Kolowsky here."

The call lasted about five minutes and Frank's end of the conversation was mostly grunts until he finally ended with, "Okay, thanks for keeping me in the loop."

He laid down the phone and turned his attention back to our food — leftover spaghetti and some cole slaw we had picked up at the deli. "This is great," he said. "I was really hungry."

I was hungry too, but now I was curious about the call. "Classified information?" I hinted.

"Not exactly. But didn't you say we shouldn't talk business during dinner?"

"Oh, I guess maybe I did."

It was true. After a day that had started with the discovery of a frozen corpse, then dealing with the medical examiner, EMT's and cops, and finally telling a woman that her husband was dead, I had hoped to relax over dinner — thinking that the meal might be at least restful, if not exactly intimate.

But now my curiosity was up. "Go ahead and tell me," I said. "If you can, that is."

"Okay, since you asked for it. The call was from Walker."

"The undersheriff?"

"Right. He couldn't get Chip Crawley to answer his phone, so he drove out to Crystal Valley to find him. The kid was home — looked hungover — then got all belligerent about having the law at his door. But he did agree to come in and ID the body."

"Why do you suppose he was paranoid?"

"Most people are, to some extent."

"I guess you're right. I wasn't too thrilled the first time you showed up at my door — even though I knew what it was about."

"The guy probably has some marijuana stashed somewhere. But we're not going to worry about that."

Frank smiled as he reached for a slice of bread. The smile revealed a gap between his front teeth, which probably would have constituted a flaw if we were going for movie star good looks. But I was not. My marriage had left me with a permanent distrust of the traditionally attractive male. This man, with a scar that intersected one eyebrow and his slightly off kilter nose, looked just fine to me. And he was a big man — well over six feet tall — which I liked since I had towered over my class mates ever since junior high.

I returned his smile and said, "That shirt looks good on you."

He was wearing the red and black flannel shirt I had given him for Christmas. His gift to me was clothing of a more personal nature and I was wearing that too. We managed to avoid any more talk about Vince Crawley until we were ready for dessert. He poured coffee while I dished up the ice cream — and then I was the one who brought up the subject that had been bugging me all along — like the proverbial elephant in the room.

"Frank," I said, "how much do you know about Alzheimer's?"

"Not a whole lot." The scent of mocha flavored coffee wafted up from the cup he placed in front of me. "One of my uncles had it. He wound up in a nursing home and I only saw him a couple of times after that. He didn't seem to know anybody, not even his wife." Frank sat down and spooned fudge sauce onto his ice cream. "How about you?"

"I'm pretty sure I don't have it yet."

"That's good." He smiled. "But do you know anything about it?"

"A little bit. You know I worked in a hospital before I moved to Michigan."

"Sure — but you weren't a nurse or anything."

"Right — I had no direct patient contact. I wrote press releases, ran a house newsletter and tried to make everybody look and sound good."

"So what did you learn about Alzheimer's?"

"The medical floor always had a lot of elderly people. And usually a couple of them had some degree of Alzheimer's." I put down my spoon and looked at him. "Based on my limited knowledge of the condition, Grace O'Malley doesn't seem like a very likely candidate."

"That's what I was thinking. Fiona's mother seemed pretty sharp."

"I agree. She was nicely dressed and the house was clean. People with Alzheimer's are usually more vague and disheveled."

"So what we have here is — well— an inconsistency."

I chuckled. "Is that a polite way of saying that Fiona told us a whopper?"

"I suppose her mother could be in the early stages of the disease." He looked thoughtful as he sipped his coffee. "But I just don't think someone like her would have such a complete memory lapse."

"Me neither." Then I had another thought. "Maybe Grace O'Malley deliberately lied to us."

"That's a possibility." Frank considered this as he melted a spoonful of ice cream in his coffee. "Certainly one of them is not being honest and — because of that — we don't know where Fiona was Saturday night. But there's one thing I'm pretty sure of."

"What's that?"

"She wasn't in her house Saturday night. Unless she sprouted wings and flew in through a window."

"Because all that snow around her house was pristine —."

"Yeah, the snow makes detective work a breeze. That's why I stay in the north. Geez, maybe I should have taken a picture of the place."

"Can't you find out if her mother does have Alzheimer's? Talk to her doctor or something?"

"It's a lot harder these days than it used to be," he said. "Patient confidentiality and all of that. First we'd need evidence that a crime was committed. And then we would probably need a subpoena."

"And by now, Fiona has probably talked to her mother —."

"Yeah, she's probably convinced her mom that she did stay over Saturday night."

"I don't like this at all," I said. "We're talking about Fiona like she's some kind of criminal."

"So let's not get ahead of ourselves. There may not even be any crime."

"I hope not."

Frank gave me an appraising look. "How well do you know this woman
anyway?"

"Not very well. Our contacts have been book club meetings and a few exchanges when we meet on the street. But you know, I've always liked her. It's hard not to like someone who is so consistently cheerful."

"You were with her when she got the news," he said. "What did you think of her reaction?"

"As near as I could tell, she was genuinely shocked. The tears were real." I looked at him. "But you do more of this stuff than I do. What did you think?"

"She looked like a grieving widow to me. She didn't get totally hysterical, but then — people all react differently."

"So where do you suppose she was on Saturday night — while her husband was freezing to death on the lake?"

"You're assuming that he froze to death. It could have been a heart attack or even a stroke. And the freezing took place later." He scraped the last of the ice cream from his bowl.

"When will you know for sure?"

"After the autopsy."

"And when will that be?"

"If Chip Crawley does the ID tonight, the body can be shipped to Grand Rapids in the morning. If they're not backed up, the autopsy could get done tomorrow. Earliest results would be sometime Tuesday." He stretched and yawned. "And there's one more thing that I need."

"What's that?"

"I need an official statement from you." Frank pulled a small spiral notebook from his shirt pocket and flipped it open. "Okay, Tracy Quinn of 248 Maple Street, about what time did you reach Arrowhead Lake this afternoon?"

Monday was cloudy with snow falling on and off throughout the day. After work I bought a few groceries and, by the time I got home, daylight had given way to darkness. I was navigating the steps of my front porch when I heard a car approaching and I turned to see a familiar vehicle pulling up behind mine. The driver's door opened and a woman emerged, her blonde hair framed by a blue scarf.

"Hi Tracy," she called. "I hope this isn't a bad time."

"It's never a bad time for you, Jewell. Come on in. We need to catch up."

Jewell Lavallen is my closest friend, a person whose company never fails to improve my bad moods or magnify my good ones. An old college chum, she was now director of nursing at the hospital in Wexford and her husband Paul sold insurance in Stanford.

Jewell followed me inside and within minutes we were settled on my sofa with cups of hot chocolate.

"Did you get down to Ann Arbor to visit Sarah?" Her daughter was a student at U of M and getting close to graduation.

"Sure did. I spent the night with Sarah and Mark at their apartment. They presented me with sonogram photos." She reached into her purse and produced the grainy photos of her future grandchild.

"Ah, the new baby pictures." I peered at the shadowy figure. "Did Paul go with you?"

"I didn't even invite him. He would have spoiled the whole visit."

"Oh — because he disapproves."

"He can't reconcile himself to the fact that they're not married and don't see any reason to get married before the baby comes. I don't really like it either, but I've decided to accept their decision. I want to be close to Sarah during this special time."

"Does Paul accept your position?"

"He has to. And I'm glad I went. Sarah and I had great fun shopping for maternity clothes. We went out for lunch and got a case of the giggles when I told her about the box of faded smocks that my mother and her friends used to pass around the neighborhood. Anyway, Sarah's just starting to show and they are both as proud as peacocks. All of their friends act as though it's the most natural thing in the world."

"For them to be having a baby —."

" — out of wedlock, as we used to call it."

"I think Paul will come around eventually."

"I expect that he will. They have all kinds of plans and somewhere in there are plans for a wedding — but it doesn't seem important to them. Times have changed, I guess. But enough about me. How was your weekend? Did you and Frank do anything special?"

"As a matter of fact, we did." I gave her a quick rundown of Sunday afternoon, beginning with my discovery of a body on Arrowhead Lake. "The dead guy was Vince Crawley. His wife is Fiona — you know — from the book club."

"Fiona? Oh that poor girl."

"When Frank found out that I knew her, he enlisted me to go with him to give her the bad news."

"So she just found out yesterday?"

I nodded.

"Well, that explains why they were short handed today in the ER."

"What do you mean?"

"Didn't you know? Fiona works at the hospital. She's an RN and a very good one. She rarely misses work."

CHAPTER SIX

"Tracy, you're five minutes late and I need to see you in my office."

My editor Marge Enright was never one to waste her breath on small talk — or even normal greetings for that matter. And this being Tuesday, she was more abrupt than usual — because Tuesday is deadline day for our weekly newspaper.

"I'll be right there," I said, "as soon as I get my coat off."

I walked down the hallway and wondered which version of Marge I would encounter. When I first started the job, my editor had appeared as a large, badly dressed woman who never hesitated to give me fashion advice. During my eighteen month tenure I had experienced the gamut of Marge's moods, which varied from inscrutable and demanding to erratic and mean.

So dealing with Marge had always been a challenge — but recently the situation had become even more unpredictable. Our boss had morphed from a critic in bad clothing to an adult undergoing adolescent changes. Her moods now ranged from irritable, because she was on a diet, to positively ditzy because she had found a bright orange blouse to match her latest hair color.

We, the employees, had floundered through several weeks of confusion until we discovered that Marge had acquired a boyfriend. Of course she never breathed a word of this to us and we did our best to play dumb. When you work for Marge Enright, the best policy is not to rock her boat.

Minutes later I was in her office waiting for Marge to finish a telephone call. Her hair, now strawberry blonde, was twisted into ringlets and piled high on her head. Finally she hung up and acknowledged my presence.

"Good morning," I said. "Nice sweater."

She ignored my compliment. "I heard that somebody froze to death out on Arrowhead Lake over the weekend. Know anything about that?"

"Well, I do know a little." I struggled to remember which events of that chaotic day I was at liberty to share.

"Wasn't it you who found the body?"

"Umm, actually, I guess I did."

"You guess?" Marge cast me a look which suggested that she had made the grievous error of hiring an imbecile.

"Yes, it was me."

She waited, tapping a pencil on her desk so I threw her a bone. "The guy's name was Vince Crawley."

"Never heard of him." She jotted down the name. "Was he local?"

"Yes, he was. Lived in a subdivision just north of town."

The pencil kept tapping so I cast about for a few more details that I hoped were safe. "His truck was in the parking lot at the Boat House — you know, that bar down by Long Bridge." Then I stumbled on a way to change the subject. "I saw some signs out there," I said. "The signs said *NO MORE CONDOS.* Have you seen them?"

She snorted. "Can't miss them. Apparently some folks are riled about that big development across from the marina. Any idea who's behind the protest?"

"Might be Larry Joslin."

"Joslin — that figures. I hear he's planning to run for council. I also heard that Erwin Dukes, the village attorney, is out of commission. Know anything about that?"

"I covered the council meeting last week and Dukes wasn't there. The mayor said he was ill."

"I'm pretty sure it's something more serious than a case of the flu."

"I think you're right. Want me to call his office?"

"I already did — tried to talk with his son. But Dukes junior doesn't return my calls and the secretary won't tell me anything."

"I could try Jim Mcneely."

"Good idea," she said. "The village manager should know something — if anybody does."

"Maybe I can talk to Jim this morning. I need to get some figures from him on the new wastewater plant. That project is beginning to sound expensive."

"But what about this dead body? Did anything look suspicious?"

Darn. She was back to the body again. But just then my salvation arrived, heralded by a melange of Old Spice and cigar smoke — our news editor Jake Billington. Dressed in a heavy topcoat, his bulk nearly filled the door way.

"Good morning ladies," he said.

"Hello Jake," said Marge. "What about this dead guy on the lake? Have you talked to the sheriff?"

Jake pulled a wrinkled handkerchief from his pocket and blew his noise. "Damn cold out there."

"We already know that." She started tapping the pencil again.

Jake raised a hand. "I'm getting to it. Just spent an hour with Sheriff Dupree. Went over all the reports. Dead man was Vince Crawley. His son came in last night and identified the body. Guess the kid is a piece of work himself. Got all cantankerous with the officers when he found out they had impounded the truck. Said he and his dad ran a snowplowing business and he needed the truck right away."

"Or maybe there's something in the truck that he's worried about," said Marge. "What about the autopsy results?"

"Still pending."

"Anyway, the story needs to go on the front page."

"Will do," said Jake.

"And Kyle is down there taking pictures of the ice shanty. Put that on the front too."

"Not much room left," he said.

"Then move something."

Jake nodded and took his leave.

"Are you finished with me?" I said.

"Yes, but you'd better call Mcneely right now. I think he's going to Stanford this afternoon — some kind of ambulance meeting."

"I'll call him right now."

Marge waved me out and turned to her computer. Back at my desk I placed a call to Jim Mcneely, our village manager, who told me to come on over. I put on my coat for the walk to village hall, which was only a block away. Our small town is convenient that way — newspaper, bank, police station and village hall are all contained within two blocks of our main street — along with a couple of bars.

Stepping outside, I discovered that the sky was clear and so was the sidewalk.

All in all, I was in a pretty good mood. The fact that the sun was shining was cause for celebration in itself, but I must confess that I am always happy to call on our village manager. Jim Mcneely is cute, thirty-something and single. We seem to hit it off nicely and on a couple of occasions have managed to sneak away to have lunch together.

"Good morning, Helen," I said to the village clerk. "I'm looking for Jim."

"Hi Tracy. He's expecting you so go on in." Helen waved a blue veined hand toward the door of Jim's office. "He'll be back in a minute."

I stepped into Jim's office and looked over the walls. There were a couple of water color paintings I hadn't seen before — one featured the bandshell on the village green and the other was the Point Sable lighthouse. Minutes later Jim appeared, all five and half feet of him, looking sharp in a navy blue sweater.

"Tracy, it's good to see you." Jim's smile created a pair of serious dimples. He dropped a stack of papers on his desk, sat down and started shuffling through them. "Somewhere in here are the numbers I promised you about the wastewater plant."

"Marge said it's going to cost almost four million dollars."

"Unfortunately, she's right." He handed me a pack of papers in a plastic folder. "Here are the details. The engineers have projected the cost and the finance people have explained how we're going to get the money — plus how long it will take to pay it back. No one is happy about it."

"But we have no choice?"

"None at all. The state has been after the village for years. I don't know how we've managed to slip by this long. The current facility has a laundry list of violations. If we don't act soon, we'll be facing some hefty fines."

"Okay," I said, taking the papers. "And thanks. Got time for one more question?"

"Sure."

"What's the word on Erwin Dukes?"

"It's official now." Jim shook his head. "Erwin won't be back."

"What happened?"

"He had a stroke — a pretty bad one, from what Kevin told me."

"Kevin's the son?"

"Right. I talked to him yesterday — after I got the resignation letter."

"Could I have a copy of the letter?"

"Sure. I had Helen make up copies for the council meeting." Jim reached into a tray, extracted a sheet and handed it to me.

I scanned the page. The letterhead read 'Dukes and Dukes, Attorney at Law'. In the second paragraph I found words indicating that Erwin was "incapacitated to the extent that he will not be able to continue his duties as village attorney."

"Do you know how long he had been with the village?"

"Long before I got here," he said. "Talk to Helen. She might remember."

"Sure. Helen knows everything. Do you think his son will step in as village attorney?"

Jim shook his head. "I asked Kevin already. In fact I begged a little, but he said no — not even temporarily. After all, he's got double the work load at his office. Not to mention a sick father."

"So what will you do?"

"We'll run an ad and then look over the applicants."

"Think there will be much interest?"

"Frankly, no." Jim stood and began to stuff papers into his briefcase. "The job doesn't pay very much. And besides, nobody wants to deal with that guy over on Rash Street."

"Rash Street? Oh, the pack rat."

"Right. The guy who keeps collecting junk in his yard. We go to court and get things cleaned up and then in a few months the place is a mess all over again."

"He sounds obsessive."

"I'm sure he does have mental problems. But we can't lock him up so we have to deal with him." Jim closed the briefcase.

"Okay," I said. "I'm out of here."

"Sorry I'm on such a tight schedule."

"No problem. We are too. Paper goes to print today and Marge is on everyone's case. So thanks for working me in."

"Always my pleasure," Jim said, flashing that killer smile of his.

Back at work, I wrote a couple of paragraphs about Erwin Dukes and then found Larry, our graphics guy, and asked him if he could locate a photo of Dukes. On my way out of the graphics room, I met Jake in the hallway.

"If you got a minute," he said, "come on in my office."

"Sure, just let me get some coffee."

Minutes later, coffee in hand, I joined Jake in his office. Jake's presence goes a long way toward making my job bearable. His bald pate, surrounded by a fringe of hair, gives him a monk like appearance, though his vocabulary of swear words definitely leans away from such a vocation. Since I barely remember my dad, I suppose Jake might be some kind of father figure for me.

"Anything new on Crawley?" I said.

"Just a couple of things and the sheriff promised to call me as soon as —."

He was interrupted by the telephone ringing. He picked up and said, "Okay, great." He reached for a pen and started writing. I resisted the temptation to scoot around and look over his shoulder.

The call lasted only a couple of minutes and, when it was over, Jake said, "Cause of death was hypothermia."

"That's pretty anticlimactic. And I suppose he was intoxicated."

He shook his head and his brows knit together. "There was a certain level of alcohol in his bloodstream — but it was less than the legal limit for driving."

"So — not enough to make him pass out?"

"Not nearly enough."

"No heart attack?"

"Heart was fine — no stroke either."

"Then why did he —?"

"Now here's the interesting part. His blood showed a pretty high level of chloral hydrate."

"Chloral hydrate?" My thoughts raced back to hospital days. "Isn't that a sleeping medication?"

"Yes. And it looks like that's why he went to sleep — and didn't wake up."

"So how did he ingest the chloral hydrate?"

"Good question. The whiskey bottle is at the lab. If the bottle shows traces of the medication, then we'll know where it came from."

"But how did the stuff get into his whiskey?"

"That is the big question. But not a word of this, you hear?"

"Of course. The story will say — what — suspicious death?"

"The story will say the situation is under investigation."

I had a thought just then but I kept it to myself. Fiona Crawley worked at Wexford General — and I was pretty sure the hospital pharmacy would have chloral hydrate in stock. But I didn't like the way that line of thought was leading.

CHAPTER SEVEN

Tracy...let's do lunch — I have big news!!!.

The note was scrawled on a ripped off corner of notepaper, slipped inside a pamphlet and passed to me during a county board meeting.

I regarded the invitation with mixed feelings. The writer of the note was sitting only a few feet away from me, sharing the table reserved for the press at Cedar County Board meetings. My friend Ivy Martin wrote for the Manistee Chronicle, a daily paper in the city forty miles to the north. Our parallel jobs had the effect of putting us into proximity on a regular basis and assured that we always had one thing in common — the pursuit of breaking news.

Initially, the situation had been fine. Ivy was smart, funny, and single — free with news tips or gossip and good for a Friday night foray into one of the local bars. Our friendship had never been really close but it never presented any problems either — until the night she confessed to a dalliance with Jewell's husband. That unhappy incident created a whole lot of fallout and afterward I gave her the cold shoulder for a while. But our work threw us together in such a way that it was impossible for me to avoid her completely.

And now here she was with this promise of *Big News*. I had to admit that she had piqued my curiosity. Knowing Ivy, the offer represented a wide range of possibilities — maybe a public figure had embezzled funds — maybe some official was being recalled — or maybe it was just a new boyfriend in her tumultuous love life.

There was only one way to find out.

I scribbled *Okay — at Schooners?* and sent the note back. She pushed back her long dark hair, cast a sideways glance in my direction and winked. The date was on.

We were in Stanford, the county seat, which offered half a dozen acceptable restaurants but I had chosen Schooners because there was less likelihood of being spotted there by someone who knew us. Marge, my editor, refers to my cohort as Poison Ivy and has all but forbidden me to socialize with her. Marge has this old fashioned idea about rival newspapers, but Ivy and I trade information freely — most of the time.

Ivy was waiting for me at Schooners, replete in high heeled boots and a long gray coat.

"Tracy," she purred, "so glad you could make it. It's been ages."

"Good to see you too," I said, "and yes, it has been ages." I felt that niggle of guilt that I get whenever I socialize with Ivy — the feeling that I am being disloyal to Jewell. I did my best to ignore that feeling as we made our way to our favorite corner table.

We claimed the spot, eased out of our coats and Ivy slowly peeled off her leather gloves. The waitress brought coffee and we placed our orders. As we made small talk, I saw Ivy doing her usual survey of the male population. But the men at the bar were oblivious to our presence, focused as they were on the ubiquitous television sets.

As soon as our food was delivered and the waitress was gone, I said, "Okay, what's the big news?"

Ivy smiled and sipped her coffee. I knew she was delaying her reply in order to prolong the drama. But finally she couldn't wait any longer. She leaned forward and said, "Greg is moving in with me."

I almost choked on my sandwich. "Really?"

"Really. And we're having a party at my place Saturday to celebrate. Of course you and Frank are invited."

"Ah, great," I hedged. "But I'll have to talk with Frank first."

"Tell him I insist."

"He might be out of town."

"Then come by yourself."

I took a swallow of water to gain a few seconds to think. "Sooooo —-." I stretched out the syllable while I chose my words. "It sounds as though you and Greg are — doing well at the moment?"

The subject was a minefield and I was treading cautiously — because I had put my foot in my mouth on more than one occasion while discussing this particular relationship. For as long as I had known her, Ivy's relationship with Greg Wetherell, a lawyer from Whitehall, had been in constant flux. The affair swung like a pendulum, from blissful getaway one weekend to catastrophic meltdown the next. I had learned to temper my responses. If the pair was in break-up mode, I assured Ivy that he was not worthy of her — in reconciliation mode, I offered congratulations.

"We're doing more than well," she said with a satisfied smile. "I think you could say we are serious."

"Sounds like it. I mean, sharing a house — that's a big step."

"Yes it is — a giant step." She picked at her salad, wearing an expression which suggested that the cat had finally caught the canary.

"Well, I hope it works out for the two of you." I tried to picture Greg making room for his suits in Ivy's jampacked closet. "But what about his job — won't this about double his commute?"

"That's the exciting part," she replied. "He's going to work right here in Stanford."

"In Stanford? No kidding?"

"Yes. With Kevin Dukes."

"Oh — Dukes Junior. How did that happen?"

"Well — you probably know about Kevin's dad."

"Sure, I just talked with Jim Mcneely. Apparently the old guy won't be working any more."

"Yep, Erwin's all finished. But, after all, the guy was pushing eighty — should have retired long ago. But anyway, Kevin has known Greg ever since law school and he asked him to step in and be his partner. And Greg said yes. What could be better? He's going to live with me and put his house in Whitehall up for sale."

"It would appear that things are working out nicely for both of you."

"Yes they are." She waved her fork in the air. "And I'm having this party so he can meet my friends. I just know you will all make him feel welcome."

"I'll check my calendar and I expect that I can make it. But I wonder —-." I stopped mid-sentence.

"You wonder what?"

"Oh nothing." I shifted gears. "I wonder what we should bring to the party?"

"Just bring a bottle of —- whatever you like to drink. I'll have lots of food and plenty of mix."

"Sure. I'll talk to Frank and we'll make a decision."

Ivy looked at her watch. "Ohmigosh," she said, " I had no idea. Forgive me, Tracy, but I've got to finish up fast. I've got a two o'clock appointment with Wertz."

"The drain commissioner?"

She nodded. "None other."

"Well then, be on time. Leroy Wertz does not like to be kept waiting."

"That guy scares me — even when he's in a good mood."

Ivy ate a few more bites and finished her coffee. Then she pulled out her wallet and handed me a bill. "Use this to pay for my lunch and I'll see you Saturday — eight o'clock." She grabbed her coat and made for the exit.

I finished my sandwich and, when I went to settle the tab, discovered that I was coming out a little short in the transaction. This came as no great surprise. Ivy was never very good at math. But as I drove back to work, I was not thinking about the discrepancy on the lunch check. I was pondering just how this new domestic arrangement was going to play out.

Because, if I remembered correctly, almost all of the Ivy /Greg eruptions had been the result of his dalliance with some other female.

And now he was moving in with her? Obviously she was delighted to have him on such a short leash. But I could imagine her living in a state of hypervigilance, alert for the single strand of blonde hair on his collar. I didn't envy either one of them. And I should likely be prepared for more fallout.

Friday proved to be a long day at work. Marge would give me directions, change her mind and tell me to do something else, then wonder why I didn't have both jobs finished. My patience was wearing thin. But then I reminded myself that Frank was coming to my house with takeout from the Mexican restaurant. That got me through the day.

I arrived home and was still hanging up my coat when Frank arrived, bearing food as promised. We opened the boxes and were treated to the aromas of salsa, shrimp tacos and chicken enchiladas. Frank and I lost no time getting into the food. For a while we ate more than we talked, sharing tidbits about our work lives, vehicle problems and the possibility of a serious blizzard within the next few days.

I was telling him about my day at work when the conversation came around to Vince Crawley. "Jake said it was chloral hydrate that put him to sleep. Do you know where it came from?"

At first Frank didn't answer — he was busy crunching a taco. Finally he said, "The lab reports came back — and the whiskey bottle showed traces of chloral hydrate."

"Aha — so we know that's how Crawley ingested the stuff."

"Right. But what we don't know is who put it there."

"What about fingerprints on the bottle?"

"The lab is checking on that. But remember, several of the fishermen told us they had been to Vince's shack and shared a snort with him."

"So how do you sort that out?"

"Walker and I will compare notes again and see which guys said they drank with Crawley." He reached for a tamale. "Then we'll ask them to come in and have their fingerprints taken — for elimination purposes."

"What if you can't find all of the guys?"

"If anyone has left the area, well, that would look suspicious in itself, wouldn't it?"

"Yes it would."

I poured two cups of coffee and we carried them into the living room. We sat on the couch and I took off my shoes, stretching out to put my feet in Frank's lap. He started massaging my toes. It was heavenly. But my brain wouldn't stop working.

"Chloral hydrate is a pretty common sleeping med," I said, "but it does require a prescription. What do you know about the drug?"

"I did some research. It's odorless and tasteless. In fact, it was the Mickey Finn that used to appear in old detective novels. Put a few drops in your cocktail and you're out like a light. It works pretty fast."

"In the detective novels the victim usually woke up with a bad headache."

"Yeah. The difference here is that Vince froze to death before he could wake up. But there's something else to think about."

"What's that?"

"If Fiona had been home Saturday night, it seems like she would have come looking for her husband."

"You're right. And she might have found him before he died."

"Unless, of course, she was in on it," said Frank.

"Or maybe the person didn't plan to kill Vince — just knock him out and what — steal something?"

"It's a thought." He was quiet for a minute, switching to my other foot. "But what could the guy have on him that could be so important?"

"Good question. Ice fisherman don't usually carry much cash."

"Or any secret documents."

"What kind of work did Vince do?"

"We know he did snow plowing in the winter. We finally let his son Chip have the truck back so he won't lose his regular customers. Chip said in the summer he and his dad ran a charter fishing business."

"Sounds like Chip pretty much depended on his dad for employment."

"Looks that way. And neither enterprise is exactly steady."

"So apparently Fiona was the one who brought in the regular paycheck. I wonder how she felt about that?"

"It's not that unusual," he said, "especially in these parts."

"No, I guess not. And, as liberated women, we're not supposed to measure a man's worth by his paycheck." He smiled at that one. "But I see another problem."

"What's that?"

"The guys who drank with Vince — out of that bottle," I said. "If they had their gloves on, they wouldn't leave any prints. And the gloves might have obliterated prints that were already there."

"Good point. That's where cold weather makes this detective work a little harder."

"I just thought of something else. Did the guys who drank with Vince have any symptoms — did they get sleepy?"

"Nobody mentioned that — but it's a good question. I guess we'll ask them when we take their fingerprints. I definitely have some more questions for the family." He leaned down and took off his own shoes. "But I usually wait until after the funeral. Do you know when that is happening?"

"Jewell said it's going to be Monday or Tuesday."

"Is she going to the funeral?"

"No, but she said a lot of staff at the hospital would be wanting to go."

"Why is that?"

"Fiona works at Wexford Hospital. Didn't you know?"

"No, I didn't know that." His eyes narrowed. "Is Fiona a nurse?"

"Yes she is. Jewell said she's been there almost ten years."

"Now that makes things interesting."

"Yes it does." Now his feet were in my lap. They didn't smell very good, but, hey, mine probably didn't either. "Anyway," I said, "enough about this Vince Crawley business. We have a decision to make."

"A decision?" He looked wary.

"Don't look so nervous," I said with a laugh. "It's nothing scary. We're invited to a party tomorrow night. To go or not to go?"

"Where is it?"

"About five miles out of town. My friend Ivy wants us to meet her boyfriend Greg. The guy is moving in with her."

"So it's a shacking up party?"

"Such a crude term." I giggled. "You have to promise to be nice."

"Sure, I can be nice."

"So we're going then?"

"Sure, why not?"

His ready agreement surprised me. But then, it was early February. In the midst of Michigan's long winter, even the most stoic soul feels a touch of cabin fever, a condition which makes us receptive to almost any kind of diversion.

CHAPTER EIGHT

"You need to brief me," said Frank, "about your friend Ivy. Have I met her?"

"Yes you have. Remember, we sat with her at the pub a few weeks ago. She has that long dark hair and wears a lot of silver jewelry."

"The skinny one with all that mascara?"

"That's her." I chuckled at Frank's description of Ivy, who aspired to setting fashion trends in Shagoni River. Frank and I were in his Blazer on our way to Ivy's house. The promised blizzard had gone south of us and we were traveling under a cloudless sky with light from a three quarter moon.

"Okay," said Frank. "And who's the guy?"

"Greg Wetherell. He's a lawyer who had a practice in Whitehall, but now he's going to work in Stanford."

"Wetherell — now that name sounds familiar. Have I met him?"

"No. Or at least, not through me. Ivy's been keeping him all to herself."

"Oh wait. I'm pretty sure I have met him."

"Really — when?"

"Last summer," he said. "Remember that dead woman who got washed up on the dunes?"

"Of course I remember. She was my friend."

"Working the case, I had reason to talk with Greg Wetherell."

"What reason?"

"Because I found some calls to him on her phone bill."

"Oh, now I remember. So what was your impression of Greg?"

"Pleasant enough guy — under the circumstances. We met in a bar and he was half loaded by the time I got there."

"Maybe he was nervous about talking to a detective. How did he explain the calls?"

"He admitted to having — I think he called it — a little fling with the victim."

"No surprise there. Greg is prone to little flings. Ivy has cried on my shoulder more than once."

"So he's a horndog?"

"I'd call him a womanizer."

"Same thing, I guess. So how is this new arrangement going to work out, I wonder?"

"Ivy is definitely possessive — so it looks like he'll have to change his ways — or face her wrath when he comes home smelling of the wrong perfume. Turn left here," I said. "First house on the right."

Four cars and two trucks were already lining the circle drive that fronted Ivy's house. Yellow light poured through a bay window making golden rectangles on the snow. The place was a fifties style ranch house with a small portico, still decorated with the tiny white lights that Ivy tended to put up in November and leave until spring.

We shed our coats and entered a living room with a fireplace at the far end where a real fire crackled behind a metal screen. People were standing around with drinks in hand, their multiple conversations blending into one continuous buzz. A woman laughed loudly. The noise almost, but not quite, drowned out the haunting sound of John Coltrane's saxophone playing his raga-like rendition of *Favorite Things*. Clearly Greg had brought his CD collection with him. Ivy's taste leaned toward the Dixie Chicks and Willie Nelson.

Our hostess appeared, looking sleek in a gold dress with a draped neckline. "So glad you could come," she said, giving me a brief hug. "And you too, Frank." Ivy reached up to put her arms around his neck. "Especially you. I'm so pleased that Tracy managed to pry you away from your work to have a little fun."

She spotted the bottle Frank was holding and grabbed him by the arm. "Bring that right over here," she said as she led us to a table that offered gin, whiskey and bourbon, along with soft drinks and tonic. An ice bucket sat next to a tray of tumblers and stemware. A huge dome of cheese centered a ring of crackers and a variety of creamy dips showed tracks where they had been gouged by chips and pretzels.

I couldn't help but notice a woman standing nearby in a clingy red dress that offered a view of some serious cleavage. She was talking to a dark haired man in gray slacks whose cashmere sweater covered a nice pair of shoulders. Ivy grabbed the man's arm and turned him toward us.

"Greg," she said, "these are my friends. Tracy Quinn is a fellow reporter, and her friend Frank — I can't remember his last name but he's a detective. Anyway folks, this outstanding specimen of manhood is my very own Greg Wetherell."

"Pleased to meet you," said Greg as he clasped my hand and flashed some very white teeth. "And you too," he said to Frank as they indulged in a manly handshake.

"Nice to meet you," Frank said, tactfully pretending that this was their first encounter.

"I hope you won't suffer from culture shock living in Cedar County," I said to Greg. "There's not much excitement here — especially in the winter."

"Well, I'm from Detroit," said Frank, "and I love this place. So it all depends. Do you do any hunting?"

Greg shook his head. "I'm not much with guns. I had a BB gun when I was a kid and it cost my brother his left eye. But I do like fly fishing."

"Then you're in the right place," said Frank. "I live right on the river and I'll be happy to share a couple of my secret spots."

"Sounds good," said Greg. "But it's little cold for fly fishing right now."

"There always ice fishing," said Frank.

"I've never tried it. My winter sport is skiing."

"Downhill?"

He nodded. "I try to get out to Vale at least once a year and the rest of the time I go to Boyne."

Ivy started tugging Greg away from us. "You two help yourselves to goodies and a drink," she said to me and Frank. "I've got some new people for Greg to meet."

We opened our bottle of vodka, found some orange juice, and Frank made screwdrivers. Minutes later, fortified with alcohol and food, I spotted Jane Minor who owns the book store in town. Or, rather, she spotted me and came over to thank me for writing a piece in the paper about her business.

"Your story brought in quite a few new customers," she said. "The month of January was far better than I expected."

"Well, adding that coffee shop was a great idea," I said. "Looks like your store became a gathering spot for winter mornings. Do they buy any books?"

"Once in a while. At least a magazine or newspaper."

As Jane and I continued to chat, I saw Frank talking to Marty Feldon, owner of the 'Bait and Boat' store in town. I figured those two would have plenty to talk about.

The next arrivals were on the boisterous side, and whatever they said set off laughing from everyone within earshot. I looked around and was delighted to see my friend Gavin and his partner Leon. Gavin had been one of my favorite people ever since the day I wandered into his antique store and discovered that we were both new in town. Now he had a friend named Leon who boasted an enviable job. As I understood it, Leon acted as a buyer for a number of art and antique dealers so he got to travel abroad several times a year.

These two approached the drinks table and Leon offered up a bottle of German wine called *Liebfraumilch.*

"This," he said, brandishing the bottle, "translates as *milk of the virgin.* Very rare German wine."

Gavin gave me a hug and whispered, "We bought it at the grocery store in town."

Leon proceeded to uncork the bottle and then poured drinks for himself and Gavin and a few other oenophiles. He and Gavin moved toward the fireplace and I joined the little group which gathered around them. Peering through his coke bottle glasses, Leon regaled us with stories about his recent trip to France. He told us that hotel rooms in Paris are cold in the winter and his room offered a bidet for which he had no use; that the food is good if one knows what to order; but Parisiennes, especially waiters, take every opportunity to intimidate American visitors.

I was on my second screwdriver when Ivy sought me out and asked if I would help her in the kitchen. I said yes, of course. The project involved wrapping strips of dough around some little wieners, getting them ready for a trip to the oven.

She pulled a cast iron skillet out of the oven. "I hate this monstrosity," she said, "but Greg insisted that I find space for it. He refuses to use Teflon, says it causes cancer, but so far he hasn't done any cooking so I don't see why it matters."

Ivy continued her monologue as we worked. "I do hope Greg will like living here. Things are a little tight right now — but it will help when I get rid of some of my stuff. Trouble is, I don't want to part with — oh — it looks like the Nelsons are leaving. I'd better see them out." She dried her hands on a towel. "Would you pop these in the oven and set the timer for ten minutes? Please."

She was gone before I had a chance to say yes, which I would have, of course. So I put the pans in the oven and decided it would make sense for me to stay in the kitchen until the baking was finished. Frank found me there just as the timer went off so we both put on oven mitts and rescued the trays. We sampled the little hot bites, then put them on serving dishes and took them out to the table.

The warm croissant tasted so good that I decided to have another, along with a cup of coffee. The entire lot of baked goods was gone within fifteen minutes, and guests continued to make their exits. Ivy was busy seeing them out so I refilled my coffee cup and took a seat on the sofa. Greg stirred the fire with a poker, then replaced the screen and sat next to me. I noticed that his hair was beginning to thin, but he had soft gray eyes and a nice jaw line. I could see why Ivy found him attractive.

"I understand you're going to work with Kevin Dukes," I said.

"That's right. I'm starting next week."

"You must have made a quick decision. How did that happen?"

"It didn't take long," he said, lighting a cigarette. He held out the pack to me and I shook my head. "Sorry, bad habit, I know. Where were we? Oh, Kevin called around two weeks ago, told me about his dad, and asked me if I wanted to take over. I told him I'd think about it. Two days later I had made up my mind. I've always liked Kevin and I think we'll probably get along."

"He does mostly real estate, doesn't he?"

"Right — and that's what I've been doing — along with personal stuff like wills and probate."

"Kevin's dad was village attorney for Shagoni River. Are you interested in that position?"

"Actually, yes. I'm planning to put in my application."

"No kidding — you are?" I remembered what Jim Mcneely had told me about the difficult duties and scant rewards of the job.

Greg shrugged. "I guess it's because I went to high school there — so I have an affection for the town."

"You went to Shagoni River High? I did too. Just my senior year."

We compared notes and found that he had been two years ahead of me. So he was gone by the time I started. By now Frank was sitting in an armchair near Greg and apparently he had overheard us reminiscing about high school.

Frank directed a question at Greg. "Did you ever know Vince Crawley?"

"Vince who?"

"Vince Crawley," I said. "He died recently."

"Oh that," said Greg. "Ivy told me about it. What a shame."

"So did you know him?" said Frank.

"Sure. We called him Vinnie. He was a year ahead of me and we both played basketball, but that was about the extent of it. We ran with different crowds."

Ivy approached and I slid over to make room for her between me and Greg. The four of us were the only ones left. I was tired but also feeling mellow from the food and drink. The fire had burned its way down to embers.

"What about your house in Whitehall?" I said to Greg.

"I've decided to put it up for sale. It came to me when my mother died, but I never did like the location, or the layout."

"So when that gets sold," said Ivy, "we're going to look for a bigger place. We're a little cramped here."

"I'd like to find a place on the lake," he said.

"It'll be lovely," Ivy said as she kissed his cheek. "Won't it, honey?"

He put an arm around her and said, "Yes it'll be lovely."

I saw Frank stifle a yawn. "Guess it's time for us to go," I said. " Never thought we'd be the last ones out of here."

We took our leave with lots of good cheer and promises to get together soon.

But something was bothering me. On the way home I aired my discomfort.

"Frank," I said, "when I take you to a party, I don't think you should start questioning the guests."

"What do you mean?"

"You know what I mean. I suppose you asked everybody there if they knew Vince Crawley. Can't you ever stop working? I don't like the way you turn a social function into an investigation."

"Gee Tracy, I'm sorry. But you and Greg were talking about high school and I knew that Vince had gone to school there —."

"I'm surprised you haven't quizzed me about him"

"Well, do you know anything?"

"Of course not. I never met him before the ice shanty."

"Well, I'm sorry. Hope I didn't spoil the evening."

"Oh I guess it didn't bother them. They're too busy being in lust. Do you think it will last?"

"Haven't a clue," he said. "Isn't that your department?"

"Well, Ivy's over the moon. But I kind of wonder about Greg. Maybe he's just using her as a stopover."

"Could be. When he buys that lake house, he might want to be a bachelor again."

"That's what I'm afraid of. And if Ivy gets dumped, she'll be not only crying on my shoulder — but also ranting and raving."

He chuckled. "Isn't that what friends are for?"

"Easy for you to say. Any guys ever dump their problems on you?"

"Only my cousin Arnie."

"Oh right, poor Arnie." Frank's cousin had recently endured an acrimonious divorce. "How's he doing?"

"Better, I'd say."

"So, for therapy, you guys get together and go deer hunting."

"Right. It solves everything. Too bad it only comes once a year."

CHAPTER NINE

Frank stayed overnight and we indulged in a leisurely breakfast. He used my washer to do his laundry and then took the soggy mass to the laundromat for drying. The lovely old house I had inherited from my grandfather did not include a clothes dryer, so I had learned to live without one.

Shortly after Frank left, I got out the vacuum and tackled the living room carpet. The noise I was generating nearly drowned out the sound of the telephone. When I finally picked up, I heard Jewell's voice.

"Hang on a minute," I said, as I reached to turn off the vacuum.

"I don't mean to interrupt if you have company," Jewell said tactfully.

"My company is drying his clothes right now — and probably having a beer down at the Belly Up."

Jewell laughed and said, "Vince Crawley's funeral is Tuesday. I won't be able to attend but I'm planning to go to visitation Monday night. Would you care to join me?"

"Sure, I'll go." My response was automatic because I'm always happy to spend time with Jewell. But then I had a second thought. "Would it seem weird because I've never actually met the — ah — deceased?"

"Except for that time in the ice shanty."

"I don't think it counts if the person is already dead."

"In any case, you do know Fiona. That's reason enough. Your presence would be a gesture of support for her."

"You're right. What time shall I be ready?"

"I'll pick you up at seven."

When Frank returned I asked him to move the sofa and recliner so I could vacuum those long neglected spots. We found seventy five cents in change and started a collection jar for some future treat. Our relationship was getting downright domestic. In the kitchen, I washed dishes while he cleaned the counter tops and swept the floor.

Chores done, Frank and I decided to have a game of chess before he went home. I had learned the basics of chess while I was in college — but since then it had been difficult to find an opponent willing to play against such a rank amateur as myself. Anyone I did play usually wiped me out in less than a minute and that didn't help me at all toward improving my meager skills.

But Frank said he wasn't very good either (I didn't believe him) and he would treat the game as a lesson. We set up the board and started moving our pawns. I played defensively, always wary of his knights because those pieces are so sneaky. For some reason the knights have been granted the ability to make obscure moves which I can never foresee. So I watched his knights carefully, but could never figure out how to use my own.

Ten minutes into the game I used my bishop to take one of his pawns which made me feel very clever.

"Jewell called while you were gone," I said. "Vince's funeral is Tuesday at St. Simon's. I don't know what time."

"It'll be in the morning." He used his knight to take my bishop.

I said a bad word, then asked him how he knew the funeral would be in the morning.

"Catholic funerals are held in the morning. It's a mass for the dead and, with few exceptions, masses are held in the morning."

"I guess you learn that stuff growing up."

"Yeah — it tends to stay with you. Are you sure you want to put your rook there?"

I studied my rook's new position and he let me change the move. Finally I said, "Visitation will be Monday and I'm planning to go with Jewell."

"That's good," he said. "Keep your ears open."

"You think I'll pick up a clue?"

"Maybe, maybe not." He shrugged as he moved his queen. "Sometimes a little detail about the family turns out to be helpful."

Frank won the game but it took him an hour to do it and, by the time it was over, I felt that I had learned a few things about chess. He promised me a rematch but said it would have to be another day because he wanted to get home before dark. We raided my refrigerator, made sandwiches and had an early meal before he left.

On our way to the funeral home Monday evening, I told Jewell that the lab tests on Vince Crawley had revealed chloral hydrate in his blood. "I know chloral hydrate is a sleeper," I said. "Is it hard to get?"

Jewell slowed to navigate around a five-foot bank of snow on a street corner. "It's a controlled substance," she said, "so the pharmacies keep it locked up. But anyone can get it at a drug store with a prescription."

"Is it common? Something people would have in their medicine chest?"

"It's not used as much as it used to be, because there are so many new drugs on the market. But chloral hydrate comes in liquid form so it's good for elderly people who have trouble swallowing."

I debated before I asked my next question. "Do you ever wonder about Fiona — having anything to do with this?"

"I'd rather not think about that. At least not right now."

"You're right. I'm sorry I brought it up."

Jewell edged her car into the nearly full parking lot. Inside, we signed the guest book. Then we joined the line of visitors making their way into the visitation room which was already crowded with people, many of whom I recognized. Jewell merged with the crowd that was moving toward the casket. I decided not to follow her since

I had already seen Vince Crawley dead and didn't care to repeat the experience.

The room was warm so I shrugged off my coat and looked around until I spotted a coat rack in an alcove. I walked over to the rack. While searching for an empty hanger, I heard voices coming from an adjoining room where the door was slightly ajar.

I froze and listened, because one of the voices was Fiona's. She seemed to be in a heated discussion.

"You know dad would want me to have it," said a male voice.

"How can I give you the boat?" said Fiona. "The thing's not even paid for."

"I can make the payments."

"Like hell you can. The creditors will be after me."

"You never did like me."

"Don't be silly. I'm giving you the truck. And remember you've got two sisters. What are they getting?"

"That's different. Dad and I were in business together. I need the boat —."

"Chip, this is not the time or place for us to have this argument. We have to get out there. Now either act like an adult, or go home." The sound of footsteps indicated that one of them was heading for the door.

Anxious not to be caught eavesdropping, I hung up my coat, scooted away and struck up a conversation with a total stranger. Seconds later Fiona emerged. The widow looked sad but composed in a dark green suit, her mass of curly hair swept up on her head and held in place with combs. She headed straight for an elderly couple and greeted them warmly, making me think they might be Vince Crawley's parents.

I kept an eye on the doorway and, minutes later, saw a young man emerge from the room that Fiona had recently vacated. Vince Crawley's son Chip was short and stocky, dressed in faded blue jeans with a clean white shirt, making me think that Fiona must have ironed — or possibly purchased — the shirt for him. His hair cut was an outdated style usually called a mullet, crew cut on top and long in back. Chip also greeted the elderly couple, hugging the frail woman whose powdery cheeks revealed streaks of tears.

Looking around, I spotted Jewell standing in front of a bulletin board covered with photos. I joined her there and we perused the display. We saw Vince as a toddler, followed by a series of grade school photos and then a family snapshot that included a sister. As a young man, Vince showed off a string of fish, then his baseball uniform and finally his date at the prom.

Then there was a wedding photo with Vince in a tux and the bride in a long white dress. But the bride had light brown hair.

"That doesn't look like Fiona," I whispered to Jewell.

"It isn't," she whispered back. "He was married before."

"Oh, of course." That's when I remembered Fiona mentioning Vince's children from a previous marriage.

Jewell and I moved to another bulletin board These photos showed Vince with his own growing family — holding a little boy, then playing Santa to a pair of girls. The most formal portrait showed Vince with his wife and all three children. After that, there seemed to be a time lapse. Then a somewhat older Vince, wearing a suit, stood on the steps of a large building next to Fiona in a blue dress.

"Do you think that's their wedding?" I whispered.

"I'll bet it is. Court house steps somewhere."

"Not near as formal."

"Second marriages are usually that way. "Oh, hello Fiona," Jewell said, raising her voice to let me know that the widow was close behind me.

I caught my breath, turned around and gave Fiona a hug. "I'm so sorry," I said. "This must be a difficult time for you."

"In more ways that one," she said hoarsely. "But thanks for coming."

"It was good of you to include the first wife," Jewell said, nodding toward the photos.

Fiona shrugged. "It would have been dumb to leave her out," she said. "Dixie was married to him longer than I was. She was the mother of his kids."

"Is Dixie here tonight?" The words were out of my mouth before I could decide whether or not the question was politically correct.

CHAPTER TEN

It was too late to swallow my words. Apparently my mouth had been working faster than my brain when I asked Fiona if her deceased husband's ex-wife was at his visitation.

But the widow answered my question without any apparent discomfort. "No, Dixie's not here. We tried and tried to reach her and never had any luck."

"That's too bad — I guess." Or maybe not. Maybe Dixie wouldn't want to attend. Would I want to attend my ex-husband's funeral? Moot question.

"It's not just her," Fiona continued, "but the bad part is that we can't find his daughter Rose."

"His daughter too?" said Jewell. "Where is she?"

"Last we heard Rose was living in san Francisco. She moved out there right after Vince and I got married. Said she wanted to be a writer — but she didn't write home."

"Is she still there?"

"As far as we know. Rose only came home once. And then she didn't even stay with us — spent all of her time with her friends."

"Did you ever meet his ex-wife?" I said.

"Dixie? Oh yeah, we got along okay. But then about a year ago Dixie went to California to visit Rose — and she never came back."

"So many loose ends," said Jewell.

Fiona nodded. "We tried everything we could think of. I called her number and left a message. But I couldn't even tell if it was her phone or somebody else's — it was one of those automatic voices. Anyway, no one ever called back. We tried information but there was no listing."

"Maybe she got a cell phone."

"That what Charlene said. She's the other sister. Chip and Charlene, they asked around, talked to all the kids who knew Rose. One of them had an e-mail address but when we tried that, it bounced back with a fatal error — ha. That was a good one."

Fiona then turned her attention to a young woman approaching her who wore a black sweater and long skirt that hid any curves she might have possessed.

Fiona reached out to take the girl's hand and introduced us, saying, "Ladies, this is Vince's daughter, Charlene."

Charlene acknowledged us with a silent nod. Unlike her brother, she was tall and thin, with straight brown hair pulled into a lanky pony tail. Nothing like Fiona, I thought. Well of course, dummy, Fiona was not her mother. Charlene's face was blotchy and she peered at us with reddened eyes from behind a fringe of long, sparse bangs.

"Charlene, you look beat," said Fiona.

"It's these damn heels," she said, indicating her brown pumps. "I don't know why I even bothered. Dad certainly doesn't care about my shoes."

"Why don't you go sit down for a bit," said Fiona, indicating a nearby love seat.

"Would that be okay?"

"Of course," said Fiona. "Go ahead."

Charlene headed for the velvet settee.

"I'll go keep her company," I said, and went over to sit beside her. We were both silent while I struggled for something to say.

"It's too bad —," I began.

Charlene shook her head, took out a handkerchief and blew her nose. She stuffed the handkerchief into her sleeve, and looked straight ahead.

"It's too bad your sister couldn't be here," I said.

"Rose. Oh yeah, my big sister. What a bitch. Two weeks after Dad married Fiona she took off to California. Guess she figured it was her last chance to be a hippie."

"Was she upset when your dad — ah — remarried?"

Charlene stared at me, as though considering whether this was any of my business. Then she shrugged. "Not really. By then we didn't care. The hard part was when they first split up."

"Were you living at home then?"

Charlene looked down as though studying the pattern of the rug. "Yeah, I was the only one left at home. I was a junior in high school when mom basically kicked him out. Maybe he had it coming — I don't know. I know he was drinking a lot, but he never, like, mistreated us or anything. So it was just me and mom for a while. We didn't get along very good so I got out as soon as I graduated. Moved to Muskegon and got a job with the telephone company. Bright lights and big city — hah!!"

"What about Chip?"

"He was in the service. Then Rose got divorced so she moved back in with mom for a while."

"Were you and your sister close?"

"Hardly. Mom and Rose always made me feel left out. And later, they had that in common — being divorced. Finally Rose goes out west, hardly ever comes home. Then, wouldn't you know it, mom goes out to see her and never comes back either. Like the rest of us don't matter. Then Dad gets sick and — uh oh — I'd better see what my idiot brother wants."

Across the room, Chip was motioning to her. She stood and left me without a backward glance. I was not offended. The girl had a lot on her narrow shoulders.

Jewell and I stayed a while longer, talking with people we knew — and listening to others. I recognized a couple of Vince's fishing buddies, cleaned up for the occasion. They talked about fishing with Vince and drinking with Vince (the two activities seemed inseparable) but I didn't hear any speculation about his death.

On the way home I told Jewell what I had overheard — Chip arguing with Fiona about the disposition of the boat. "And Charlene seems sort of angry at everybody."

"You have to remember," said Jewell, "that a death in the family brings out the worst in everyone."

"Guess you're right about that. I was a real brat after my mother died. I'm not sure how my grandparents put up with me."

"People do what they have to. Learn anything else from Charlene?"

"She thinks her mother and Rose are both in California, but nobody knows for sure."

"That seems a little strange," said Jewell. "I mean about them being totally out of touch."

"Yes, it does. Especially with her own kids." Then I remembered something else I had overheard. "Charlene started to say something about her dad being sick — but she never quite finished. Do you have any idea what that was about?"

"Yes, I do. Fiona told me that Vince had been diagnosed with cancer — pancreatic cancer."

"So that was it." I thought for a moment. "But isn't that diagnosis pretty, um, grim?"

"Grim is an understatement. Nobody lives long with cancer of the pancreas. Usually about a year."

"So why would anybody want to kill a dying man?" I wondered.

Jewell spent a few seconds framing her response. "Don't repeat this," she said at last, "but — to me at least — it's starting to look more like suicide."

"That's what I was thinking too."

"Except for one thing."

"What's that?"

"Vince was Catholic. I gather he rarely went to church, but he was raised Catholic. And suicide is considered a mortal sin."

"Do you think he was in a lot of pain?" I said.

"They aren't, usually."

"Maybe he had the prescription for chloral hydrate — and just decided to OD."

"I guess Frank can find out from his doctor," she said.

"But I wonder — how many people knew about Vince's diagnosis?"

"Not very many, I gather. Fiona said he didn't like to talk about his problems."

"I guess Vince's problems are over now."

"That all depends."

"On what?"

"On whether you belief in the afterlife."

"So maybe we should light a candle for him?"

"Guess it wouldn't hurt."

Early Wednesday morning Marge accosted me in the hallway. Some time over the weekend she had re-colored her hair, leaning more toward blonde, and her yellow blouse had a big drooping bow at the neck. The effect was that of incipient jaundice. Marge issued a curt good morning and asked when I was going to do the business profile on that sandwich shop in town.

"I've scheduled a visit for later this morning," I said. My plan was to interview the owner and have lunch there when I finished.

"Good," said Marge. "Holly can go with you and try her hand at some photos."

I swallowed hard and bit my tongue — because what I really wanted to do was scream.

Holly Nagel was back.

At least this time I knew what to expect — but that was part of the problem.

Holly was a high school senior taking something called a 'work experience' class. It must have been a plum course for the instructor because all the teacher did was assign students to spend time at any business in town where folks were willing to put up with them.

Last fall Marge had made our newspaper part of the program.

So during that term, someone on staff usually had Holly duty one morning per week We were supposed to rotate the task, but Jake had enough seniority to opt out completely — probably his tendency toward foul language helped his cause. That left three of us — Marge, myself and Kyle, our young sports reporter. Since Kyle didn't mind an adolescent female mooning over him, he usually had more then his share of Holly time.

As it turned out, Holly had proved somewhat helpful last fall, providing me with the crucial information about Marge's boyfriend. Still, I was relieved when the semester ended. But Holly had liked us — or perhaps she liked the easy credit. In any case, she had signed on for another term — this time with a camera.

Lucky us.

I bowed to the inevitable with as much grace as I could muster. "Okay then," I said. "I've got some work to do before we go." I retreated to my office and got busy on my computer. When Holly arrived, Marge took her into the graphics room to talk with Larry about photos. That was a blessing. I managed to finish two stories before I went to the break room to grab a cup of coffee.

That's where Holly found me. She greeted me with a big smile while I stared at the ring piercing her left eyebrow. Was that new? I wasn't sure.

"Hi, Ms. Quinn," she said. "I'm so excited that Marge — I mean Ms. Elliot — is letting me do photos. We've got a school newspaper now and — can you believe it — I'm the editor? I'm getting pretty serious about journalism. I've applied to MSU but my folks say it's too expensive. They want me to go community college for a couple of years and I said I will if I have to, but I refuse to live at home. I told them I can get a part time job and find someone to share an apartment. So how have you been?"

"I'm fine," I said, smiling in spite of myself. The girl was a bit of a pain but it was hard not to be affected by her enthusiasm.

Holly had the long, straight hair I remembered and a sweet round face that she tried to dramatize with blue lipstick and various piercings. Her jeans were tucked into high heeled boots that boasted a row of buckles. The boots didn't look very weatherproof or functional.

We were about to find out.

"We're going to walk," I told her as we retrieved our coats. "It's only about two blocks from here."

"Oh cool," she said. "Fresh air."

We stepped outside. The temperature was fifteen degrees according to the sign on the bank. My coat was fleece. Holly had a denim jacket. I wore gloves and a neck scarf. Holly had neither and seemed unconcerned. Snow had fallen overnight and we were confined to a narrow, icy path on the sidewalk. But Holly and her boots managed the walk without incident.

Within minutes we reached a shop on the corner where yellow lights were visible through steamed up windows. As we entered we were engulfed by yeasty cinnamon smells that came wafting from the kitchen. There were half a dozen round tables, only one of them occupied by a pair of men drinking coffee. The menu was written on a blackboard and claimed to offer the "Best Reuben this side of New York."

Seeing no one behind the counter, I walked back to the kitchen where I found Jennie Miller kneading dough on the counter. Jennie is probably about forty but she always makes me think of Raggedy Ann because of her braids and the faint sprinkle of freckles across her cheeks.

"Hey, good timing," she said when she saw me. "I have to leave this to rise for an hour." She gave the dough some final pats, covered it with a dish towel, and took off her apron.

I introduced Holly and explained that she would be taking some photos.

"Fine," said Jennie, "let's go up front. There's plenty of room right now."

We went to the front where Jennie checked on her two customers, then directed us to a table covered with a flowered oilcloth. She produced a soda for Holly and mugs of coffee for us.

We talked for about half an hour and I made a few notes but most of it was easy to remember. Jennie told me it was difficult to keep a business afloat in a tourist town where July and August are the only profitable months. As a result she had turned to mail order sales, making jams, jellies and pickled asparagus to sell through her website. She said her holiday sales were increasing every year.

When the interview was over, Jennie went to check on her bread dough and I worked with Holly on taking photos of the place. With their permission, we included the two customers who were all excited about having their picture in the paper. When that was finished, I told Holly I was planning to have lunch there and asked if she had time to join me.

"Well yes," she said, "I have time but —."

"But what?"

"All I have is about a dollar."

"I'll take care of it."

As it turned out, our lunch was on the house because Jennie said she appreciated the publicity she would be getting from the newspaper feature.

So I tried the Reuben sandwich and Holly took a long time debating before she ordered a hot dog. Holly looked with suspicion at the cole slaw that accompanied her order, but had no problem with the potato chips.

We had chosen a table up front near a window so we had a good view of people walking by on their way to the post office. The lunch crowd came straggling in and now numbered close to ten people.

The sandwich was good. I didn't have to think about making conversation because Holly was in her chatterbox mode. But then she fell silent. I realized that she had stopped eating and was looking at me, twisting her paper napkin. It began to look as though she had something on her mind — either that or indigestion.

"Um, Ms. Quinn—," she said at last.

"You can call me Tracy."

"Okay. There's something I'm worried about. And I haven't been able to tell anyone."

I felt like yelling — *so don't tell me!*

But I just nodded and tried to look receptive — expecting to hear about some kind of problem with puppy love. Then I had a scary thought and hoped she wasn't pregnant. But she had never even mentioned a boyfriend. Still, what did I know about the mating patterns of today's adolescents?

"Well you see —." She coughed, took a drink, looked at her plate.

I waited. Now I was frozen too, holding my sandwich in midair — stopped on its trajectory toward my mouth.

"The thing is — it's about my dad." She fell silent again.

"So — what is it about your dad?" I began to wonder if maybe he beat her or even molested her? My mind raced over unpleasant possibilities.

"I think maybe my dad — well, it looks like maybe —." She stopped, sighed and began again. "I'm not sure, Ms. Quinn, but it looks like — maybe he's, um, like, having an affair."

CHAPTER ELEVEN

Holly's confession left me, literally, speechless.

I stared across the table into her black rimmed eyes and wondered why she had chosen to tell me, of all people, about her father's possible infidelity.

I was not prepared for this. As an only child raised by a single mother, I hadn't a clue about family dynamics — and certainly no training as a counselor. Did this kid have an overactive imagination? I was completely flummoxed. But there she was, waiting for an answer, with that expectant look on her face.

"Umm, Holly, what makes you think that your dad might be, ah, doing what you think he's doing?"

She chewed her lower lip before she answered. "If I tell you, will you promise not to laugh?"

"Of course. I mean of course I won't laugh."

"Okay. I saw something — on Homecoming night."

"Homecoming? When was that?"

"After the basketball game. It's always the second game after Christmas break."

"Oh sure, I remember now."

Shagoni River High had such a small student body that it had never been able to field a football team. As a result, Homecoming festivities were scheduled around a basketball game, making it a bright spot in midwinter — provided the whole thing didn't get canceled by a blizzard. So this event had been fairly recent. I recalled a picture in the *News* of the Homecoming King and Queen wearing their lopsided crowns with the girl glowing and the boy looking thoroughly embarrassed.

"So I had a date for the dance," said Holly, "and then there was a party after the dance. But the party was lame, so four of us left early — Tiffany Clark and me and two guys. We had some beer in the car and we needed somewhere to go and drink — but, well, all of the usual places down by the lake were snowed in. You know how it is in the winter—". She twisted the packet from her drinking straw.

"Well, yes, I do." I had gone to Shagoni River High School myself and apparently some things hadn't changed much in twenty-five years.

"Right." Holly took a swallow of her root beer and glanced around the room, checking for surveillance. Apparently satisfied, she leaned toward me and continued. "So we had to find another place. Joel, that was Tiffany's date, he was driving, and he said we should try the parking lot at the Best Western Motel."

"That new one out by the highway?"

"Right. It's out of town, the lot is plowed, and there's nobody around after midnight. So that's what we did — for a while."

"Okay. But what does this have to do with your dad?"

"I'm just getting to that part."

"Okay, sorry."

"So then, just as we were pulling out of the lot, I saw my dad's car parked at the motel. I knew the car was his, but I was so spooked that I didn't say anything to the others kids. I just said I didn't feel good and wanted to go home. Even though it was only a little after three."

"But Holly, how can you be sure it was him? Maybe it was someone else —with a similar car."

She shook her head. "A couple of things. First of all it had a bumper sticker that said *Visit the Mystery Spot.* Dad was kind of angry when that got pasted on two years ago at some tourist trap in California."

"Still, there could be others —."

"And then I recognized my stuffed elephant in the back window."

"Oh. Guess there aren't too many of those around."

"And I couldn't see the whole license plate but the first letters were ER. He ordered that special."

"Okay, it sounds like the car was his. But maybe he was — what — there with your mom? Does the place have a bar or restaurant?"

"I don't think so. And anyway — my mom was waiting up for me when I got home."

"And your dad — ?"

"My dad wasn't home."

"Was your mother upset about — your dad not being home?"

"Well, that's the thing. My dad is gone a lot because he's a doctor and works in the emergency room — so it's no big deal for him to be gone overnight."

"I see. But it's hard to figure out a reason for his car being at the No Tell Motel."

Holly nodded, her eyes brimming. I was afraid her mascara might start running. "What should I do?" she said. "Should I tell my mom?"

Talk about a rock and a hard place. Any answer I could provide seemed fraught with horrible consequences. I really needed to talk with Jewell about this. Then I had a thought. "Holly, what hospital does your dad work at?"

"The one in Wexford."

"Okay, good. I have a friend who works there. Maybe she can find out about his schedule."

"That would help. I don't want to cause any trouble — but I just feel bad when I'm with my mom. Like I'm lying to her by keeping this a secret."

"Do you have any brothers or sisters?"

"My sister's only eight years old. I don't think I should tell her."

"No, you're right about that." Stalling seemed like the best option. Hopefully Jewell could give me some advice on handling this. "Look Holly, just keep this to yourself a little while longer. I'll see what I can find out. I should know something by next week."

She smiled as though a huge burden had been lifted from her. "Thanks Ms Quinn, uh, Tracy. Thanks a lot. I feel so much better now that I've talked about it."

Well, maybe Holly felt better — but I sure didn't.

Back at work, I was relieved to find that Marge was out of the office, and not expected back any time soon. As a result, I had a stretch of uninterrupted time at my computer, my only company being Kyle at his desk on the other side of the newsroom. The click of keys was our only conversation. While some have labeled our youngest reporter anti-social, I am not offended by his lack of small talk. Maybe Kyle is that way with everyone, or maybe he just can't converse with anyone over thirty — which includes all of our staff.

It was a few minutes after four when Kyle closed down and grabbed his coat, gruffly informing me that he had an evening basketball game to cover.

"Enjoy the cheerleaders," I said.

He made a noise that was likely intended as a derisive snort and slammed the door behind him.

Twenty minutes later I started to think about going home. Heaven knows I had put in enough extra time to justify an early departure. Propelled by this rationale, I reviewed my latest story, tweaked it and got ready to close down.

But then I heard the front door open. Marge came in and started issuing directives.

"Tracy, there's some kind of flap going on over at Rash Street. I need you to go check it out."

"Oh great," I said. "The usual?"

"Looks that way."

I didn't even need to ask for the address. I was only too familiar with 525 Rash Street, the home of Woody Pucket, whose primary purpose in life seemed to be causing maximum irritation to his neighbors and the village officials.

"So what's the problem this time?"

"The lady across the street called Chief Bridges because she saw a big dump truck pulling into Woody's driveway. She's afraid he's going to dump another huge load of slab wood — like he did last winter. Hopefully Bridges will get there in time to head off the delivery."

"I'll go over and take a look," I said, "and then I'll just go home."

Minutes later I was zipping up my coat and then added the knit cap that I use for serious outdoor assignments. Out in the parking lot, I discovered that my Honda had a new coating of ice, but I didn't take time to find a scraper and launch a proper attack on the windshield. Instead, I drove through town half blind, with the driver's side window down to increase my visibility. Unsafe, of course, but I only had a few blocks to go.

My destination on Rash Street was a two-story frame house that might have been white at one time — but now the paint had flaked so much that it was hard to tell what the original color might have been. One of the upstairs windows had a pane missing and the hole was plugged with cardboard. The house sat on a long narrow lot and the driveway was occupied by a large truck. The truck was backed into the driveway and had the words Schimmler Saw Mill on the driver side door.

A small convoy seemed to be gathering. A rusty pick-up truck with a snowplow was parked in front of the house, and right behind that was a black and white Shagoni River Police car. I parked across the street behind a gray sedan that had just pulled in, and saw a man in a black leather coat emerge from the car. When he started across the street, I recognized Greg Wetherel.

"Hey Greg," I said, running a few steps to catch up with him.

He slowed mid stride and looked at me. "Oh hi — Tracy, right?"

"Right. Are you here in your — official capacity?"

"Afraid so," he said. "The council met yesterday and appointed me as acting village attorney. As luck would have it, I was at village hall today when Chief Bridges got the call. Mcneely's out of town so I got the duty. I guess there's some kind of restraining order against this guy — to stop him collecting more trash in his yard. What's his name anyway?"

"Woody Pucket," I said, "more commonly known as the Trash Man."

I fell into single file behind Greg so we could squeeze through the narrow space between the truck and the piled up snow. The truck had its engine running so the air was thick with diesel fumes. I slipped and nearly fell, but steadied myself against an oversized fender. When I finally rounded the back end of the truck, I saw four men. One was our chief of police, Owen Bridges, his nose and cheeks red from the cold as he stood facing off against the owner of the house.

His adversary, Woody Pucket, wore a khaki jacket which hung loosely on his stoop shouldered frame and a sparse gray beard that failed to hide the pock marks on his gaunt cheeks.

"Who the hell says I can't buy a load of slab wood?" Pucket said to Bridges, punctuating his statement with a stream of tobacco juice directed onto the snow at their feet.

Standing next to Woody in head-to-toe camouflage was a shorter man who looked vaguely familiar. "Yeah, who says?" echoed the sidekick. That's when I recognized Chip Crawley, whom I had last seen at his father's visitation.

"Well, there's been a complaint," said Bridges, trying to maintain an authoritative posture while trapped between the two men and the back of the oversized truck.

Now the fourth man weighed in. Hank Schimmler was a large man with a bushy red beard. "Look," he said to Bridges, "this guy ordered some slab wood and I'm here to deliver it. It don't come cheap to drive this big rig around. Now can I dump it or not?"

"There's a restraining order," said Bridges.

"Against what?" said Woody. "You got the order?"

Chief Bridges glanced at us, the newcomers to this little fracas. "This here is our village attorney," he said, indicating Greg. "He can tell you."

"There's a restraining order," said Greg, "against the depositing of any litter, trash, garbage, refuse or other material on the property where it is visible to a neighbor or general traffic." As he recited this, he reached inside his coat and pulled out a thick envelope.

"Well this ain't no trash," said Woody. "This here is my fuel."

"Then you should keep it in a woodshed," said Bridges.

"It's goin' in my garage," said Woody, "just as soon as it gets unloaded."

"Let's see this garage," said Bridges.

"Right here." Woody pointed to a building behind him that looked like a small garage, built when cars were a new idea.

"Let's take a look inside," said Bridges.

Woody kicked aside some snow and managed to pull the door of the building open a couple of feet. Greg and Bridges looked in first and, when they were finished, I went to have a look for myself. The only light came through one dirty window, but I made out shoulder high stacks of crates and boxes that leaned at odd angles against two of the walls. The third wall featured a work table nearly buried under metal parts that must have come from old lawnmowers, bicycles, and perhaps a motorcycle or two.

"How you gonna get the wood in there?" said Bridges.

"Plenty of room," said Woody. "Just needs to be arranged."

"Yeah," said Chip "I'm gonna help him get organized in there."

"In the meantime," said Bridges, "the pile of wood is going to sit out here and be an eyesore. Just like before. Can't let you do that."

"I'll stack it on the back porch to start with," said Woody.

"Nope," said Bridges, "that's a fire hazard."

"Damn, you folks won't let a guy live his life." Woody's hands tightened into fists, opened slowly, then clenched again. "There's no law against heating with wood. That's how I live."

"You guy are discriminatin'" said Chip. "We'll sue you guys — that's what we'll do."

"This is wasting my time," said Schimmler. "What's the story? Do I unload or not?"

Greg eyed the business end of the dump truck, which loomed well above our heads. "Do you think you could unload part of it? Then we'll keep an eye out and see how long it takes him to get it out of sight."

Bridges said, "Yeah, can you do that?"

"Guess I can," said Schimmler. "Got a woman out in Elbridge who called yesterday. She can take the rest."

Chief Bridges nodded his acquiescence to the plan and finally Woody did too. Nobody was completely satisfied but the immediate crisis had been averted.

Schimmler walked to the cab of his truck and climbed in. He leaned out the window and said, "You folks best clear out."

"Sure," said Greg. Bridges and I nodded our agreement. None of us was eager to get buried under a load of slab wood. We started to leave but then were stopped by Schimmler who had changed his mind and climbed down from the cab. We stood aside to make room for him while he approached Woody Pucket.

"Woody," he said, "you got to pay me first. And I want it in cash."

"Damn," said Woody. "Don't nobody trust nobody any more?"

If there was another comment I didn't hear it, because the scream of a fire siren filled the air.

CHAPTER TWELVE

Reacting to the fire siren, I trotted to my car, climbed in and managed a U-turn, just in time to see two fire trucks moving north on Hancock Street. I followed the trucks at a respectable distance and when I saw them make a right turn onto Plum Street, I was pretty sure I knew where we were heading.

Sure enough, the trucks had stopped at the home of Grace Morrisen, a one story brick house with a large stone chimney at one end. That chimney was the center of attention now as it belched black smoke and sparks that fizzled out on the snow.

I parked and got out, joining the small knot of neighbors who had gathered. We stood across the street from the action as two firemen hauled a ladder from one of the trucks and leaned it against the house. A third firefighter clambered up the ladder with a hose, pointed it down the chimney and yelled to someone at the tanker truck. Seconds later a stream of water blasted down the chimney causing a volcano of smoke and steam to erupt, along with a few gouts of flame.

Now there were three firefighters on the roof. A bulky figure in fire gear emerged from the house, yelled something to the men on the roof. Then he stood by, watching. After a few minutes I realized that this was our fire chief, Milt Jackson. When I judged that I wouldn't be interfering, I walked over to him.

"I see the press is here," he said.

"And this looks like another chimney fire — right?"

Jackson chief nodded. "We keep telling her it's not a good idea to burn her Christmas tree in the fireplace, but she won't quit."

"Maybe it's some kind of ritual from her home country."

"Yeah, maybe that's how they do it do back in Slovenia."

"Off the record," I said, "does this kind of thing upset you?" He didn't respond so I continued. "I mean — getting called out for something like this. Isn't it a waste of everybody's time and money?"

"It's what we do," he said noncommittally. Then his fleshy face betrayed a grin. "Besides, it gives the men a little exercise — actually the men and the new girl — ah woman."

Now I smelled a story. "You have a female fire — person?"

He nodded.

"Is she the first?"

"Definitely the first for Shagoni River — although it's fairly common elsewhere. I mean in the big cities."

"How is she working out?"

"She's learning as fast as anyone — better than some. But — off the record, okay?" I nodded. "Well — some of the guys are having a problem getting used to the idea."

"They think the fire brigade is a boys' club?"

"Right. But I've told them — we don't have much choice. We're all-volunteer so we need people who live in town but can drop what they're doing when the whistle blows. The young men aren't signing on because they work out of town. So when a couple of the ladies applied, I decided to give them a try."

"Well, I'd like to do a story on it sometime. If that's okay with you."

He grimaced, but said nothing.

"Not a good idea?" I said.

"Actually, I'd rather you wait awhile before you do that. The guys are just getting used to it and putting this in the paper would just — I don't know —."

"Rub it in?"

"Something like that. You know how the guys at the bar chew a subject to death

82

— until they get a new one."

"Okay," I said, thinking I'd never make a hard-nosed investigative reporter. "I'll check with you later — maybe next summer."

"Thanks Tracy, thanks a lot." As he spoke Milt Jackson raised a hand to greet someone who was coming up behind me. "Well look who's here," he said.

I turned to see a big guy in a brown canvas jacket and my heart gave a little thump. It was Frank Kolowsky whom I hadn't seen for three days.

Frank linked his arm through mine while he exchanged a few comments with Jackson. Although everyone in town knew that we were an item, we tried to limit our public displays of affection. Then the chief left us, heading for the tanker truck where firefighters were reeling in the hose.

"Are you working?" said Frank. "I don't see your notebook."

"I followed the fire truck, but Grace Morrissen's chimney fires don't make the news any more. What are you up to?"

"I drove to Lansing today and the roads were nasty. But I'm glad to be home. And I'm hungry — how about you?"

"Starved."

Half an hour later we were at the Belly Up chugging a pair of longnecks while waiting for pizza. I told Frank about being sent to Woody Pucket's house.

"Greg Wetherel showed up about the same time I did. He's already acting as village attorney."

"So how did Greg do?"

"Pretty good, I'd say. Sort of cooled things down so nobody got hurt."

"Is he going to get the job?"

"It looks that way. But the village still has to go through the whole process — advertise and review applications. But Mcneely said earlier he didn't think anyone else would be interested. He's probably relieved that Greg showed up when he did."

We fell silent as our waitress set the pizza on the table, all hot and steamy with the cheese still bubbling. While we tucked in, our conversation was limited to comments on the flaky crust, the spicy pepperoni or the fact that one of us had a string of cheese decorating a cheek or chin.

There were only two pieces left and we were considering a second round of beers when I said, "Frank, there's something I've been wanting to ask you."

"What's that?"

"About the Vince Crawley situation."

"Okay. I'll answer if I can."

"Did you ever talk with Fiona Crawley's mother? About that Saturday night?"

"Oh that. Yes I did and —."

"Oh shit — wait a minute—." I interrupted him because I had a view of the front door and wasn't thrilled by what I was seeing.

"What?"

"Greg and Ivy just walked in."

"Oh. And does that mean they're going to — ah — join us?"

"Probably. She just saw me and waved."

He turned to look. "And they are moving in our direction. What's the plan? I mean do you want to —?"

"No I don't. I don't want to become a foursome with those two. I'm almost sorry we went to the party. But —."

"The party was your idea."

"Oh, I know. Look, how about we were just getting ready to leave — right?"

"Right. Just leaving."

The pair bore down on us. Ivy was pulling off her gloves and hat, shaking out her hair. "Tracy and Frank," she cried. "What a nice surprise."

I put on something resembling a smile and we all said hello. "Greg and I had a little adventure this morning," I said. "Did he tell you about it?"

"Why no," she said, rolling her eyes in Greg's direction. "But I'm sure he will. Won't you honey?"

"Of course," said Greg. "I'll tell you the whole story. Just haven't had time yet."

"So — do you mind if we join you?" Ivy was already reaching for one of the empty chairs at our table.

"You're welcome to sit here," I said, "but —."

"Unfortunately, Tracy and I can't stay." Frank can be authoritative when he wants to. "We really have to go."

"Oh, that's too bad," she said, batting her eyes. "Can't get you to change your mind?"

Frank shook his head, drained his beer. "Nope," he said. "But you're welcome to the last slice of pizza."

Ivy's face got all pouty. "But why are you running off?"

"Business," said Frank.

"Id love to stay and visit," I lied, "but Frank's got to go. And besides, I'm expecting an important phone call."

"I keep telling you to get a cell phone," she said.

"Guess I'm just technology challenged," I slid into my coat. Frank already had his jacket on. "Well, nice seeing you guys," I said with all the sincerity I could muster.

Once we were outside I started giggling. "I'm afraid we're not very good liars."

"You know what they're probably thinking?"

"What?"

He gave my arm a squeeze. 'They think I just can't wait to get you home and ravish you."

"Actually not a bad idea. But —."

"But what?"

"How about some coffee first?"

"Sounds good. Maybe ice cream too."

I was already in my car when Frank appeared with a scraper and gave my windshield the thorough cleaning that it needed. When we reached my house, Frank grabbed the snow shovel and made a nice path from my driveway, up the steps and right to my front door. There are times when it is nice to have a man around — winter is one of those times.

Inside, I was taking off my boots when I saw the light on my answering machine. I ignored it until we had our coats hung up and Frank was in the kitchen putting on water for coffee. That's when I pushed the play button.

The message was so polished that I thought at first it was a telemarketer. Then I recognized a voice I hadn't heard it a long time. "Tracy," it said, "I know it's been a long time but this is Steven and — I really need to talk with you. Call me at —- ."

I deleted the message.

Frank came into the living room a minute later. I couldn't tell if he had heard the message or not, but he didn't ask me about it. He probably didn't even remember that Steven was the name of my ex-husband. Why should he?

CHAPTER THIRTEEN

I joined Frank in the kitchen where we dished up bowls of ice cream and I did my best to forget about the telephone call from my ex-husband. But then, with coffee mugs in hand, I forgot what I was doing because I couldn't figure out why Steven would call me after all this time. I mean, how long had it been since we had even talked, much less seen each other? Well over five years, likely closer to —.

"Are we ready?" said Frank.

"Oh — sure." I snapped out of my reverie and poured the coffee.

In the living room we made space on the coffee table for our cups and once again I tried to rein in my wandering thoughts. Then I realized that Frank was speaking to me. "Oh, sorry, what did you just say?"

"There was something you wanted to ask me."

"There was?"

"Yes. Just before Greg and Ivy walked in."

"Oh right. That. I was wondering if you ever went back to talk with Fiona Crawley's mother."

"Yes, I did."

"Did she shed any light on Fiona's whereabouts — that Saturday night?"

He shook his head. "Not really. I drove up to Manistee and had another visit with Grace O'Malley. She fed me cookies and told me about her son who is a cop in South Haven — and her two other daughters."

"So much for small talk. What about the Saturday night when Fiona's husband died?"

"It was pretty much what we expected. She reported that Fiona had, in fact, spent the night with her — because the weather was bad. Fiona's mother acted as though she didn't remember telling me a different story a week before."

"Great," I said with a sigh. "Either way she can plead bad memory."

"But I did ask her what she meant about Vince. Remember she said that she had told Fiona not to marry him."

"I almost forgot about that. What did she say? Criminal past?"

"No. Just that he drank too much and had no regular job. She said Fiona attracts freeloaders because she's a nurse and always has an income."

"I guess that's entirely possible."

"But there's been another development — something that might render the whole question of Fiona's whereabouts — not all that important."

"Like maybe Vince committed suicide?"

He turned and gave me an appraising look. "So what have you heard, Nancy Drew?"

"That Vince had cancer. Specifically, pancreatic cancer which is pretty much a death sentence."

"And you heard this — where?"

"Vince's daughter Charlene mentioned it at the visitation. Then Jewell confirmed it on the way home."

"And the autopsy findings indicated the cancer was spreading to his liver. So suicide is a distinct possibility. Except —." Frank fell silent and stared straight ahead, holding his coffee mug in both hands.

"Except what?"

"It's a hard sell — for me anyway — to believe that someone who was raised Catholic would commit suicide."

"That's what Jewell said too. And I guess you would know about that."

"Yes I do. From the time you're a kid, it gets drummed into your head that suicide is a mortal sin. And no matter how old you are, that stuff tends to stick — like super glue."

"So tell me — about this mortal sin business."

If Frank was surprised at my ignorance, he had the tact not to mention it. "The church says there are two kinds of sin — venial sin and mortal sin."

"And the difference is — ?"

"Sort of like the difference between a misdemeanor and a felony."

"And the mortal sin is God's felony?"

"Right. With eternal bad consequences. No release, ever."

I was quiet for a moment, thinking this over. Then I said, "I'm almost certain that Vince was buried in the cemetery behind St. Simon's Church."

"I checked that out and, yes, he was interred in the Catholic cemetery."

"But isn't there some big deal about where suicides can be buried?"

"Yes, but nowadays the church is more relaxed about that issue. I guess it's pretty much up to the local priest. Besides, at this point nobody knows whether it was or not."

"What's your gut feeling on this one?"

Frank looked thoughtful. "Like I said, it's a little hard for me to believe that Vince would commit suicide."

I reached out and stacked our empty bowls. "Can you find out if Vince had a prescription for chloral hydrate?"

"I'm working on that. Fiona said no, he didn't take any meds except codeine for pain and not much of that. But Vince had at least three doctors and we're contacting all of them to see if he had a prescription that Fiona didn't know about."

"But even if he had the drug — it doesn't mean that he's the one who put it in the whiskey."

"True. But it would have to be someone close to him — like maybe his wife."

"Why do you persist in picking on Fiona?"

"I'm just being objective. The spouse is always the prime suspect."

"Don't forget his son Chip. He seems like a loose cannon. Today he was over at Woody Pucket's house complicating the situation. Does Chip have his dad's truck now?"

"Yes, we let him have it. We searched it but didn't find anything helpful."

"Then I saw the truck today. And I'm pretty sure there was a gun mounted across the back window."

"The gun is a new addition. But it's legal to carry a rifle that way."

"And Chip seems to have a lot of anger." I stood and headed for the kitchen. "At the visitation, I heard him arguing with Fiona because he wanted the boat."

"I've already had a talk with Chip," Frank said when I returned to sit beside him. He stretched his legs and kicked off his boots. "Chip insisted that he didn't see his father at all on the Saturday in question. Said he was out snowmobiling with friends."

"You think that's true?"

"I tracked down one of the friends. And he backed up the story."

"Well, sure — but friends will always alibi —."

"I also talked to the bartender at the Crystal Valley Tavern. She said that Chip was in there with two buddies late Saturday afternoon, all wearing snowmobile gear. They ate hamburgers, shot pool, hung around a couple of hours."

"Okay then. I suppose the CVT bartender is a pretty reliable source."

"One of the best."

"And I suppose you had a beer during this investigative visit."

"Seemed the friendly thing to do."

"Hey, isn't the bartender that woman with the big —?"

"Yes, it was Annie. So what?"

"Oh nothing. But think about this. Chip could have doctored his dad's whiskey the day before."

"Yes, it could have been Chip or Fiona or somebody else entirely. But remember this," he said. "The other fishermen drank with Vince and none of them reported feeling sleepy."

"So the question is — when did the stuff get put into the whiskey bottle?"

"I think it must have happened while he was in the ice shanty."

"Okay. And that leaves the question of who put it there."

"That's all we need to figure out," Frank said as he reached over and pulled me close. "And we'll have this case all wrapped up."

The next evening I had supper with Jewell. Paul was away so it was just the two of us having chili and cornbread and our usual free flow of conversation. We were almost through when I proceeded to unload my latest problem on her.

"Jewell," I said, "do you remember Holly Nagel?"

"I think so. Isn't she the high school girl who interned at the newspaper?"

"Yes. And now she's back for another semester."

"You sound perturbed. Is that difficult for you?"

"Not really. I can deal with Holly." I put down my spoon. " But here's the thing. For some reason she has chosen to share a family crisis with me — and I have no idea how to help her."

"So tell me about it. Let's go in by the fire."

That's what I love about Jewell. She seems to actually welcome other people's troubles. So I cleared up the table while she made cocoa. Then we took our cups to the living room where we sat facing the fireplace and watching the blue flame dancing above the fire log.

"This feels wonderful," I said. "Thanks for inviting me."

"You were going to tell me something about Holly."

"Yes, I was." I struggled a bit, not sure where to begin. "Did you know that Holly's dad is a doctor?"

"Guess not. What's her last name?"

"Nagel. So he would be Dr. Nagel."

"Why that must be Todd Nagel." Jewell's voice registered surprise as she made the connection. "He's one of our Emergency Room doctors."

"So — does he work long hours?"

91

"Sure. The ER doctors work forty-eight hour shifts. That doesn't mean they're awake all that time. There is a doctors' lounge with a bed and they get to sleep a few hours when things are quiet."

"Holly thinks her dad might be having an affair."

"Oh dear. What makes her think that?"

I stared into the fire for a moment, again searching for the right words. "Okay," I said at last. "It all has to do with a Saturday night when he told the family he was working. But Holly was out late that night and she saw his car parked at the Best Western Motel."

"Oh! And where was Holly's mom?"

"Home alone, waiting up for Holly."

Jewell shook her head and sighed. "You know, Todd has a great sense of humor and sometimes gets flirtatious. But he's professional and there has never been a complaint about him. If there was I would definitely know about it."

"Okay. But can you check the schedule for that night and see if he was at the hospital?" I gave her the date. "I guess there's always the chance that he let someone use his car while he was on duty."

"Or maybe someone took the car without his consent? If it was back by morning he might never have noticed."

"I guess we shouldn't condemn him until we know something more definite. But anyway, will you check it out for me? I promised Holly I'd try to find out something."

"Sure, I'll check it out. There are four doctors in the ER and they have a pretty regular schedule. But let's not start any rumors."

"Of course not. I haven't said a word to anyone but you."

"Excuse me a minute," said Jewell. "I think that's Hamlet at the door." She rose and went to open the back door. Seconds later a brown cocker spaniel made his way to the rug in front of the fire where he flopped down with a groan of pleasure.

"But anyway," said Jewell. "About your friend Holly."

"I just don't understand why she chose me to confide in. I never had any kids and I'm not very good with young people."

Hamlet raised his head and started to chew on the chunks of snow that had frozen onto his legs.

"Tracy, you may not have kids of your own but I think you did very well with Brooke last summer."

"Thanks to your help. Remember, we had our share of crises."

"It was kind of fun though, wasn't it?"

"Yes it was, in a way."

I smiled at the thought of my summer with Brooke Quinn. As the daughter of my ex-husband, the girl shared a last name with me but no blood ties. After being out of my life for a matter of years, she had reappeared as a college student who desperately wanted to spend her summer in Shagoni River — and so came to live with me.

During that eventful summer she had become almost inseparable from Jewell's son Derek. Now both of them had gravitated to Arizona. Derek was living with his uncle in Phoenix and Brooke was going to school in a town called Prescott.

"Have you heard anything from Brooke since she moved?" said Jewell. "I wondered how she would cope with moving so far away to a town where she didn't know a soul."

"She's doing okay, as far as I know. I had a few e-mails and a couple of postcards — all indicating that she's glad she made the switch. She wanted a college that focused on the environment and that is just what she got. Her orientation was a three week camping trip in the Grand Canyon. I answered her last e-mail but got no reply. Guess she's busy with her classes. Do you hear from Derek?"

"Derek called Sunday," she said, reaching down to stroke the dog who had moved closer to her chair. "We talked for almost an hour. He's working full time and taking EMT classes two nights a week. He said he can't wait to get some hands-on experience."

"He may change his mind when things start to get bloody."

"We'll just have to wait and see. But he's managed to buy himself a car and a couple of weeks ago, he drove up to Prescott to see Brooke."

"Great. So she's okay?"

"Better than okay. She took him all over town and he said it was a hoot. Apparently the place is full of coffee houses, art galleries, cowboys and hippies."

"Bars too, no doubt."

"Oh yes. They went to Whiskey Row."

"Sounds like a lot more fun than Shagoni River," I said.

"Especially now. Derek said the weather in Phoenix hits the seventies most days and a cold day is in the sixties. Did I tell you that I'm planning to visit him for a week if I can get the time off?"

"Oh, lucky you."

"Why not come along?"

"Thanks for the invite, but I don't think I can afford it."

Jewell got up and went to the kitchen, returning with a plate of peppermint cookies. "So what else have you been up to?"

"Not much," I replied, feeling suddenly awkward because I didn't want to say anything about Ivy's party. So I told her about the incident at Woody Pucket's house and the chimney fire at Morrisens' where I ran into Frank. "And then, when we got to my house, there was a call on my answering machine from Steven."

"Steven? That would be your ex?"

"None other."

"What did he want?"

"He didn't say. Just asked me to call him back." Hamlet was sniffing my feet so I reached down to scratch his ears. "Maybe I should get a dog — but I'd want one exactly like Hamlet."

Jewell wasn't about to let me change the subject. "So — did you call Steven?"

"No, I didn't. In fact, I deleted the message without taking down his number."

"Why?"

"I'm not sure. Maybe I didn't want to waste my dime on a long distance call." I took a bite of cookie. "Or maybe I did it because Frank was in the kitchen."

"Oh, come on. I can't see Frank as the insanely jealous type."

"I know. It was just my gut reaction. Maybe I don't want Steven rocking my boat. I'm pretty happy with my life right now."

"Tracy. Steven can't rock your boat — unless you still have feelings for him."

94

I had no reply for that so our conversation drifted away onto other topics.

But as I drove home, cautiously, through flurries of swirling snow, my thoughts drifted back to Jewell's comment about my ex-husband. What had she said?

Steven can't rock your boat unless you still have feelings for him.

Jewell is usually right about things like that.

CHAPTER FOURTEEN

"OUTHOUSE RACES?"

"That's what I said." Marge handed me a brochure. "The outhouse races are a new feature this year for the Winter Festival."

It was Friday morning and I was getting the details of my weekend assignment — which was to cover the third annual Shagoni River Winter Festival. The brochure listed a full roster of events — an ice sculpture contest, cross-country ski races, sleigh rides and beer tasting.

"This is so pathetic." I shook my head. "Don't people understand that this is a beach town — and no amount of effort will make our summer visitors show up in February?"

"Let's think positive," she said. "The goal is to make our town a Four Season Destination."

"Right. And so far, the most successful events have been the wine and beer sampling. Last year the town was filled with tipsy people, almost all of them locals."

"That's why the chamber is adding this new event," she said. "In case you haven't heard, Outhouse Races have become a midwinter highlight in a number of towns up north. Some of them even got TV coverage. So Jill, down at the chamber, got approval from the board to add the races to our winter festival —- and I'm planning to feature the winners on our front page. So we want photos, of course."

"Of course," I said, accepting the inevitable. I read through the schedule again — and this time an item popped out that I hadn't noticed before. The ice fishing contest. Oh crap.

"Anything else?" Marge turned to her computer.

I cleared my throat. "The ice fishing contest — could you ask Kyle to cover that for me? I mean I've done him plenty of favors —. "

"Ask him yourself," she said. "If he wants to, that's fine with me."

"Okay," I said. "Thanks a lot."

"Outhouse Races?" Frank looked at me in disbelief.

I nodded.

"You're kidding, right?"

I shook my head and passed him the brochure. "It's really happening and I'm really assigned to cover it." We were in my kitchen heating up some venison stew he had brought over.

Frank opened the pamphlet and read the schedule. "Yep, that's what it says — Outhouse Races. So, would you care to enlighten me? What happens during this event?"

"Honestly, Frank, I don't know." I put two bowls on the table, started looking for bread. "I talked with Jill, down at the chamber, and she told me that she saw it last year on the evening news. So she went on the internet, got some information, and decided that an Outhouse Race would be just the thing to generate excitement for our town."

Frank shrugged. "Well, whatever works. Are you covering the whole weekend?" He moved to the stove and began to stir the stew.

"Everything except the ice fishing. I begged Kyle to take that and he agreed."

"And you did that because —."

"Because I have a strong aversion to being anywhere near an ice shanty right now."

"Darn," he said. "I suppose this means I'll never get you to go ice fishing with me — or even bring me a sandwich."

"You're right about that," I said. "But there is good news."

"Tell me."

"I have two complimentary tickets for the beer tasting on Saturday night."

"It's nice to know somebody with connections," he said.

"And it's nice to know a man who can cook."

"I guess we're about to find out."

The venison stew was tasty. Along with the meat he had used garlic, onion, carrots and potatoes, plus stuff like turnips and rutabagas.

"I thought turnips and rutabagas didn't exist any more," I said.

"My mother used them a lot. But my wife hated them. So next summer I'm going to plant a garden. Beets too."

"Don't get carried away," I said. "I'm not fond of beets."

Saturday night brought a mini blizzard with six inches of new snow — but by morning the sun was peeking through the clouds. I left home shortly after lunch wearing my warmest coat, equipped with camera in one pocket, notepad and pen in the other. I stepped outside and was nearly blinded by the brilliance of sun on new snow.

I went back inside and found a pair of sunglasses, put them on and set out again. Since my destination was only a few blocks away, I was traveling on foot. Most of the sidewalks were clogged with snow so I had to walk in the street, but the few cars I encountered were moving slowly enough that we shared the road without any danger.

Approaching downtown, I saw that the business district was blocked off, all the way from Third Street to the village marina at the south end of town. The sidewalks here were cleared of snow, and people were beginning to gather. A lady clown was handing out colorful balloons. Some parents had brought their bundled up toddlers who took occasional falls onto well padded behinds. The light poles were wrapped with crepe paper and the street had been cleared of all vehicles.

With one exception. A rusty orange pick-up with a snow plow attached was parked in front of the Antler Bar. The truck looked like the one that belonged to Chip Crawley so, when I saw police chief Owen Bridges examining the vehicle, I headed over.

"I think I know who owns this truck," I said.

Bridges glanced up, acknowledged me with a nod and continued punching in numbers on his cell phone. "Got to get it moved," he said.

"Oh yeah. For the Outhouse Races."

He glared at me as though daring me to laugh. "Yep," he said, "for the Outhouse Races."

Shortly after Bridges finished his call, a tow truck appeared. Bridges waved to the driver who proceeded to swing around the barricades. The truck approached, the driver hopped out and Bridges went to give him instructions. Minutes later, the rusty orange pickup was being towed away.

Jill Townsend, the chamber of commerce director, came by and exchanged a few words with Bridges. Then she grabbed my arm and said, "Tracy, come on down and meet our contestants."

"Thanks," I said. "Marge told me to get a lot of photos."

I walked with Jill to the marina parking lot where a couple of odd looking structures sat waiting and another was being unloaded from a flat bed trailer.

"Here's my favorite," said Jill, leading me to an outhouse with a tropical theme. It had a thatched roof and artificial flowers stuck all over the sides. The little building was mounted on a pair of skis and the hinged door hung open revealing that it was a one-seater. There were signs on both sides indicating that it was sponsored by Doralee's Hair Creations. I was busy adjusting my camera when Doralee herself appeared, sporting flowers in her hair and a turquoise lei over her parka.

She laughed and said, "Happy Winter Festival," as she put an plastic lei around my neck. I thanked her and asked if she would pose for pictures beside the outhouse.

"Oh sure," she said, "but let me get the rest of the girls." She disappeared behind the building and returned with three women, all of them wearing grass skirts over their blue jeans and one with a coconut shell bra on top of her sweatshirt.

They mugged for the camera, laughing and dancing. I thanked them, wished them good luck and was then accosted by Jane Minor from the book shop.

"Come see mine," she said and proudly led me to her outhouse, and opened the door to show a straw man sitting on the seat holding one of her books. I adjusted the lighting on my camera to get a picture of the avid reader. Next I got photos of the Antler Bar outhouse which was predictably decorated with the horns from various unfortunate animals. Their sign declared, "The Horniest Bar in Town," and four guys stood around it, hooting and hollering.

No less raucous were the racers surrounding the Hunting Shack, a little house painted in splotches of green and brown that nearly disappeared behind the half dozen men in camouflage gear who were arguing about which of them was going to sit inside and who would be the pushers.

Jill was moving through the group handing out numbers and explaining the rules. As near as I could gather, the contestants would first parade down the street to the starting area and then race back, one at a time, while the mayor stood by the finish line with his stopwatch.

Jill turned to me with a worried look. "We're already running late," she said, "but there's supposed to be one more." Then she started waving wildly to an approaching truck. The latecomer was backed into place, and an army of volunteers hopped up to unload the last entry.

This outhouse resembled nothing so much as a psychedelic van of the seventies. The walls were splashed with a combustion of butterflies, comets, flamingos, and stars, with a door that featured a king on his throne holding a roll of toilet paper. From another vehicle, four androgynous people appeared, all wearing paint spattered smocks and black berets.

"It's the artists' co-op," Jill said with a laugh. "You can depend on them to be late."

Diego Jones, a tall black man, gave her a hug and apologized for their tardiness. "It's our artistic temperaments," he said. "Plus we thought the race was at the other end of town."

Jill rolled her eyes as she handed him a number and a list of the rules. "You'll be number five," she said. "First you all parade down to the other end, then wait your turn to race back. The best time wins."

I took some pictures of the psychedelic outhouse and then walked back to mingle with the crowd on the sidewalk who cheered as each of the outhouses slid down the snow covered street. After about ten minutes, it seemed the race was under way in earnest. The starting gun went off and people started yelling as the Antler Bar outhouse came down the street propelled by two men on each side, red-faced from the cold and exertion. Then came Doralee and the hula girls, shedding flowers as they ran.

After that nothing happened. There seemed to be some confusion at the starting area. At the finish line I saw the mayor, Clancey Fredericks, holding his stop watch and looking impatient. Then it looked as though he was telling one of his minions to go to the other end and see what was happening.

That's when I noticed a man and a woman across the street who didn't quite fit in with the carefree scene. They were standing in the doorway of a gift shop talking and gesturing while paying no attention to the race. From where I stood, I could have sworn the guy was Woody Pucket. But who could the woman be? She had her back to me and I couldn't figure out who she was. But the exchange with Woody continued.

Risking the wrath of the race officials, I sprinted across the street.

I reached the curb and pushed my way through the crowd until I was a few feet behind Woody and that's when I recognized the woman as Charlene Crawley. I wondered what had brought those two together.

"Hello Charlene," I said as I approached the pair. "Remember me?"

Charlene frowned, her pinched face showing no sign of recognition.

"I'm Tracy Quinn," I said. "We met at your dad's visitation."

"Oh yeah," she said. "Hi Tracy. You know Woody?"

I nodded. Woody looked my way and grunted.

Charlene's expression relaxed a bit as she apparently decided to confide in me. "We're trying to figure out what happened to my brother Chip," she said. "Have you seen him lately?"

"Not since —well, over at Woody's house a couple of days ago."

"He's not home and we can't find him anywhere," she said. "We think something must have happened to him."

"Maybe something bad," said Woody, eyeing me with a disgruntled look that suggested maybe the whole situation was my fault.

CHAPTER FIFTEEN

"How about you tell me what's going on?" I said.

The fact that Charlene Crawley's brother was missing, just two weeks after his father had died, suddenly seemed a lot more interesting than the outhouse races.

So the three of us, Charlene, Woody and I, went into a huddle in the alley between the Sweet Things gift shop and the police station. Woody, now in close proximity, gave off an odor of wood smoke and tobacco. Charlene wore a wool hat that smelled slightly of moth balls.

Now that she had my full attention, Charlene seemed unsure about trusting me. "This isn't going in the paper, is it?" she said.

"Of course not," I assured her. "Right now I am not a reporter, just a friend."

"Okay. Well, you tell her, Woody. Tell her how this started."

Woody coughed and cleared his throat. I was afraid he was going to spit on the ground but he didn't. "Well, me and Chip was supposed to go snowmobiling today. I keep my machine out at his place." Woody kept his eyes on the ground as he spoke. Clearly talking to strangers was not his forte. "So I went out this morning but nobody was there. His truck wasn't there either but his snowmobile was in the shed. No tracks in the snow anywhere."

He fell silent, glanced at Charlene who picked up the narrative.

"So Woody called Fiona to see if she knew anything. I've been staying there, so I was the one who answered. But Fiona and I couldn't help much. Neither one of us had seen Chip since he came by the house on Wednesday. Fiona said she had seen his truck downtown last night so I came down to look."

"Me too," said Woody. "Got here just as the law was hauling it away. Damn stupid cops."

"It was right in front of the Antler," she said. "So I thought maybe he drank too much and someone gave him a ride home."

"But he ain't home," said Woody.

"Maybe he's at somebody else's house," said Charlene.

"Do you think maybe it was, um, a girl?" I suggested

Woody smiled, revealing a gap where his two front teeth should have been. "As a rule," he said, "Chip don't get too lucky in that department."

"How about we go over to the Antler and talk to the bartender?" I motioned across the street. "Bartenders usually notice things."

Charlene looked at Woody. "What do you think?"

He shrugged. "Guess it wouldn't hurt."

"Let's check things out," I said, unsure whether the races were over or not. We all looked at the street. There were no outhouses in sight, either moving or stationary.

But then there was hooting and laughter from the crowd indicating that another outhouse was on its way. I pulled out my camera and elbowed my way to the curb, just in time to get a photo of the artists as they ran by, propelling their colorful outhouse. If there were a prize for creativity, I thought, that group should get it. It soon became apparent that the race was over. The audience began to disperse into any business that offered them warmth or a hot drink. I figured it would be a good day for Jennie and her sandwich shop.

I decided that I could wait to find out who the winners were. Right now, I wanted to stay with Charlene and Woody.

"Let's go," I said, and the three of us crossed the street together. We reached the bar, Woody grabbed the deer horn that served as a handle and held the door open while Charlene and I walked in. The place was nearly deserted but for a plump fortyish woman in a Spartan sweatshirt working behind the bar.

Woody leaned close to me and whispered, "I think her name is Hilda."

But neither he nor Charlene made a move. So finally I went up to Hilda and asked her if she had been working the night before.

Hilda shook her head. "I only work days," she said and started to walk away. But then she turned back. "If you want to wait, you can talk to Stanley when he comes in. I think he worked last night."

The three of us were debating our next move when a short, swarthy man emerged through the swinging doors that led to the kitchen. He was tying a blue apron over his bulging midsection.

"That's him," said Hilda.

We filed down to the other end of the bar where Stanley was standing behind the cash register shuffling papers. Apparently Charlene knew him because this time she took the lead.

"Stanley," she said. "You know my brother, don't you?"

Stanley looked up. "Sure, I know Chip. He was in here last night."

"We thought maybe he was," she said "cause his pick-up was still parked out front this morning."

"Just got towed away," said Woody.

"But we can't find him," said Charlene. "Do you remember anything? Who he was with? What time he left?"

The front door opened and the Antler's noisy race team poured in along with a group of boisterous fans. Stanley glanced at the newcomers and then back to us. "All I know is that he was here. Sat right over there." He indicated a long table between the bar and the booths.

"Do you know what time he left?" said Charlene.

"Hell no, I don't babysit these folks." He glanced at the pack who were lining up on the barstools. "So I'm a little busy here. You gonna order anything?"

"Um, no, I guess not," Charlene glanced from me to Woody. "But thanks," she said. Stanley probably didn't hear her because he was already heading for the other end of the bar.

Another group arrived, pushing up the noise level, so the three of us went back outside. Woody, Charlene and I talked for a few minutes, but no one had any idea what to do next. For me, it seemed like a good time to locate Jill and find out who had won the races, but she was nowhere in sight. The chamber office was right across the street and I figured maybe I could find her there. So I told Charlene and Woody I wasn't deserting them, but I wanted to pop over and see if I could find Jill. I was still talking to them as I started across the street and collided with a rather large man.

"Hey, watch where you're going," he said as he grabbed my arm.

Dismay turned to pleasure when I recognized the familiar bulk and remembered that I had plans to meet Frank Kolowsky after the race.

"Frank," I said, "am I ever glad to see you."

"Likewise. Who won the race?"

"I'm not sure — but — oh heck. I can find out later."

"Great. Have you had lunch yet?"

"No but — I need to tell you — I'm sort of involved in a situation here." I nodded toward Woody and Charlene. "That's Chip Crawley's sister over there. The guy with her is Chip's friend, Woody. Chip seems to be missing and nobody knows where he is. I tried to help but we've run out of ideas. Could you — well — talk to them?"

Frank grimaced a little but then he said, "Oh sure. Why not."

I grabbed Frank's arm, led him to the sidewalk and introduced him to Woody and Charlene. I didn't say anything about Frank being a cop or a detective, just said he was a friend of mine. Taking turns, the three of us gave Frank a quick summary of the situation.

When we finished, I looked at Frank and said, "Got any ideas?"

"Maybe," he said, "but I haven't eaten today and I don't think too well on an empty stomach. Can we go inside and get a burger?" He nodded toward the Antler. "Maybe we'll run into someone who knows him."

So the four of us went back inside and claimed a table. Frank and I ordered hamburgers and coffee. Woody looked uncomfortable, ordered coffee and so did Charlene.

"If you two want anything to eat," said Frank, "I'm buying. Just won the lotto." I knew that was a lie. Frank never buys those tickets.

So then Woody ordered french fries and Charlene got a chili dog.

"Okay," said Frank, when he was half way through his burger. "How about any other friends where Chip might have spent the night?"

"Fiona and I called around before I left home," said Charlene. "We left two messages and talked to Jimmy Therow. Jimmy said he saw him two days ago but not last night."

"Can we report him as a missing person?" I said.

"You mean the police?" said Charlene. Woody frowned.

Frank shook his head. "It really hasn't been long enough. He's an adult so he's entitled to disappear if he wants to. Needs to be three or four days before anyone will file a report."

"And then they would probably search his place, wouldn't they?" said Charlene.

"Chip wouldn't like that," said Woody.

"No he wouldn't," said Charlene.

Around us, business was picking up. A trio of women sailed in and settled into a booth, talking and laughing. Now that we were paying customers, it seems that Stanley the bartender decided to cut us a break.

Stanley came over, leaned down with his hands on our table and said quietly, "See that girl that just come in? Green coat and blonde hair. Her name's Tanya. She was sitting with Chip last night. She might be able to tell you something."

So now we had a lead. But we weren't sure about the best way to approach Tanya.

"How about you girls do it," said Woody.

"That might work best," said Frank. "If a guy walks up to a girl in a bar, she could get the wrong idea."

So that's how Charlene and I got the job. We waited until the women at the booth had placed their orders. Then we walked over together.

"You do it," whispered Charlene, like we were in junior high approaching a teacher. So I did.

"Are you Tanya?" I said to the girl, who looked to be about twenty-five. She looked at me and nodded slowly.

I smiled my best non-threatening smile. "You don't know me, but my name's Tracy — and this is Charlene. She's a sister to Chip Crawley and — well — he left his truck out front last night and now nobody knows where he is. Did you see him last night?"

"Yes, I saw him," Tanya said softly.

"Can you tell us anything? Like what time he left?"

Tanya thought for a moment. "He was still here when I left about ten-thirty. I had to get home because my sister works nights and I was watching her kids."

"Did Chip say anything about where he might be going?"

"Sorry," she said. "I can't think of anything. He wasn't talking very much."

Charlene looked at me, shrugged. "Okay," she said, "thanks anyway."

"I hope you find him," said Tanya. "I hope nothing has happened to him."

"So do we," said Charlene.

We went back to our table where Frank and Woody were talking about that male common denominator, fishing. Charlene and I relayed what little we had just learned.

The four of us mulled over the same bits of information, without coming up with any new ideas.

"Maybe we ought to drive out to his trailer again," said Woody.

"Yeah," said Charlene. "Maybe he'll be sitting there with a beer and he'll laugh at us for worrying abut him."

"Or he'll be sound asleep."

"Do you think the trailer is locked?" said Charlene.

"It wasn't," said Woody. "This morning I opened the door and yelled inside."

"Did you look in the bedroom?"

"No, I didn't go in."

"I'd just feel better," she said, "if we went out there and looked around."

"Sounds like a good idea," said Frank. "Call me if you find him." He scratched his cell phone number on a scrap of paper and handed it to Charlene.

Charlene pocketed the paper and the two of them took their leave. Charlene left a bill to pay for her food and Woody left some change for a tip.

Frank and I ordered refills on our coffee. Apparently word about Chip's disappearance had made its way around the room because pretty soon a tall, skinny guy in an orange hunting coat ambled over to our table.

"Tanya says you two are looking for Chip."

"That's right," I said. "Do you know anything?"

"Did you see him last night?" said Frank.

"Yup," said our informant, whose Adam's apple bobbed while he talked. "We was sitting at that table right over there." He pointed to a table. "Chip had three or four beers but he don't hold it very well. After a while he got all riled up — talking about that fishing boat and how he was afraid it was gonna be sold now that his dad was dead."

"Were you still here when he left?"

"Yup."

"About what time was that?"

"Sometime after midnight."

"Was he with anybody — anyone who might have given him a ride?"

"Nope. Just paid up and walked out. Alone."

"Okay," said Frank. "Thanks for your help."

"No problem."

As the guy walked away, Frank drummed his fingers on the table. "So Chip was talking about the boat," he said.

"And wherever he went, he didn't take his truck."

"Where is the boat stored?"

"I don't know."

"Let's call Fiona." He pulled out his cell phone. "Do you know her number?"

I nodded. "You go ahead." He handed me the phone.

I placed the call and Fiona answered. "This is Tracy," I said. "I've been with Woody and Charlene and we're still trying to find Chip."

"I got a call back from one of his friends," she said. "But they weren't any help. Have you found out anything?"

"Only this — he was talking about the boat before he left here last night."

"That damn boat. He's obsessed with it."

"Can you tell us where the boat is stored?"

"Jerry's Marine. You know, at the south end of town."

"Ask her the name of the boat," said Frank.

"What's the name of the boat?"

"The *Night Crawler.* Clever, huh?"

"Okay. Good. I'll let you know as soon as we find out anything."

I handed over the phone and said, "The boat is the *Night Crawler* and it's stored at Jerry's."

"That's not far away," he said as he pocketed the phone. "Are you up for a walk?"

"Sure, I guess. What are we going to do?"

"Just look around. See if we can find any tracks."

"Great," I said. "Winter makes this detective work a breeze."

So we paid up, left the Antler and walked to the south end of Hancock Street, past the lot where the last of the outhouses was being loaded, and around the corner to Jerry's Marine Storage.

There was no sound here except for the wind soughing off the lake. The ground was buried under two feet of snow, with some drifts reaching twice that high. Above us loomed several large boats, wrapped in white canvas and looking like sea monsters out of their element. Away from the road, near the lake, were two large storage barns.

"Did Fiona say if the boat was in a barn or not?" said Frank.

"Sorry, I forgot to ask."

The wind had started to come in off Lake Michigan with a knife like ferocity. I covered my face with my hands and began to think this venture was not a very smart idea.

"Hey, look here," said Frank who had wandered away from me.

I shuffled over to where Frank was standing and he pointed out a disturbance in the snow. The wind had blown new snow into the footprints but we were looking at an unmistakable path leading into the marina property.

"Let's go," he said.

CHAPTER SIXTEEN

Without another word, Frank set off through the snow, following the faintly visible set of foot prints.

"Aren't we sort of, umm, trespassing?"

"Jerry won't mind," he said. "I've done him some favors."

I was curious as to what those favors might have been, but this didn't seem like a good time to ask. The wind was finding its way down my neck so I zipped up my coat and wished that I had one of those wooly neck scarves my grandma used to knit.

The snow was so deep that it sifted in over the top of my boots and felt like razors against my bare skin. But I just followed Frank, walking in his footsteps, while he walked in the windblown tracks. I was keeping my head down so it came as a bit of a surprise when we found ourselves up against a wall. Literally. It was a sheet metal wall of the storage building nearest the lake. Closer inspection revealed that the wall was actually a large sliding door and Frank quickly located the padlock that held it shut.

"Should we go find Jerry?" I said.

"Jerry's in Florida."

"Oh great. So what now? You carrying a hack saw?"

"No, but we'll get in."

"Are you going to — maybe — shoot the lock off?"

"Nothing that dramatic," he said. I started wondering how much illegal activity I was pursuing and how much excuse it would be that I was just following Frank around.

"This kind of door is not very hard," he said. "I'll show you."

I followed him to the far end of the sliding door, the end that wasn't padlocked. There was a hook hanging on the door but it wasn't connected to the latch on the side of the building.

"All we have to do is dig a little," Frank said as he bent down and started scraping snow away from the door.

"You think Chip is in there?"

"What I think is that last night somebody did exactly what I'm doing right now."

The door was well over eighteen feet high. After a few minutes Frank stood and pulled the bottom of the door away from the wall. This created a triangular opening, wider at the bottom and narrowing to the point where the door hung on the track.

"I'm going in," he said, crouching down to slide his bulk through the narrow opening. "You coming?"

"It's awfully dark in there."

"Don't worry, I've got a penlight."

"Oh great. A penlight."

"You don't have to come if you don't want to."

"Well I'm not going to stand out here in the cold."

"So come on in."

So I did. I turned sideways, slid through the opening and bumped into Frank because I couldn't see a thing. Finally Frank produced a penlight which made a tiny point of pale illumination.

"That's not much light," I said.

"Your eyes will adjust."

"I hope so. Damn I'm cold."

Frank wrapped his arms around me. It was an unexpected moment of intimacy — as much as one can get through several layers of clothing — and after a minute or two I felt warmer. Also my pupils had dilated so that I could see vague outlines of more huge boats, looming high above, balanced on their keels.

"How come they're all so big?" I said.

"When you see them at dock, all this is under water."

"Okay. That makes sense. Do you think Chip came in here last night?"

"Somebody did. So let's look around."

I stayed behind Frank as we walked between the rows of boats that towered above our heads. The way those huge boats rested on their keels made me think of ballerinas, with all their weight on the point of one toe. I stuck pretty close to Frank, occasionally grabbing his coat. When we approached the stern of each boat, Frank raised his penlight and tried to read the name. Sometimes the light wasn't strong enough. Other times we were treated to some overly clever puns. *Idle Ours, Son of a Beach* and *Nautical Lady.* But so far, no *Night Crawler.*

The chill of the cement floor came up through my boots. "I'm colder here than I was outside," I said.

Frank ignored my whining. "I'm starting to think that whoever came in here, went out the same way. But I want to check that last row over in the back."

"Isn't that where we started?"

"Maybe, but I'm not sure."

"Probably Charlene and Woody have found him by now." I said. "I don't think we're doing much good in here."

I was so busy complaining that I didn't notice when my foot tangled with something on the floor. I screamed as I grabbed the air and pitched forward.

"Tracy," said Frank, "are you all right?"

I was down. And I fully expected to be scrabbling on the cold cement floor. But I wasn't.

"I'm not hurt," I said. "Something cushioned my fall."

"What is it?" He knelt next to me. "What's this underneath you?"

"No idea. I can't see a thing."

"Me neither," he said. "But it feels like maybe — ."

"It feels like maybe it's a body."

114

CHAPTER SEVENTEEN

"It's a good thing you folks found this guy when you did." The doctor had the bluest eyes I had ever seen. "He's had a concussion and he's suffering from hypothermia."

Frank and I were in the emergency room of Cedar County Hospital where bright lights reflected off hard surfaces and voices murmured from behind green curtains. Mechanical equipment hummed and buzzed, punctuated by the occasional human moan or groan.

The body I had stumbled over in the boat storage unit had, in fact, been that of the missing Chip Crawley. So after Frank called village personnel to come and disable the padlock, and the emergency medical service to carry out the rescue, we had followed the ambulance to the hospital.

"Do you think he will be okay?" I said to the doctor.

"There's a fair chance he'll make a full recovery."

"Is he talking at all?" said Frank.

"Just starting to mumble a few words."

"I'd like to ask him some questions." Frank pulled out his wallet and showed the doctor his sheriff's department ID.

The doctor glanced at the ID, then at Frank, before he replied. "I guess that would be okay. But we're just getting ready to move him to a hospital room. Could you wait and talk to him there?"

Frank nodded and the doctor walked away. Minutes later, two people in scrubs pushed a loaded gurney down the hallway and into an elevator.

"Is either of you a relative?" The question came from a woman in a navy blue jacket carrying a clipboard. "There's a lot of admission paperwork," she said apologetically.

"No," I said, "but his, ah, somebody will be in shortly."

"Somebody?"

"Either his sister or stepmother."

"I guess I'll have to wait," she said. "When they get here, tell them to come to the admission desk first thing." She flashed a perfunctory smile, turned and disappeared through a door.

"Who's coming?" said Frank

"It'll probably be Charlene," I said. "I called Fiona but she didn't sound very willing to drive over here on her day off."

"Not surprising, considering that she and Chip are not on the best of terms."

Then two things happened. The nurse at the desk told Frank he could go up to Chip's room just as red- haired Fiona burst in through the sliding doors.

"Fiona," I said as I walked over and gave her a hug. "Thanks so much for coming."

"Good to see you," Frank said as he shook her hand. "How about I leave you ladies here while I go upstairs?" He left without waiting for an answer.

Fiona shook the snow out of her hair. "Good lord, Tracy, isn't it just one thing after another?"

"It seems that way." I mustered a smile. "I guess the admitting people want to see you."

"Oh, of course. They always want to know who's going to pay the bill. What do I know — he's not my kid. I don't even know his social security number."

"Hopefully he's got his wallet on him."

"Unless somebody stole it while he was knocked out."

"I guess that's what Frank is trying to find out," I said.

116

"Do you know who the emergency room doctor is?"

"I didn't get a name, but he's about six two with blue eyes."

"Oh. Him." Fiona cast a searching glance around the waiting room where a woman sat with a crying child and an old man was slumped in a wheel chair. "I'd better get over to admitting. You want to come with me?"

"Might as well." I followed her into the main lobby and took a seat.

I found a copy of People magazine and had time to read about the infidelities of several Hollywood couples while Fiona dealt with the admissions clerk. I was just starting to review the Oscar nominations when Fiona came to sit by me.

"I told them all I know," she said. "I wonder what I should do next."

Before I could answer I saw Frank exit an elevator and come walking toward us.

"Was Chip talking?" I said. "Did he tell you anything?"

"Let's go over there." Frank nodded toward an alcove on the other side of the lobby. Fiona and I followed him to an area that featured several potted plants.

"Okay," he said. "Here's what we've got so far." Frank sounded like he was briefing some fellow officers. "Chip told me that somebody followed him into the storage barn and whacked him over the head. That's all he remembers until he woke up in the ambulance."

"But how did you two know where to look for him?" said Fiona.

So Frank and I told her how the bits of information we had picked up led us to Chip lying unconscious on the floor of a locked storage barn.

"We figured he had to be on foot," I said, "because his pick-up was still parked outside the bar on Saturday morning."

"And his buddy said he was agitated, talking about the boat," said Frank. "So we just decided to follow the trail, so to speak."

Fiona shook her head. "Chip just seems to be one problem after another. He never could hold a job — so Vince ended up providing employment for him. The fishing boat and the snow plowing."

"Was that enough?" I said.

She shook her head. "I'm sure he slipped him some cash in between. One of the many bones of contention between me and Vince. I don't know what Chip will do now. I gave him the truck but I can't give him the boat. He's got no license to take charters anyway."

"Frank," I said, "did Chip explain why he went to the boat in the middle of the
night?"

"Said he had some personal stuff on the boat. He wanted to get it off before Fiona went ahead and sold it."

"Yeah," said Fiona . "Like anybody's going to buy a boat in the middle of the winter."

"Did the guy who bumped him steal his wallet?"

"Chip wouldn't have enough money on him to make it worthwhile," said Fiona.

"Especially after a few hours in the bar."

"Well, his wallet was still on him," said Frank. "So it looks like robbery wasn't the motive."

"It really doesn't make any sense," said Fiona. She glanced out the window. "For heaven's sake, look who's here."

Through the window I saw two figures approaching. As they drew closer I recognized Charlene Crawley and Woody Pucket. The two of them pushed through the front door, then paused as though unsure what to do next.

"I'd better go talk to them," said Fiona. She left us and headed toward the new arrivals.

Frank and I stayed put, watching as Fiona greeted Charlene and Woody. Then she took them to the woman at the desk who apparently gave an all clear for the visitors to go up and see Chip Crawley.

Fiona came back to where Frank and I were standing. "I think I'd better go up with them for a few minutes," she said. "Just in case Woody starts to get Chip riled up. That guy is so wacky there's no telling what he'll make of this business."

"Want us to come along?" I said.

Fiona shook her head. "I'll handle this. I work here, so if things get out of hand, I'll have the charge nurse call security. The visits are limited to ten minutes anyway."

"We'll hang around down here for a little bit," said Frank.

"You really don't need to," she said. "You've both done a lot already."

"Well then, go on upstairs. And let me know if you find out anything new." He handed her a card with his cell phone number.

"Right," she said, giving us a strained smile. "I'll do that."

Frank and I stayed in the lobby a little longer talking about Chip's bizarre accident and unlikely rescue. But neither of us came up with any new ideas, and there wasn't any word from Fiona, so we decided to leave.

We were in Frank's Blazer about two miles out of town when his cell phone rang.

"Oh darn," I said. "That might be Fiona."

Frank took the call, looked at me and shook his head. He listened for about two minutes and said, "Great. That's good news." Then he ended the call.

"What's the good news?" I said. "Anything you can share?"

He kept his eyes on the road as he answered. "This is strictly classified, okay?"

"Top secret," I promised. "No press."

"Okay. We may have caught a break in the Vince Crawley case. One of our boys found a bottle on the edge of the lake, close to the parking lot for the Boat House Bar."

"What kind of bottle, another Jim Beam?"

"Nope. A small one. About the size and shape for a prescription drug."

Back at my house, Frank and I sat at the kitchen table and tucked into food we had picked up at the deli. "These meatballs are pretty good," he said between bites.

"So's the potato salad."

We munched for a few minutes in silence, but clearly Frank's brain was working as hard as his jaw. "You know," he said, "the more I think about Chip Crawley, the more it seems like the whole business doesn't add up."

"Well, I sort of assumed that his personal stuff on the boat could be marijuana. Why else go traipsing down there at midnight?"

"I agree with you on that. But still — who would follow him and whack him over the head?"

"And why would they do that?"

"All we have to go on is what Chip told me — and it wasn't much. But I'm going to take a look around the boat tomorrow."

"Do you think this could have something to do with his father?" I said.

"You mean maybe somebody killed Vince — and now they're trying to kill Chip?"

I nodded vigorously, my mouth full.

"Possible I guess."

"But why, for heaven's sake?"

"Something to do with the boat?" he said. "Maybe a smuggling operation?"

"Cigarettes to avoid the Michigan sales tax?"

"I don't believe any of this was done by a stranger. Maybe we should ask Fiona where she was last night."

"Oh please, not Fiona. I can't believe she would follow Chip from the bar with a baseball bat. It doesn't seem her style."

"No, it doesn't. But still — something's a little off."

I brought out a package of cookies for dessert. "I'd like to know more about that bottle they found by the lake," I said.

"Me too. The deputy said the bottle still had a piece of the label on it. I'll see what I can learn from that. But the bottle may have nothing to do with Vince."

"But then again, there might be traces of chloral hydrate in it."

"That would be very helpful."

Frank and I retired to the living room where we cuddled up on my sofa and indulged in a prolonged kiss. That's when my telephone decided to ring. I let the machine take it.

It was a male voice and this time I recognized it. "Tracy, this is Steven and I really need to talk to you. Call me at ——." the number that followed had an unfamiliar area code.

Frank shifted position and held me at arm's length. "Maybe it's not my business but — is somebody stalking you?"

"Nobody is stalking me. In case you forgot — Steven is the name of my ex-husband."

"Okay. Not my business, I guess."

And we let it go at that.

CHAPTER EIGHTEEN

Monday morning I found a note on my computer indicating that Marge wanted to see me in her office. I went to her office but found it difficult to keep my mind on the business at hand.

While my editor issued instructions I stared at her hair which was piled into an odd arrangement that I had never seen before. Anywhere. On anyone.

Eventually I decided that last week's ringlets had started to droop so badly that Marge was trying to hold everything in place with an oversized gold headband — the effect was not flattering.

"Tracy, did you hear my question?"

"Oops, sorry —."

"I need to know who won the Outhouse Races."

"Oh that. I guess it's not a sure thing yet." *So if Marge's hair had suffered over the weekend, did that mean that she and her boyfriend had —?*

"Why not?"

"Why not what?"

"Why don't you know the winners?"

"Oh that." I stopped thinking about Marge's hair. Tried to stop looking too, but that was impossible. "I just talked to Jill at the chamber and she said there was some confusion." Marge's pencil started tapping. "See, the guys from the Antler Bar had the best time, but they had a ten-year-old kid sitting inside their outhouse — and the rules said there had to be a person inside but didn't specify that the person had to be an adult."

"So someone could have used a midget."

"Nobody thought of that. The bookstore used a straw man so they were disqualified. The hunters had the second best time but one of the officials claimed that they jumped the gun. Which, of course, the hunters deny, so now Jill is looking for witnesses."

"Oh for heaven's sake." Marge took off her glasses and rubbed the bridge of her nose. "Is there money involved?"

"Prize money? Yes, at least two hundred dollars. People need some kind of incentive to go out cavorting in that kind of weather." Marge's eyes looked red. *Could she possibly have a hangover?*

"Okay then. I guess the best we can do is run pictures of all the contestants. Maybe Jill will have this sorted out in time for next week's paper."

"Sounds good to me." Back at my desk I considered offering Marge a couple of aspirin but decided that the gesture might overstep the boundaries of our relationship.

I went home for lunch and found the message light on my answering machine blinking. *Steven again?* I felt a little trepidation as I pushed the play button, but this time it was Jewell's voice.

"Tracy, I need to see you — it's important. I'll stop by after work and hope to find you at home."

The cryptic message caused my imagination to run wild with possibilities while I ate lunch. Then I forgot the whole affair back at work where I had to focus on the business of creating a newspaper. On my way home, however, I started wondering again what Jewell had to tell me.

The suspense didn't last for long.

As it turned out, I had just finished making coffee when Jewell arrived. I filled two cups, brought them into the living room and put them on the coffee table. But Jewell ignored the coffee. She opened her purse and pulled out a black rectangular object.

"What's this?" I leaned closer to examine the object.

She looked at the box, hesitated and then looked at me. "Tracy," she said, "I'm breaking all kinds of confidentiality rules — but I wanted you to hear this first. So you can help me decide what to do."

"Sure. This feels exciting." I realized that I was looking at a small tape recorder.

"What's on it?"

"It's our change-of-shift report tape."

"I've heard that some hospitals use them now. Tell me how it works."

"Okay. You know that when the shift changes, say at three p.m., the day nurse gives a report to the oncoming nurse, summarizing the condition of every patient on the unit. About six months ago we started putting the report on tape."

"Why?"

"For a number of reasons. First of all, it allows the oncoming nurse to replay the tape if there's something she wants to check. Also it allows me to review any part of the report."

"Makes sense."

"And there is another big reason. The system shortens the report time because it eliminates a lot of personal trivia and, well, just plain gossip."

"Which is not a productive use of time?"

"Exactly. Small town residents know entirely too much about one another."

"So what have we here?" I said, touching the box. "Some juicy gossip?"

"In a way — but the speakers never knew they were being recorded."

"This could be interesting."

"The night nurse brought the tape to me. She said she played it by mistake and thought maybe I should hear it."

"Now I'm really curious. Somebody stealing towels or scrub suits?"

"Nothing like that. But first you have to understand the setting. The shift report is given in the nurse's lounge. The room has a coat closet and a bathroom, chairs and magazines for break time. Personnel is largely, but not entirely, female."

"I think I've got the picture."

"Okay. Apparently here's what happened. After the eleven p.m. shift change, the nurse thought she turned the tape off, but she accidentally left it on record function. Everybody went out and the tape was still running." Jewell set the recorder on the coffee table. "Okay now, I'll just play this for you."

The tape started running and I heard about lab values on someone named Ed Oglethorpe. Then there was silence; door opening, door closing, toilet flushing, more door action.

Jewell pushed the pause button. "Here it is," she said. "See if you recognize the woman talking." She started the tape again. There were two voices, one male and one female.

The man's voice: *I don't see why you're doing this*

The woman's voice: *If you don't see, then you're absolutely mad*

The man: *I can understand that you're upset but couldn't we just—-*

The woman: *No, Todd, we can't. Not now and not ever again*

"It's Fiona," I gasped.

Jewell nodded. The tape continued.

The woman: *My husband is dead and I'm having an affair. How do you think that looks? I've already made my mother lie for me and I hate that*

The man: *Are you a suspect?*

The woman: *Of course I am. The spouse is always a suspect. So please, don't contact me — at home or work or anywhere*

The man: *Can't we just —*

I never heard the rest of the sentence because the tape ran out. "So who is Todd?" I said.

"There's only one Todd in the hospital and that is Doctor Todd Nagel in the emergency room."

"Oh — Doctor Blue Eyes. He was the one who took care of Chip Crawley when he came in."

"That's him."

"Well, I can understand the appeal but — wait a minute—." I finally made the connection. "Todd Nagel would be Holly's father." Jewell nodded. "That means poor Holly was right about him. Oh — it also means that Fiona was probably with Todd at the motel the night that Vince died."

"It certainly looks that way."

I stared at the incriminating little box. "What should we do now?"

"I'm not sure. Any ideas?"

"Maybe we should call Frank."

Jewell pursed her lips, the way she does when she's thinking hard. "Maybe we should," she said. "Otherwise we'd be guilty of — what—?"

"Withholding evidence — or something like that."

"I wish I could see another way out of this."

"At least Frank is someone we know."

"Thank goodness for that. So will you call him?"

"Of course."

I made the call. When Frank answered I didn't give him any details, just said that Jewell had a tape she wanted him to hear. He said he was in Stanton finishing up some paperwork and would drive over shortly. Jewell decided to wait. She called home and told Paul that she was at my house. She was talking to a machine so she didn't have to give any further explanation.

I reheated our coffee and we drank it while we waited. Frank arrived about half an hour later. He kicked off his boots, sat in the recliner and I brought him a beer. Jewell explained the context of the tape and then she played it for him.

Frank listened carefully.

When it was over he said, "So that's where Fiona was the night her husband died."

"Looks that way," I said.

"What do we do now?" said Jewell. "I'd like to keep this as quiet as possible. I don't want to embarrass Fiona any more than absolutely necessary."

"I understand your position," he said, "but Fiona has created her own mess. This tape is evidence in a murder case and I need to take it with me."

Jewell bit her lip as she looked at Frank. "I shouldn't let you take it until I share it with the hospital administrator. I know I should have gone to him first — but he wasn't in today. Plus, I just feel so conflicted about the whole situation."

I didn't hear Frank's next comment because I was on my way to my front door to answer a persistent knock.

I opened the door to find my neighbor, Les Tattersal, standing on the porch with a broad smile on his worn face. His white hair was flecked with snow and his glasses were slipping down on his nose.

"Come right in, Les," I said. "I'm sorry I haven't been over to thank you for all the times you've cleared my driveway."

Les ignored my apologies. He stepped into the living room and looked past me to Frank and Jewell. "Well, isn't it great you're all here," he said. "Because I have an announcement to make."

Frank and Jewell stopped talking. We all looked at my elderly neighbor who had removed his glasses and was attacking them with his handkerchief.

"Daisy and I are getting married," he said, squinting at his bemused audience. "Next Saturday. And you are all invited to help us celebrate."

CHAPTER NINETEEN

My neighbor's announcement left me temporarily without words. I gave him a big hug and finally managed to say, "Les, I am so happy for you — and for Daisy too."

Jewell and Frank joined me in congratulating the beaming little man whose presence had brought an unexpected grace to the demise of a gray winter day.

The news banished from my mind all thoughts of the audiotape lying on my coffee table. Les Tatersall, who was eighty if he was a day, had been a widower for nearly twenty years. And Daisy Fritzel was a delightful lady who ran a tea shop in town when she wasn't handling a spinning wheel nearly as tall as herself.

So I gave Les a cup of coffee, brought out some fruitcake and we all quizzed him on the wedding plans. The reception was to be at his house the following Sunday, a small and unpretentious affair.

"And for heavens sake, don't bring us any presents," he pleaded. "Daisy and I already have far too much stuff. She's going to keep her own house rather than try to fit all of her belongings into mine."

"But she'll be living with you, won't she?" I was already anticipating the pleasure of having Daisy as a next door neighbor.

"Oh yes. She's moving in with me — my house is certainly bigger than hers. But then, if she gets in a mood where she needs to be alone, she'll have somewhere to go."

I refilled coffee cups and the four of us exchanged pleasantries for another half hour. It was dark by the time Les said goodbye, so I turned on the porch light to show him out.

Jewel looked at her watch. "I really need to get home," she said. "But — we haven't decided what to do about this tape business." All three of us looked at the little black box where it sat on the coffee table like a viper at a tea party.

Finally Frank spoke up. "If you let me take it now — I'll get it transcribed first thing tomorrow. Then I'll drive straight to the hospital and return it to you."

Jewell listened to his offer and nodded slowly. "If you get it to me by noon," she said, "I can take it to the administrator and let him hear it. Hopefully he won't be too upset with me for coming to you first."

"Okay," said Frank, "let's do that. And when I come to the hospital, there's somebody else I want to see."

"And who would that be?"

"Todd Nagel. Will he be there tomorrow?"

"I don't know but I can find out." Jewell pulled out her cell phone and made a call. When she was finished, she said, "You're in luck. Todd will be there all day tomorrow. Shall I tell him you're coming?"

"Oh no." Frank showed the merest hint of a smile. "I want this to be a surprise."

"Are you going to question him about the motel business on Saturday night?" I wondered.

"It all depends," he said. "I need to talk to Fiona about that first."

"Oh sure. I guess that makes sense. Poor Fiona."

"Maybe I should talk with Fiona," said Jewell. "Tell her the cat's out of the bag, so to speak."

"No way," Frank said quickly. "I want to get to her first — maybe yet tonight. Otherwise, early tomorrow."

"So, back to Todd Nagel," I said. "What's your other business with him?"

"I have some questions about Chip Crawley's condition. We know he had a concussion — but I'd like to know more about the exact nature of his head injury."

"You think there's something fishy there?"

"I'm not sure," he said, "but something, somehow, doesn't feel right."

I thought about that later, after everybody was gone and I was getting ready for bed. If someone had followed Chip Crawley into the boat storage shed, wouldn't we have seen another set of footprints?

Tuesday I covered the village council meeting which promised to be fairly quiet, based on the agenda. And it was for a while. But then a couple of irate citizens showed up to complain about the property on Rash street — the property belonging to Woody Pucket.

"There's a huge pile of wood in his backyard," said a woman who identified herself as Woody's neighbor to the north. "That big truck backed in and dumped it out and there it sits. Same thing happens every winter and nobody does anything about it." The woman sat down wearing a scowl that slowly changed to a smile when a small ripple of applause moved through the audience.

The mayor looked around the room and spotted our chief of police. "Chief Bridges," he said, "would you care to speak on this issue?"

Owen Bridges stood, blushing all the way to his bald head. "When the stuff got dumped," he said, "Woody promised he would put it out of sight, inside his garage. But so far he hasn't. I went to his house yesterday to check on things but nobody was home."

"Well there's somebody home now," said a white haired man. "I live right across the street. When I left home tonight, there was two trucks crammed in his driveway and one of them was blocking the sidewalk. Couldn't see around the trucks to tell if the wood was still there or not."

"It's still there," said a small woman whose speech was punctuated by the wheeze of her portable oxygen tank. "That's the view out my kitchen window and I have to look at that mess every day."

Bridges looked cornered. "Okay. I'll go see Pucket again tomorrow."

"I'll go with you, if you like." The offer came from village attorney Greg Wetherell.

"Okay," said Bridges, with a grateful glance at the lawyer. "Let's do that."

After the meeting, I found Greg talking with Chief Bridges in the manager's office. I waited at a respectful distance until they acknowledged my presence.

"Would it be okay if I went with you to Pucket's house tomorrow?" I said.

"That might be a good idea," said Greg. He looked to Bridges for confirmation.

Bridges shrugged. "Guess it wouldn't hurt anything."

So it was decided. The intervention was scheduled for eleven the next morning and the three of us were to meet at village hall.

When I arrived at village hall the next day, Greg was already there. But he told me that Bridges had been called away with no indication as to when he might be back. I asked the clerk if Jim Mcneely was available but she said he was out of town for the day.

"What do you think?" I said to Greg.

"We promised to make a visit so I think we should do it. Are you up for it?"

"Might as well," I said, considering that the alternative was being in the office with Marge.

"Why don't you just ride with me?" said Greg. So I climbed in his town car and buckled myself into the soft leather seat which was just getting warm by the time we arrived at Woody Pucket's house on Rash Street.

I saw that there were, in fact, two trucks in the driveway and one of them extended well into the walkway, which probably didn't matter much since the rest of the sidewalk was buried under snow. Woody's house had a small front porch where the snow was drifted right up to the door, a clear indication that nobody used the front entrance, at least not during the winter.

So Greg and I made our way around to the back of the house, single file, our steps confined to the narrow strip of space between the trucks and the piled up snow. The odor of freshly cut wood was unmistakable. I slipped once and steadied myself by grabbing the door handle of a pick up truck. Then I looked and saw a pile of slab wood as tall as I was. Greg was heading around the pyramid shaped pile.

I followed him and the next thing I saw was the old garage. The door to the building was open and Greg disappeared into the shadowy interior. Before I could see anything inside, I heard Greg talking and a female voice answering. Curious, I entered the dimly lit space and saw a woman clutching a cardboard box filled with magazines and newspapers. She wore a navy pea coat and had long straight hair that hung down from under an orange stocking cap.

When I realized that I was looking at Charlene Crawley, I gave her a little wave but she more or less ignored me as she continued talking to Greg.

"You guys ought to cut Woody some slack," she said. "My brother got hurt, you know, almost killed, and now he's staying here. Woody has his hands full so I'm trying to help out. He's gonna move the wood inside as soon as this place gets organized. But guys aren't very good at that kind of thing, so that's what I'm doing — helping them get things organized."

As my eyes adjusted, I looked around. The stacks of junk I recalled from my last visit seemed to have shrunk a little. "Looks like you're making some progress," I said.

"Oh yeah." Charlene acknowledged my presence with a nod. "I took back all the bottles and cans yesterday. And today I'm putting glass and plastic in the recycle bin."

"What about all those newspapers?" said Greg.

"These are going over on the work bench and then we can stack the wood against that wall." She turned and shoved the box she was holding into the dark recesses of a shelf.

"What the hell's going on here?" The question, delivered by a growling male voice, came from the direction of the house.

Greg and I turned to see Woody Pucket standing on his back porch, shivering in a worn gray tee shirt and holding a lit cigarette.

"Just checking on the progress," said Greg.

"Well, I been busy. You know someone tried to kill my friend."

"Yes, we know about that," I said. "It was good of you to take him in."

"Well, the damn hospital kicked him out and it's for sure he can't be alone."

"Fiona did offer to take him," said Charlene.

"He ain't on very good terms with Fiona right now," said Woody.

"So how's he getting along?" I said.

"He's all right."

"I think there's room to start stacking the wood now," said Charlene.

"Well okay," said Woody, "but we gotta eat first. Ain't had no breakfast. Did you buy some bread, Charlene?"

"Yes I did," she said. "Turned in all those bottles and got enough money for bread and Velveeta cheese. Chip really likes grilled cheese sandwiches."

"Well, ain't you something," said Woody.

Charlene walked up onto the porch and stood next to Woody. They both leaned on the railing, causing it to shift a little.

Woody fixed his gaze on me and Greg. "You guys can see I got my hands full here."

"I know that," said Greg. "I'm just trying to keep your neighbors happy. They keep showing up at council meetings."

"Well, screw them."

"Don't worry," Charlene said as she patted Woody's knuckles. "We'll take care of it this afternoon."

"Chief Bridges will be here tomorrow to see how you're doing," said Greg.

But Woody probably didn't hear this because a gust of wind carried away the words, and the next blast sent him scurrying into the house. Charlene followed him inside.

As the door closed behind them, Greg and I looked at each other — then laughed as we shrugged simultaneously.

"All we can do," he said.

"I agree. All we can do."

"So how about some lunch? I think they might have grilled cheese down at the pub."

We both laughed again. "Grilled cheese does sound kind of good, doesn't it?"

"But we have to make sure it's Velveeta."

At the pub Greg ordered a BLT and I went for the grilled cheese. We both ordered coffee. I was starting on the second half of my sandwich when Greg said, "Looks like that girl might actually get something done over there."

"Charlene? I think you're right. She seems to be just what they need. Someone to get them organized."

"Women are good at that."

Was that a comment on his co-habitation with Ivy? I had no desire to explore that minefield. Instead I turned the conversation back to the situation at Woody's house. "How much time will you give that bunch?"

"I'll tell Bridges to check in again Friday. If nothing happens by Monday I guess we'll have to get tough."

"Like take him to court?"

"Something like that."

Greg was insistent about paying for lunch so I gave up my feminist principles and let him take the check. I didn't think I could win an argument with him — he was, after all, a lawyer.

Back at my desk and waiting for the computer to kick in, I mentally replayed my time with Greg. He was a good replacement for Dukes and I had enjoyed his company. Even so, there was something about the morning's adventure that made me uncomfortable. Maybe I was wondering what Ivy would think about our lunch date. Would he tell her about it?

Then again, why should I care what Ivy thought? She wasn't exactly my best friend.

But the fact was — I didn't want her as an enemy either.

134

CHAPTER TWENTY

"Did you talk with Fiona Crawley yet — about Todd Nagel?"

I asked the question as I came out of my bedroom but Frank didn't answer. I soon discovered that he was standing in front of my hall mirror, all of his attention focused on his necktie.

"Goodness," I said, laughing at his grim expression as he ripped out the knot and started over again. "A person would think you didn't wear a tie very often."

"Have you ever seen me wearing one before?"

"Come to think of it — no."

"I think I've done this twice in the last five years — and both times I was a pallbearer."

"Well, at least this is a more cheerful occasion. Besides, the necktie was your idea."

"I know." This time his maneuver with the tie was more successful. He stood back and started sliding the knot into place. "The fact is, I think these folks are old enough to appreciate a gesture."

"I agree. And that's why I've made an effort concerning nylons and a skirt."

Frank finished with his tie and turned to look at me. His gaze traveled up and down, taking in the lavender skirt I had paired with a crocheted sweater. I wore a necklace that had belonged to my grandmother which featured an intricate pattern of silver and pearls.

"You look nice." He pulled me close for a hug.

"And so do you." Frank was wearing a pale blue shirt, along with a navy blue jacket and dress slacks. I took a deep breath. "You smell good too — sort of like lime and spice."

"Better than my usual sweaty self, I guess."

"Oh, I kind of like your sweaty self — at times."

"That's good." He planted a brief kiss on my forehead and we turned to the mirror for a final inspection.

"I guess this is what passes for formal wear in Shagoni River," he said.

"Especially in the winter. It's hard to get all frilly when dealing with the ever present danger of frost bite."

"At least we're not going far. Are Paul and Jewell coming tonight?"

"Yes, and they plan to stop here first."

"Great."

"Would you like some wine while we're waiting?"

"Sounds good. I'll try not to spill any on us."

"That's why I bought Reisling. It won't show up if we get clumsy."

When we were supplied with drinks and a plate of cheese cubes, I led the conversation back to my question. "What about Todd and Fiona — how did all of that go?"

Frank stared at the cheese as though trying to decide which color looked more appealing. He grabbed a piece of cheddar and took some time chewing before he answered.

"With Fiona, it was — well — it was difficult. We were alone in her kitchen when I played the tape and she didn't say a word — just looked sort of shell shocked. When the tape finished she broke down crying and admitted to the affair. In a way I think she was relieved that now she could tell the truth about where she was on the night her husband died. So the next day she came into the office and made an official statement."

"What about Todd?"

"I caught up with him at the hospital. Jewell put us in a conference room. Once I told him we had evidence on tape, plus his car had been spotted, he admitted to the affair. He confirmed that he had been with

136

Fiona at the motel that Saturday night and part of the following day. He asked me to keep things as quiet as possible to protect his family."

"Hah, that's a joke. It was his daughter who gave him away."

"Guess that part of it will be his own problem."

I took a sip of wine and looked at him over the edge of the glass. "Does this mean that Fiona's in the clear now?"

"Not by a long shot."

"Why not?" Surprised, I almost spilled wine on my dress.

"Isn't it obvious? A married woman having an affair has a good reason to want her husband out of the way."

"Well maybe, but still —." He was quoting Fiona's own words — but this was an angle I didn't want to think about.

But why? Why on earth was I always trying to protect Fiona? Then I remembered the phone call Frank had received as we were leaving the hospital. It seemed a safer topic.

"Frank, you said there was a bottle found by the edge of the lake. Have you learned anything from that?"

"Yes. First of all, there were traces of chloral hydrate inside."

"Aha! What else?"

"Not much. There was a tiny piece of label with a few readable letters. The lab is trying to lift some fingerprints."

I had more questions about this bottle, but our attention was diverted by the arrival of Paul and Jewell. Frank took their coats while I produced two more glasses of wine. The four of us sat down, traded a little small talk and then Frank asked Jewell for an update on Chip Crawley.

"I thought we should keep him at the hospital another day," she said, "but he wanted to go and the doctor said it was okay, so out he went. Not much time for discharge planning. Doesn't he live alone out in Crystal Valley somewhere?"

"He does," I said. "But right now — well, at least a few days ago — he was staying in town with Woody Pucket."

"Woody Pucket!" Paul said with a derisive snort. "I'm not sure if being with Woody is any better than being alone. That guy is always in some kind of trouble."

"So you've had dealings with Woody?" I said.

Paul nodded. "Pucket had homeowner's insurance with us at one time. Our inspector looked at his house, decided the place was a fire hazard and told me to make him clean up or cancel his coverage."

"What happened?"

"I tried. Over the course of several visits, I explained to him what he needed to do. Install smoke alarms, get newspapers out of the house, clean the stove, move the chimney. But he kept getting more belligerent and finally wouldn't allow me inside. So eventually I had to cancel his coverage."

"Bet he didn't like that much."

"Not a bit. He called me some names I won't repeat, accused me of discrimination, but in the end there was nothing else I could do. The guy is his own worst enemy."

"So now Woody and Chip are together," said Frank. "What a combination."

"Frank, did you ever talk to Chip Crawley again?" I said.

"I interviewed him a second time while he was still in the hospital. The guy is convinced that someone is trying to kill him."

"If that's true," said Jewell, "maybe it's just as well he's staying in town with Woody."

"I've had dealings with Woody myself," Frank said with a shake of his head.

"Those guys being together is not a good combination. They're both so full of conspiracy theories there's no telling what they might dream up next."

"Chip's sister Charlene has been over there helping out," I said. "I think maybe she's a civilizing influence on those two."

"Let's hope so," said Frank. "Chip is convinced that whoever killed his father is after him now."

"Think it's possible?" I stood and picked up the wine bottle.

"Have to consider all possibilities."

"Any idea who whacked him?" Paul held out his glass for a refill.

"I'm working on that," said Frank. "I went back to the boat storage, got the lights turned on and found some footprints on the foredeck of the *Nightcrawler.*"

"So somebody was up there? Recently?" Jewell waved me away from her wine glass.

"Yes, I'm sure of that."

"Nosing around the boat maybe?" I turned to Frank. "And Chip surprised him?"

"Can't be coincidence they were there at the same time," said Paul.

"How about this?" I said, my mind racing. "Maybe Chip was set up. Someone lured him down to the boat shed."

"Lured him down to the boat shed and whacked him? It would have to be someone he knew."

"Did you search the boat?" said Paul. "They have all kind of cubby holes, you know." Paul was speaking from experience since he had a fishing boat of his own.

"I searched it," said Frank. "And didn't find anything incriminating."

"Not even girlie magazines?" said Paul.

"Well sure," said Frank, "but it wasn't kiddie porn or anything illegal. But I have a question for you, Jewell. Does the hospital pharmacy have a supply of chloral hydrate?"

Jewell looked a bit startled. "Yes, of course."

"How well secured is it?"

"Pharmacy is locked when no one is in there. Only the pharmacists and the nursing supervisor have keys. And chloral hydrate is a controlled substance — so it's in a locked cupboard inside the pharmacy and a record is kept of all usage. Same thing on the patient units."

"Chloral hydrate get used much?"

"Not a whole lot. Sometimes on the medical ward. For older people who have trouble swallowing."

"And Fiona is an RN?" Jewell nodded. "Where does she usually work?"

I gave Frank a gentle kick in the shins. "Honey," I said, "this is supposed to be a social evening."

"I'm sorry," he said. "Forget my question."

But Jewell went ahead and answered. "Fiona is a float nurse. She goes to any unit that needs her. Lately she's been covering for one of the ER nurses on maternity leave."

"But what about doctor Todd?" I said. "Couldn't he have got the chloral hydrate?" Now I was ignoring my own dictate to avoid talking about the investigation.

"Truth is," said Jewell, "nurses have more access to drugs in the hospital than doctors. Doctors, however, have only to write a prescription and take it to a drugstore."

"The label on the bottle," I said to Frank. "Did it look like it was from a drugstore or a hospital?"

"Hard to tell," he replied. "Could have been either, as far as I know."

"The labels would be similar," said Jewell. "Do you want to talk to our hospital pharmacist? Have a look at our records?"

"Maybe later," said Frank.

My grandfather clock began to chime.

"What time are we supposed to be next door?" said Jewell.

"Right about now," I said. "Although I understand that the actual ceremony took place at the court house yesterday. Still, this is not a time to be fashionably late."

We finished our drinks and got into our coats. When the men were out on the porch I grabbed Jewell's hand and asked her to wait for a minute.

"Jewell," I said, "would you please tell Todd Nagel to have a talk with his daughter?"

"His daughter?"

"Remember I told you about his daughter, Holly? She asked me to find out about her dad and the motel business — and now I've done it. But I don't want to be the one to break the news."

"Oh sure. Now I remember," she said with a sigh.

"I realize it's not your job."

"Oh, I'll tell him." She flashed a grim smile. "It seems like a lot of the things I do never showed up in my job description."

We laughed together and joined the men. The four of us walked through a gentle snowfall to the house next door where lights beckoned through multiple layers of lacy curtains.

CHAPTER TWENTY ONE

"What a lovely old house," said Jewell as we entered Les Tattersal's living room. "Have you been here before, Tracy?"

"Many times," I said. "But things look different tonight."

And it was true. Wood surfaces had been polished to a shine, curtains were starched and a pair of rockers boasted new seat cushions. In the dining room, a crystal chandelier sent dazzling splinters of light onto cut glass vases filled with roses and lilies. The scent of flowers mingled with a spicy odor emanating from little dishes of dried flower petals.

Les and Daisy were holding court in the living room by a fieldstone fireplace, looking for all the world like a nineteenth century tintype. Daisy wore a satin dress with long sleeves and a high neck of ruffles and lace. Les stood beside her in a black suit that he might have worn for his first wedding fifty years ago.

The newlyweds greeted Frank and me with handshakes and hugs.

"You folks head right over there and get yourselves a drink." Les pointed to a corner of the room where an antique buffet had been pressed into service as a bar. "That's my son Henry playing bartender and he'll give you champagne or anything else you want."

"We have coffee too," said Daisy. "Even if you don't drink any, be sure to check out my silver coffee urn, it's almost a hundred years old."

Frank and I moved on to make room for more well wishers. Behind the bar we found Lester's son Henry, a solidly built man with a healthy crop of gray hair. While Henry served us he shared a few details of his life, mainly that he lived in Chicago, worked in finance, and had two sons in college.

We accepted two generous glasses of champagne which proved to be excellent, as near as I could tell. Moving on, we paused to admire Daisy's coffee urn which was polished to a luster and had a small gas flame burning underneath. By this time we had become separated from Paul and Jewell. Then Frank started talking to Jack Peterson who was president of the sports fishing association.

So I was on my own, which didn't bother me at all. I knew about half of the people there, at least by sight, and within a few minutes I was chatting with Daisy's hairdresser. Her name was Beulah, and she boasted that she was the only beautician in town who still did the bobby pin waves that Daisy insisted upon. Then Beulah introduced me to a petite blonde lady, who looked to be in her forties.

"This is Daisy's niece, Monica, and she lives in, let's see, Livonia, is that right dear?"

"That's right," said Monica. She extended a small hand that gripped mine firmly. "Henry and I came up to be witnesses at the wedding and help with their party. Les and Daisy don't have a whole lot of family left."

"That was very kind of you both," I said. "But it must be overwhelming to deal with a houseful of people you don't even know."

"Not at all," said Monica. "I'm used to occasions like this because I'm a writer and I have to do appearances."

"Really? What do you write?"

"Romance novels," she said with a secretive smile.

"How did you get into the romance business?"

"I studied journalism and for a while I worked for a magazine. But then I published my first book — and discovered I could make a living that way. So that's what I do. Every couple of years my publisher sends me on a tour where I sign books and talk and mingle but, by the next day, I wouldn't recognize a single person I had spoken to. Unless, of course — oh look who's here."

I followed her gaze to the foyer where a thin, bent man was slowly making his way into the room. Clearly the progress was costing him a great deal of effort. The elderly man had a cane in one hand and was leaning heavily on a younger man who supported his other side. I felt that I should know this person, but couldn't put a name to the pale, haggard face.

The crowd parted as Daisy made her way toward the two men and commandeered an arm chair for the frail newcomer.

"Who is it?" I whispered to Monica.

"He's an old, old friend of Daisy's. Or maybe suitor would be a better word since I understand he wanted to marry her —."

"Did she turn him down?"

"She told me she cared for him, but something — maybe the war — sent them in different directions. Then they both married other people."

"Oh I see. A romantic plot line."

"Of course. The world is full of them. But anyway, she's always had a soft spot for him. I'll come up with his name in a second. I know he's a lawyer."

"Then it must be Erwin Dukes," I said. "He was our village lawyer for years until he had the stroke. Poor man. I didn't even recognize him."

"That's his son who brought him. He said his dad was absolutely determined to come."

"I think I'll go say hello to him."

Monica grabbed my hand. "I'm sure he'll appreciate that —but don't expect an answer. Daisy said his speech was badly affected."

"Thanks. Thanks for telling me that."

As I moved closer to Erwin Dukes, I saw further proof of the ravages of his illness. His face was lopsided, with all expression limited to the right side while the left showed a drooping eyelid and downturned mouth.

I stood in front of him, bent down and gently placed my hand on his good arm. "Erwin," I said, "I'm Tracy Quinn — from the newspaper. I'm so glad you could come." Erwin looked up at me with an expression that may have signified recognition, or maybe just confusion. I stood up and said to his son. "It was good of you to bring your father."

"Didn't have much choice," said Joel Dukes. "Once the invitation arrived, he was absolutely determined to attend — even though everyone, including his doctor, advised against it. Dad insisted he was coming if it was the last thing he did."

As I chatted with Junior Dukes, I saw that he was a younger version of his father, who must have been a handsome man in his prime. Joel was tall and well built, with a sensuous mouth and aristocratic nose, his good looks marred only by small, dark eyes which darted nervously around the room.

"This must have been a considerable shock," I said. "To have your father change so suddenly from able and working to – ill and dependent."

Joel Dukes nodded. "It hit like a lightning storm. The worst part is that he can't even talk — to bring me and the new partner up to date on the work."

That's when I realized that this was the man who had taken on Greg Wetherel as a partner. "So how is Greg working out?" I said. Joel looked a little surprised so I felt an explanation was in order. "I know him through his girlfriend Ivy."

"Oh sure. Greg is catching on just as fast as I hoped. And he never complains about staying late or coming in on weekends."

"I'm glad things are going okay — for both of you."

"Thanks," he said. "So far there's been only one problem." Joel bent down and used a handkerchief to wipe his father's chin. "The only problem might be, actually, the girlfriend you mentioned."

"Oh, Ivy. Really?"

He shrugged. "She calls the office way too much."

"Doesn't he have a cell phone?"

"Of course. But if he doesn't answer, then she calls the office wanting to know where he is. Our receptionist is starting to call her Poison Ivy."

I wondered if the office staff included any attractive females. But I didn't say anything about that. What I said was, "I'm sure it will all work out. Ivy is probably a little insecure."

Henry appeared then with a glass of champagne for Joel and asked whether he should bring some for Erwin. Joel said that was not a good idea and the two of them fell into conversation, so I drifted away toward the food table. After a careful survey, I filled a small plate with half a dozen mints, a sugar cookie and a slice of yellow cake. I was just starting to sample it when Daisy approached me.

"This cake is wonderful," I said.

"Isn't it, though? Jennie made it for us. But Tracy, there's something I've been wanting to tell you."

"Go right ahead."

She leaned toward me and lowered her voice. "It's about the day you found that man out on the ice. Actually it was the day before you found him —."

Les appeared beside her and interrupted. "Daisy dear," he said, "I don't think you should bother Tracy with this kind of stuff. After all, she came here to relax."

"Lester, I will tell this young lady anything I please." Daisy looked her new husband in the eye. "Don't think you can start bossing me around."

I smiled. Clearly the bride had some ground rules for this marriage.

Les backed down. "Okay then," he said. "I'll leave you ladies to it."

"Let's go over there," said Daisy, nodding toward a bay window. I followed her to an alcove where deep sills held a variety of African violets. Daisy arranged her dress, then plopped down on the window seat and kicked off her satin slippers.

I followed suit, equally happy to discard the high heels I had only worn twice since moving to town. We sat together on the curved seat, our knees almost touching.

"Okay now," she said, returning to her subject. "So it was you who found the man out there."

"Yes, it was me. I was out there looking for Frank — and found him instead."

"I read about it in the paper, of course. And then, when the sheriff said it was a suspicious death, I started thinking about something I saw that Saturday — something that seemed a little bit strange. So I'm going to tell you about it — and if you think it might be important, then you go ahead and tell your boyfriend Fred."

"His name is Frank."

"Right — well, anyway, the detective. I just feel more comfortable talking to you."

"Of course. What did you see?"

"Here's what happened. I was driving back from Whitehall that day — two of my friends live down there in that condo and we get together to play cards. Now Les had invited me to meet him for dinner at the Boathouse. I don't usually go to bars but, after all, there's hardly anything open in town during the winter and they do make such good soup. Actually that is the night that Les proposed to me, so I guess you might call this a hurry up wedding." She giggled. "But not for the usual reason."

"So what was it that you saw?"

"I'm getting to that. You see, Les told me if I got there before him to just wait in my car because he didn't want me to go in there alone. So that's what I did. And I only had to wait about five minutes — but while I was waiting I saw something that struck me as peculiar. Now maybe no one else would have noticed — but you know I'm a very observant person."

"Yes you are. So what did you see?"

"I saw a man. He drove in and parked his car facing the water, as though he was going to the lake, not the bar. Now that, by itself, didn't seem unusual because there's all those shanties out on the lake. Why anyone would want to sit on the ice all day surely beats me. I'm glad Les doesn't do that any more because I wouldn't want to —-."

"The man at the lake. What did he do?"

147

"I'll tell you what he did. He got out of the car, stood there and poured out half a bottle of whiskey, well it looked like whiskey anyway — he poured it out on the snow. And then he was just getting back in his car when Les showed up so we went inside and I didn't think any more about it — at least not at the time."

"That does seem a little strange. Did you get a glimpse of his face — or can you remember what he was driving?"

Daisy started to answer, but was distracted by a babble of excited voices coming from the other side of the room.

"Excuse me," she said. Then she stood and dashed across the room in her stockinged feet. I followed through the press of bodies, noting that all normal conversation had ceased. Something had riveted everyone's attention. Finally I got close enough to see what it was.

Erwin Dukes was lying in a crumpled mass on the floor while his distraught son bent over him.

CHAPTER TWENTY TWO

"I'm sure that Erwin was dead even before he hit the floor," said Jewell. "My efforts at CPR were pretty useless."

"But the ambulance had the siren going when they left," said Paul.

"They were following protocol," she said. "But I talked to the ER supervisor this morning. She said he was pronounced dead on arrival."

I drank some coffee and thought about the previous evening. "Joel Dukes said his dad wanted to go to Daisy's party, even if it was the last thing he did."

"Looks like that's the way it turned out," said Frank, reaching for another pancake.

It was the morning after Lester and Daisy's wedding reception. Erwin's collapse had pretty much dampened everyone's spirits and the guests had begun to depart. Frank and I were among the last to leave, about an hour after the ambulance crew had carried out Erwin's body.

Now we were at the Lavallens' house, indulging in Jewell's apple pancakes with real maple syrup and plenty of butter. Our conversation covered a lot of ground, and when they spoke of their daughter Sarah's pregnancy, Paul didn't say anything about the fact that she and her boyfriend were not yet married.

"I talked with Derek yesterday," said Jewell. "He still seems pretty happy with his life in Phoenix."

"Did he say anything about Brooke?" I wondered.

"No, and I forgot to ask. I'm sorry."

"I love that girl, but I'm glad it's not my job to keep track of her," I said.

"Whatever she's doing out there in Arizona, she's certainly not interested in sharing it with me."

"Didn't you say that her dad has been trying to call you?" said Jewell.

I shot her a look. "I really don't want to deal with that right now."

Now Frank gave me a questioning look.

"No, he's not stalking me," I said, and then changed the subject. "Frank, I just remembered something — there was a piece of information that Daisy wanted me to pass on to you. It might have some bearing on the Vince Crawley case."

"Let's hear it," said Frank.

So I repeated what Daisy had told me — that on the Saturday afternoon in question she had seen a man at the edge of the parking lot pour out part of a bottle of whiskey.

"What did he do afterward?" said Frank

"What do you mean?"

"Did he head for the lake or did he get back in his car?"

"I think probably he got back in the car. Why? What are you thinking?"

"I'm thinking he could have dumped out part of the whiskey — then got in his car and poured some chloral hydrate in the bottle."

"Oh! I guess that would fit with the prescription bottle you found in the weeds at the edge of the lake."

"So what did the guy look like?"

"All she said was that the guy was pretty much average height and build — and of course you can't tell very much under winter clothes. But she did mention — one rather odd detail. She said the man wore a blue winter coat and it had little paper tags attached to the front."

"Paper tags?" said Paul.

"That's what she said."

"That is odd," said Frank. "Guess I'll need to talk to Daisy."

"In that case," said Jewell, "you'll have to wait until after the honeymoon."

"Are they going away?"

"Probably already gone," she said. "Monica told me they were leaving today for a Caribbean cruise."

"Sounds wonderful," I said.

As Paul refilled our cups, I shared the tidbit about Erwin having been Daisy's suitor. We talked about Henry and Monica and how hard they had worked to make the evening perfect for their elderly relatives.

"I wonder if those two are both unattached," said Jewell.

"A spinoff romance," I said. "Wouldn't that be spectacular?"

"I think Henry mentioned a wife," said Paul.

"Oh darn, you just killed that fantasy. Did you know that Monica is a romance writer?"

"Yes," said Jewell. "We talked for quite a while."

"I wonder if she'll be inspired to write a senior citizen romance."

"Probably not much market," said Jewell. "Anyway she gave me one of her books."

"Really? Can I see it?"

"Sure." Jewell found her purse, pulled out a paperback and handed it to me. The cover featured a young female dressed as a jockey and leading a horse, while a square jawed man looked on.

"At least it's not a bodice ripper," I said. "Can I borrow it when you're done?"

"You can have it right now. I've got three books I'm trying to finish."

It was well past noon when we said our goodbyes and headed back to my place. Frank left shortly afterward so I settled in with the book and devoured the entire thing before going to bed. At least it didn't have any calories.

Monday morning arrived on schedule. I had just started writing up a story from the council meeting when Marge came in and asked me if I was finished with the "Looking Backward" section. I swallowed hard and told her it was almost ready. The truth was I had totally forgotten about that particular assignment.

So I got busy on the project, which wasn't very difficult. The idea was that I needed to find some news story that had appeared either twenty, twenty-five or thirty years ago and prepare it for a re-run. Preferably something with a photo. So I put my other work aside and started cruising the archives for something that had happened during the month of February either twenty or thirty years ago.

Thank heaven for microfilm. I searched through headlines from the Shagoni River News and discovered that in 1972 the high school boys basketball team had been doing very well. By midseason they were undefeated and then the whole town went crazy when they took down their archrival, Baldwin, by a score of 90 to 50. The entire community rallied behind them, with high hopes for them to become Class C State Champions.

So I printed out the story and a photo of the team, turned it in and thought my assignment was done. But half an hour later Larry, our graphics guy, informed me that he wasn't happy with the quality of the photo. He said if I wanted to use the story, he needed a much better photo.

"So where could I find a better photo?"

"In the high school yearbook."

I sighed. "And where am I going to find that?"

"At the library."

"Okay. I'll try."

"By three o'clock today," he said.

So that's what I did on my lunch hour. I walked to the library and then, with a little help from one of the librarians, located the 1972 yearbook. Inside I found a pretty good photo of the basketball team, with names underneath. But when I tried to check it out, the same librarian said it was reference material and the library policy did not allow reference material to be taken out.

Using my most persuasive mode, I explained the situation and promised to have the book back the very next day. Finally she relented.

I had to fill out a special two page requisition form and let her copy my driver's license, but finally walked away with the book I needed.

Back at work I gave the yearbook to Larry and showed him the photo. He seemed satisfied. So when Marge showed up an hour later, I was able to tell her with a clear conscience that the assignment was finished. She hung up her coat, paused in front of the mirror and reminded me that I still hadn't provided the final results on the Outhouse Races.

So I called around until I found Jill, who told me that the Hunting Shack had been declared the official winner although some of the other contestants, especially the

Antler Bar crew, were disgruntled about the decision.

"It's really hard," she said. "I was trying to do something for the town and now I have a bunch of people mad at me."

"Don't let it get you down," I said. "The only way to not make anyone angry is to not do anything at all. And then someone will complain that you're not doing enough. So don't worry, Jill. By next year all the problems will be forgotten. Folks will start getting ready for the races right after Christmas, and you'll have even more contestants."

"Thanks, Tracy," she said. "I needed that."

So we ran another picture of the Hunting Shack team and provided stats on all of the race entrants. I was getting ready to leave when Larry came out of the graphics room and handed me the yearbook.

Since I had just turned off my computer, I sat for a moment and paged through the old yearbook — starting with the picture of the boys basketball team. Further investigation indicated that future lawyer Greg Wetherell had been on the debate team, the quiz bowl team and Showtime, the acting group. Turning to senior snapshots, I saw Greg with Vince Crawley showing off a string of fish. Another showed the two of them in tuxedoes with their prom dates.

But wait a minute — that night at Ivy's party, hadn't Frank asked Greg if he knew Vince Crawley? And his answer was something like — *oh we just played basketball, nothing else* —.

But then, maybe it's easy to forget adolescent friendships.

Or maybe it's only natural to want to distance oneself from a murder victim.

I headed home. But I didn't have much time to dwell on the Greg/ Vince connection. The minute I turned the corner onto Maple Street, something else drew my attention.

An unfamiliar car was parked on my side of the street. It was a white sedan which might have been a rental, and it was pretty much half way between my place and Tattersall's. I knew that Monica had gone back on Sunday. So I wondered if maybe the car belonged to Henry and he was staying on for a day or two. But if so, then why was he parked on the street?

At least the car was not blocking my driveway. So I drove on up and parked. I climbed the porch steps, telling myself I had no reason to be all paranoid about a white car on the street.

But the minute I opened my front door I knew something was wrong.

The sound of the television sent my pulse racing. I never leave the television on when I'm gone — never. Then I spotted a man's gray trench coat hanging on a hook in the foyer.

Someone was in my house. And no, I hadn't locked the door — I rarely did, except at night. So the person in my living room could be just about any one. Now I could just see the back of a man's head — he was sitting on my sofa watching the tube.

I took a deep breath and tried to calm myself.

"Frank?" I called — knowing all the while that it wouldn't be him. Maybe I wanted to make the intruder believe that I had a husband.

"No, it's not Frank," came the answer.

I held my briefcase to my chest like a shield and stepped into the living room.

The man stood and faced me, nothing about his body language offering any sort of apology. I should have known. It was nearly ten years since I had seen him but I recognized him immediately.

"Sorry to frighten you," he said. "But, damn it, Tracy, you never return my calls."

The man in my house was Steven Quinn, my ex-husband.

CHAPTER TWENTY THREE

"Tracy," he said, "it's good to see you."

My former husband greeted me with a broad smile. His demeanor suggested that we were meeting at a party, or maybe on the street, but definitely something other than the actual circumstances which felt a lot like home invasion.

I considered my visitor. The incipient wrinkles had deepened but I could still see the good looks that had been my downfall. He had gained a few pounds but for a man nearing fifty he was in pretty good shape.

Meanwhile, I struggled to find a suitable response for this guy who had divorced me nearly ten years ago and now had the nerve to reappear in my house, uninvited and unannounced.

"I see you've made yourself at home," I said, struggling to convey chilly indignation.

He was unaffected. "It was too damn cold to wait in the car. Never did like these Michigan winters."

"Then why are you here?" My grip on the briefcase was slipping. I let it slide out of my hands and land on the coffee table. A lot of thoughts jockeyed for position in my addled brain, one of them, oddly enough, was how did I look.

"I'm here because I need to talk to you."

"Really? About what?"

"About Brooke. I haven't had a word from her since before Christmas."

"In that case, I doubt if I can help you." I walked over and turned off the television. "She hasn't kept in touch with me either."

"I was hoping we could at least compare notes." He opened his hands in an entreating gesture.

"Yeah sure. Okay."

"Damn Tracy, you look good. How come I got older and you didn't?"

Ah, that old black magic. But it wasn't going to work this time. I shook my head at his outrageous compliment.

"And you've done a nice job with this old house. I thought you were going to sell it."

"I was planning to. But now I guess I'm attached to the place." I was feeling weak in the knees so I allowed myself to collapse into the recliner. Steven returned to his seat on the couch.

"I was sorry to hear about your grandfather. And your grandmother too. They were both lovely people."

Was he making this up? Did he even know my mother's parents? Then I remembered that we had made summer visits here together. "I guess you did come here a few times, didn't you?"

"Sure — you and I and Brooke. She loved the place so much when she was little. Her eyes lit up whenever she talked about Shagoni River and the Big Lake and the sand dunes."

"Probably there were some beach flirtations we never heard about." Now we were drifting into the area of shared memories.

"I wasn't surprised to hear that she came here last summer. How did that work out?"

At this point I found myself trying to steal a peek at Steven's left hand. Brooke had told me about her father going through a whole series of relationships — but I couldn't remember if he was supposed to be married at the moment or not. And what did that matter anyway? That's when I realized that Steven was looking at me, waiting for an answer.

"Sorry. Did you ask me something?"

"Just wondered how it worked out — having Brooke here last summer."

"Oh that. It was fine mostly. After we worked out the wrinkles I actually enjoyed her company."

"When I saw her last fall, she talked about you a lot. I can see that you're very important to her."

His words gave me a little rush of pride. But then — it was likely all meaningless flattery. Steven had lived in so many places, with so many different jobs, wives or girlfriends, how could he know anything about what his daughter really thought or felt? Still, I had to give him a little credit in the father department. For some reason he had agreed to finance his daughter's dream of studying ecology at some all but unknown college in the mountains of Arizona.

"I like Brooke a lot too," I said. "I just hope she doesn't regret moving out west — to a town where she didn't know a single soul."

"You spent a whole summer with her. So tell me, do you feel like she is — responsible?"

"Responsible?" I had to think for a moment. "Sure. As much as anyone is at that age. Almost twenty-one. Right?"

"Almost. Birthday this spring."

"I know she was really excited about going to Arizona. And I guess she couldn't have done it without your help."

"You're right about that. The tuition is several times what it was at a state college." He ran fingers through his hair revealing a bald spot that had previously been covered by an adroit comb over.

"I guess that means you're doing okay financially. She said you were — what — working at a radio station?"

"I did that for a while — but the station went under. Since I was already in Florida I just got into real estate. People are always coming and going, buying and selling, so there's money to be made."

"Do you like Florida?"

"Sure. Can't beat the weather."

"So what brings you up here in the winter?"

"Just to see you, sweet lady."

"Now that is a lie. I know one when I hear one."

"Okay. I had to be in Chicago to sort out some business. And since you never answer your phone and don't return my calls — here I am. What can you tell me about Brooke?"

"Not a whole lot. I got some e-mails and a couple of postcards after she got settled. She said she loved the town, and the college was everything she had hoped for. She was living in a house with three other people and working part time at a bagel shop."

"She told me the same thing. Our agreement was that I would pay tuition but she had to earn her own room and board."

"That seems fair enough."

Steven stood and started pacing. "So I've paid her tuition for this semester. The check was canceled but I haven't heard a thing from her since an early Christmas card."

"Pretty much the same for me." Then I had a scary thought. "Do you suppose something has — well — happened to her?"

"I hope not. I called the college, but they won't tell me anything except that she's enrolled there. The idiots won't even tell me if she is showing up for classes." His voice took on an angry edge that I remembered only too well.

"Well, she does have this friend Derek. He's in Phoenix now."

"Do you think they maybe ran off together?"

I laughed. "I don't think so. Derek talks to his parents every week. He drove up to see Brooke and said she was fine — but I'm not sure when that was. Maybe it was during the holidays."

"Well damn it, I need to know what's going on. After all, I'm spending big bucks on that girl and — nothing."

"Have you tried calling her?"

"Of course." Steven stopped pacing and stood in front of the fireplace. "Before she left I fixed her up with a cell phone. But the number doesn't work any more."

"E-mail?"

"No reply. Do you have a postal address?"

"There was a return address on one of the post cards. But she said she was getting ready to move — and didn't have the new address."

"Oh great. So what are we going to do?"

That was typical Steven. His problem had now become our problem. But in a way it was, because I cared about Brooke. "How about if I give Jewell a call?" I said. "That's Derek's mother. See if she has any news."

"I'd appreciate that."

So I called Jewell and got her answering machine. I explained that Brooke's father was in town looking for any information about his daughter. Did Jewell know anything? And would she try to call Derek and see if he had any recent news of her?

I hung up and said, "Beyond that I just don't know what to tell you."

"Well, thanks for trying."

We feel into an awkward silence. It occurred to me that this was the point at which I should offer Steven a cup of coffee. But I was tired and not feeling especially hospitable.

Steven resolved that dilemma. "I'm hungry," he said. "Is there some place where I can buy you dinner?"

"Ah, sure, I guess."

"Good. You decide where."

Half an hour later we were in the Antler Bar in a back booth with a gigantic pair of moose horns looming overhead. I had picked the Antler instead of the Belly Up because I figured we were less likely to run into anyone I knew. But then I wondered why it would really matter.

Maybe it was the whole idea of how I would introduce him, if the situation arose. As an old friend? My ex-husband? A traveling salesman?

Anyway the bar was quiet, as one would expect on a Monday night. We both got draft beer and hamburgers with a side order of sweet potato fries.

The juke box was playing Willie Nelson just loud enough to preclude conversation and that was fine with me because I was hungry and the beer was going down nicely. But then the music ended and a loud silence prevailed. I searched my brain for a safe topic of conversation. Finally I waved a sweet potato fry at Steven and asked what he thought of them.

"They're good," he said, "I can't believe you've introduced me to a food that I've never had before."

"Right here in the wilds of West Michigan." Then I couldn't think of anything else to say. Silence loomed again.

This time it was Steven who spoke up. "Brooke told me you were seeing someone."

I didn't respond.

But Steven wasn't about to let the subject rest "That you had a man in your life," he said. "Do you?"

"Well, yes I do."

"Good, that's good."

"He weighs three hundred pounds, works for the mob and he's very jealous."

Steven's eyebrows shot up, just before his face relaxed into a smile. "Jeez, Tracy you really had me for a second."

We both giggled. And I figured this would have been the opportune time to ask him about his personal life.

As it turned out, I never got around to asking Steven about his love life because that was the moment when the front door opened and a cold wind blew in. Along with that wind came Frank Kolowsky. Or was it him? Of course it was. I knew that man. I knew his clothes, his walk, his shape. It was Frank.

Instinctively I slid to the far corner of the booth. Maybe I could avoid Frank's notice — at least until I figured out a sophisticated way to handle this situation. But then I saw something else that turned the whole matter on its head.

Frank, my boyfriend Frank, was not alone. He was with another woman.

CHAPTER TWENTY FOUR

Or maybe Frank wasn't really *with* the other woman . Maybe she just happened to walk in behind him. But no. They were talking, gesturing, obviously deciding where to sit — at the bar or at a table.

She had her back to me but within seconds I spotted the long dark hair, the tall boots and then the cape — my god, who else in this town wears a cape? Even from behind there was no question that the woman with Frank was my colleague, Ivy Martin.

But — what was going on here? Ivy was living with Greg Wetherel. She was mad about Greg, possessive, insanely jealous, and suspicious of anything as minute as a strand of blonde hair on his person. So why was she at the Antler Bar with Frank, sitting at that table by the window, while he went to fetch drinks?

And what, if anything, should I do about it?

By this time Steven had noticed that my eyes were glued to something up front. "What's going on?" he said. "You look like you've seen a ghost."

"It's a little hard to explain."

Steven tried to lean sideways and turn around to see what had my attention.

"Don't do that," I said in a loud whisper. "Please. It's no big deal. Just some people I'd rather not see."

"Small town politics?"

"Yes. Something like that."

By this time my appetite had completely deserted me. I chewed slowly, wondering if we could stay in the booth long enough that Frank and Ivy would leave and I wouldn't need to deal with them at all. Steven was talking now, something about his plans to move to Fort Lauderdale where he could buy a boat and live on board and save money on rent — but I just nodded once in a while and kept trying to figure out what to do next. There was a back door a few feet away, a door which I knew opened into an alley which led to the street. I considered the possibility of Steven and me slipping out through that door.

But that would be childish, wouldn't it? Yes, it would. And if we did that I would never find out what was going on with those two up front. Because I didn't see how I could ask Frank about it later. That would be putting him in a bad spot — and then would I be able to believe anything he told me? I nibbled on my burger and scooted to the edge of my seat so I could see a little more of what was going on.

Were Frank and Ivy eating? Or just having a drink? It looked like he had a beer and she had one of those frothy green things she favors. I wondered if Frank was paying for that. Well, of course he was. And what business was it of mine?

I still hadn't figured out what to do when Frank stood and moved in our direction, then turned into the hallway which led to the restrooms. So far he hadn't seen me, but I knew that when he came out we would be directly in his line of sight.

If I could hide somewhere, then all he would see was a man sitting alone in the booth. And he wouldn't know who Steven was. But I couldn't figure out anywhere to hide. Except maybe behind the life-size cardboard cutout of the race car driver? But then my ex-husband would have good reason to believe that I was totally nuts. I grabbed the menu, held it up and pretended to be fascinated by something I was reading there.

Minutes later a familiar bulk emerged and started moving in our direction. I kept my eyes on the menu and just as Frank approached our table, I looked at him in mock surprise.

"Tracy," he said as he glanced from me to Steven. "Fancy meeting you here."

I gave him a big smile. "I was just thinking the same thing."

The two men studied one another.

"Steven," I said, "this is my friend, Frank. Frank this is Steven. He's visiting from out of town."

"Nice to meet you." Frank reached out and they exchanged a manly handshake.

Innocently, I patted the seat next to me. "Are you alone?"

"Believe it or not, I'm with your friend Ivy." He nodded toward the front and I saw Ivy up there, watching him closely. He put his hands on our table and leaned down. "She insisted on meeting with me here. Alone."

"Really?"

"Really. Said she had some mysterious note to show me. But so far she hasn't produced it."

"Sounds like Ivy," I said. "She loves drama."

"So look," he said, as he began to move away. "Call me tomorrow, will you? We need to talk."

"You're so busy," I said. "How about if you call me? When you have time."

"I'll do that," he said.

By this time Ivy had spotted me so I gave her a little finger wave which she returned. I knew that as soon as Frank got within range she would ask him who was with me in the booth.

What was it I had told him? *An out of town visitor.* Let her chew on that for a while.

We finished eating and Steven asked me if I wanted to play a game of pool. I decided there was no harm in a friendly game so I agreed and he ordered more beer for both of us. Now that I was over the shock of his reappearance I was starting to feel a little more relaxed. Of course the beer helped too. After all, he was an old friend — and there had been some good times.

Fiddling with my pool cue and studying the balls on the table provided me with an effective way of ignoring the couple up front —

but I had the feeling that Ivy was not going to leave quietly. And I was right. I was leaning on my cue stick and Steven was lining up a shot when Ivy appeared beside me.

"Tracy," she said. "You must introduce me to your friend."

So I made the introduction, once again referring to him as an out of town visitor and omitting his last name. Because it was the same as mine, it would have given her way too much information.

Steven abandoned his shot and gave Ivy his full attention. She looked up at him while she pulled on her gloves. "So where are you visiting from?"

He ignored the pool game to gaze back at her. "I'm in Florida right now, not far from Miami."

So then Steven joined Ivy in complaining about Michigan weather until Frank, who had been at the bar settling their tab, came over and told her he was leaving.

I'm sure she wanted to stay and flirt with Steven a little more, but she also wanted to leave with Frank, so she could bolster the impression that they were on some kind of date.

"Guess I have to go," she said. "So nice to meet you, Steven. Will you be around for a while?"

"Leaving tomorrow," he said.

"Oh, that's too bad. Be sure to come and see us again."

Ivy turned and marched to the front door and Frank held it open for her. He lingered for a moment until he caught my eye so I shrugged and waved before I turned my attention back to the pool table.

The game lasted quite a while because neither of us was trying very hard to win. We did a lot of talking and laughing at one another's bad shots. Although I didn't ask him, Steven revealed that the 'business in Chicago' had to do with his latest divorce.

"A divorce," I said. "Does that make number three or four?"

"Four, I'm afraid."

"This one didn't last long, did it?"

"Less than a year." He hit the cue ball and it went straight into a corner pocket. "Guess I'm just not marriage material."

"That's one way of putting it." I dropped the eight ball in the opposite corner.

"I realize it's not a great track record. And, in the end, there's only one thing I know for sure."

"What's that?"

"I will never, ever get married again." He chalked his cue. "It's too damn expensive."

"So that's how you reckon failed marriages? Like an expense account?"

He shrugged.

"Isn't there any emotional cost?"

He walked around the table, considering the layout. "I guess you might say that I'm emotionally bankrupt."

A moment of truth for Steven? Oddly enough, I felt a surge of sympathy for him. And that, I guess, was his deadly charm. Whether calculated or not, Steven somehow made women feel sorry for him. And then they married him? Amazing.

Our conversation moved back to less personal topics and when we had finally disposed of all the balls, neither of us had the faintest idea who might have won. We stepped outside into a blast of snow, propelled by the wind that came gusting off the lake. We reached my house and found a message from Jewell. So I called her and this time she answered.

"I called Phoenix and spoke with Derek," she said, "but he couldn't tell me much that we didn't already know. He went up to Prescott for New Years and Brooke told him she was planning to move — some kind of house sitting arrangement. Then a couple of weeks later, he got one e-mail saying that she loved her new place — but nothing after that. He gets no response from his e-mail messages. Her phone number doesn't work. He thought about getting in touch with her previous room mates but there's no house phone and he doesn't know how to reach them."

"Sounds like it's pretty much a dead end."

"At this point yes. But I have firmed up my travel plans. I'm going to see Derek at the end of the month. He said he wanted to show me Prescott so, while we're there, we could try some inquiries in person."

"That would be helpful," I said. "I'll tell Steven."

After I hung up I relayed everything to Steven.

"Seems like kind of a long shot," he said.

"Do you have any better ideas?"

He shook his head.

"We're just lucky that those two care about her enough to make the effort."

"I guess you're right."

"I'm tired," I said, stifling a yawn. "And tomorrow is a big day at work."

"And I have to be on the road early." He looked at his watch. "Can you recommend a place for me to stay?"

"We have some B and B's," I said. "But they all close this time of year."

"I saw a motel out on the highway."

"That's the Best Western. They just went into foreclosure."

"Oh great." He looked at me with that little boy expression I remembered. "Is there any chance I could maybe — um — stay here for the night?"

"Not in my bed."

"That's not what I meant."

"Of course," I said, feeling the blood rush to my cheeks. "There's the bedroom upstairs. You can have it if you don't mind shivering a little."

He smiled. "I remember that room. That's where you and I used to —. Sure, that would be fine. I hope I'm not imposing."

Was he? That was a moot question. But for some reason I didn't feel mean enough to turn my ex-husband out into a blustery winter night.

Not much later I was snuggled under my electric blanket while Steven was upstairs dealing with cold sheets. But my thoughts were not on the man in the upstairs bedroom.

I was thinking about Frank because I had an awful lot of questions for him — starting with the mysterious note that Ivy had used to lure him into the Antler. Was there really such a note — or was she playing some kind of game?

Like trying to make Greg jealous?

Or messing with my head?

With Ivy, anything was possible.

CHAPTER TWENTY FIVE

By the time I woke up the next morning, Steven was gone.

Fine with me. Now that he was out of sight, he could also be out of mind. Already his visit was beginning to feel like a movie or a dream, something that didn't fit into my real life and perhaps had never happened at all.

I was far more concerned about Frank. At work, I waited for a phone call from him — a contrite phone call — full of apologies and a good explanation as to why he had been with Ivy at the Antler Bar on Monday night.

But as the morning passed I realized that he wouldn't want to interrupt me at work to talk about anything so personal. I went home for lunch, checked the answering machine and found the red light blinking. Instantly I felt relieved and validated.

That feeling disappeared when I pushed the button and heard a man telling me that I was in serious credit card debt and his company wanted to help me out. I talked back to the voice, called the man an imbecile, asked him how he knew so much about my finances. Then I felt like an idiot for talking to a message machine.

For about five minutes I was very, very tempted to pick up the telephone and call Frank.

But then I remembered the lame excuse he had provided about being with Ivy and I got angry all over again. Surely it was his place to call me and explain. As far as my being in the same bar at the same time with my ex-husband — well maybe Frank was a bit flummoxed by that. It was all very confusing. In any case, I had to get back to work so I made myself a fried egg sandwich and ate it with a lot of mustard.

Fortunately the afternoon was busy enough that I didn't have time to think about the situation. Shortly after 5:30 I finished up and headed home feeling absolutely sure that I would find a message from Frank. But there was nothing. Not even a sales pitch from the cable company.

The temptation to call him was nearly unbearable now, and I started rehearsing exactly what I would say — how I would express my righteous indignation. Then the telephone rang. Although I was standing right over the device, I let it ring three times before I answered.

It wasn't Frank. But at least it was a real person, it was Jewell.

"Tracy," she said, "is your, ah, visitor gone?"

"Steven? Oh yes. Probably in Chicago by now. Or maybe on a plane to Miami."

"So how are you coping?" *Coping? Had she heard something about Frank and Ivy?* "What I mean," she continued, "is that Steven's visit must have stirred up a lot of old feelings for you."

"Oh that. I'm doing okay, really."

"Are you sure?"

"Jewell, I've been way too busy to think about him much. No, that's not exactly true. Because here's what I've really been thinking about — Steven and I went to the Antler for supper and while we were there Frank came in."

"That must have been awkward."

"That's only half of it. Frank was with Ivy."

"Frank and Ivy?! I don't believe it."

"I didn't either. But I saw them with my own eyes."

"This is rich. We definitely need to get together — because I have news too. How about coming over for supper? We can talk while we're getting it ready. Paul's not here yet, he's going to be a little late."

"Sounds great." I agreed quickly because I knew that if I stayed home I would break down and call Frank. "I'll bring a bottle of wine."

I didn't even bother to change clothes. I just grabbed the bottle, still in its brown paper bag, and drove straight to Lavallens' house. Within minutes of my arrival, Jewell and I were laughing and talking while I foraged through her refrigerator for salad materials.

"Our main course is shrimp curry with rice," she said.

"Sounds good. Did you make it?" I lined up lettuce, celery and carrots next to the cutting board.

"I brought it home from work. We had a lunch hour staff meeting and Doctor Ahmed brought in food. His wife loves to cook and there is always a lot left over."

"Lucky for us," I said as I began chopping. "Okay, you go first. What was your news?"

"Oh that. Well, it had to do with Chip Crawley's injury."

"Ah yes. The mysterious attack in the boat storage shed. Did they find out who whacked him?"

"Here's what Frank and the doctor figured out — nobody whacked him."

"Nobody? Then what —?" I paused with a carrot in one hand, the peeler in the other.

"As it turned out, nobody hit Chip Crawley, he just fell. Dr. Todd thought the
x-rays were not consistent with Chip's story about being hit over the head. He talked to Frank and then consulted with a radiologist who agreed. The pattern and location of the injury indicated that he fell and hit his head on the cement floor."

"So where did he fall from?"

"From the boat."

"Okay. I guess that could do it." I remembered being in the barn and asking Frank why the boats loomed so high above our heads.

"But Tracy, please, remember this is all privileged information."

"Of course."

"So then Frank talked to Chip again. And this time Chip admitted that he had climbed up onto the deck of the boat. He said he fell because he had snow on his boots and the deck was slippery."

"And of course he'd been drinking. So why did he come up with that intruder story?"

"He claims that when he woke up in the hospital, he was confused and thought somebody had hit him. So maybe that's true. But I also think he didn't want to admit to being drunk and clumsy. The story of being attacked was a lot more dramatic."

"So I guess Frank can quit looking for a deranged maniac wandering around boatyards."

"Right. But quick now, before Paul comes, tell me about Frank and Ivy."

Normally I don't talk to Jewell about Ivy Martin. Her indiscretion with Paul had done permanent damage to Jewell's trusting nature and to the marriage — so I always tried to avoid any conversation that would stir up painful feelings.

But now Jewell wanted to know what had happened Monday night.

So while I chopped celery, I told her about finding Steven at my house and how, after a few preliminaries, we had gone to the Antler for supper.

"We sat in a booth in the back and I figured I wouldn't see anyone who knew me. But I was wrong on that count. Pretty soon Frank walked in and right behind him came Ivy."

"What did you do?"

"I tried to hide but that didn't work. Frank eventually saw me and came over so I had to introduce him to Steven."

"As your ex-husband?"

"As an out of town visitor."

"I wish I could have been a fly on the wall."

"Then Frank tried to explain why he was there with Ivy and, honestly, it sounded absurd. Apparently she had called him and said she had some mysterious note she wanted to show him."

"Sounds like the Hardy Boys. Did you see the note?"

"No. Frank said he hadn't seen it yet himself. So it could all be a big fabrication on her part."

"But I wonder why she did it? Isn't she living with that lawyer boyfriend of hers?"

"Yes, she is. Greg moved in with Ivy a few weeks ago. I'm pretty sure he's still with her. Otherwise, Ivy would be on the phone to me, weeping and threatening suicide."

"Okay," said Jewell, as she slid a casserole dish into the microwave. "Enough about Ivy. I want to know about you and Steven."

"I already told you most of it. He thought I might know something about Brooke. He's furious because he's paying her tuition and she doesn't communicate with him."

"I already know that. But I want to know about you."

"About me?"

"How did you feel, seeing him again. Did your heart flutter?"

"Hah! Maybe for a minute — but only because it scared the dickens out of me to find him in my house."

"Are you sure that was all?"

"Pretty sure. Why?"

Jewell set the microwave and turned around to face me. "Because whenever I heard you talk about Steven, I always got the impression that you hadn't resolved your feelings for him."

"You may be right," I said. "After all, I was madly in love. I thought the marriage was going to last forever. And then, one day, he just changed his mind. End of story."

"You must have wondered what you did wrong."

"I tried for years to figure it out."

"Have you?"

"I understand now that Steven has a short attention span when it comes to romantic partners. That's really all there is to it."

We both had a laugh when I told her it was his latest divorce that had forced him to travel from Florida to Chicago.

"He sounds like a guy with some real problems."

"He does have problems — and I'm relieved to no longer be a part of them. Our only connection now is this business about Brooke."

"And Brooke is a valid concern. For all of us. I hope I can learn something about her when I go to Arizona."

"Me too. Steven gave me his phone number and e-mail so we can contact him. It was all on a note he left this morning."

Jewell took a stance, hands on her hips. "Does that mean he spent the night?"

"What are you," I sputtered, "my mother?"

"Oh, I'm sorry. You don't need to answer if you don't want to."

"If I don't answer — then you'll really think something happened."

"Not my business, really."

"No big deal. I let him sleep upstairs. He was gone this morning before I got up."

"Does anything feel different now?"

"Yes it does. It feels like I've finally laid that ghost to rest."

"That's great. Now maybe you and Frank can —."

Just then the dog started barking deliriously, the door opened and Paul came inside, bearing the scent of cold air and new snow. He gave Jewell a hug and then gave me one too.

"What are you ladies cooking? The smell in here is making me crazy."

Jewell told him he was about to experience authentic Indian curry and we lost no time getting dinner on the table. While we ate, I told Paul about the reason for Steven's visit — that he was worried about Brooke.

"Does Derek know anything?" Paul said to Jewell. "I'm sure he went up to Prescott to see her at least once."

"I called Derek," she said. "He's had no contact with her in over a month."

"That's odd," he said. "Brooke didn't seem like the flighty type."

"Derek and I are going to investigate when I go to Arizona," said Jewell.

"Lucky you," I said. "I bet you're looking forward to some sunshine."

"I am. But I really hate to travel alone." She cast a wistful glance at her husband.

"You know I'd go with you if I could," said Paul. "But our agent in Newaygo is off for a month with chemotherapy so I'm handling most of his work load along with my own."

"I know," said Jewell. "And right now I need to use my vacation time or lose it."

"How about you, Tracy," he said. "Why don't you go with Jewell?"

"What an idea." I reached for a piece of bread. "I've never thought about taking time off. I'm not sure we have such a thing as a paid vacation."

"Even Marge must offer some kind of vacation." Paul refilled our wine glasses. "By the way, this stuff is pretty good." He held his glass up to the light. "And thanks for bringing it. My last client today left me feeling pretty stressed out."

"Oh, I'm sorry," said Jewell. "We've been talking nonstop and never asked you anything about your day."

"My day was fine until this afternoon," he said. "My last appointment got so irate that he ended up swearing and threatening me with bodily harm."

"Who on earth was that?"

"Chip Crawley."

"We were just talking about him," said Jewell. "What problem did you have with him?"

"He was unhappy about the insurance premium for that truck he got from his dad."

"The truck with the snow plow?"

"That's the one. His dad carried a form of business insurance on it."

"You know, I remember Fiona telling Chip that she would give him the truck but she couldn't give him the boat —."

"Right. So she gave him the truck and he's got a list of customers and plenty of snow. But he's finding that it's much harder to run the business himself — instead of just working for his dad."

"So what's going on?"

"The insurance premium is due and it's higher than it was before. That's because Chip is younger and also he's had a couple of traffic

174

violations. There's nothing I can do about that. But Chip came in, along with his friend Woody, and they spent the better part of an hour complaining and threatening."

"Those two seem to feed off each other," I said.

"Chip says I'm discriminating against him."

"They love that word."

"He threatened to take his business elsewhere and I'd be happy if he did. But I'm supposed to work with him. It doesn't look good if I lose a customer."

"Maybe you need a vacation," I said. "Just run away for a week with Jewell."

"I can't, Tracy. I think you should be the one to go."

"Well, maybe. I'll look into it."

And on the way home I did think about going to Arizona with Jewell, but only for a few minutes.

Because most of the time I was thinking about Frank. Frank and Ivy. And the mysterious note? What balderdash!

CHAPTER TWENTY SIX

"That out of town visitor you were entertaining," said Frank. "Did he happened to spend the night at your house?"

"You should know," I retorted. "You probably had the place staked out."

"That's ridiculous."

"Okay, so maybe you didn't have a deputy watching my house. No doubt the village cop drove by a couple of times and figured he should let the Great Detective know that his girlfriend had an extra car at her house during the night. I know how you guys work."

"It's their job to keep an eye on things."

"And report suspicious behavior. Damn it, Frank I don't like being spied on. I should be able to have company whenever I want without answering to you."

"Tracy, I'm not accusing you of anything."

It was Wednesday. Without the courtesy of a phone call, Frank had arrived at my house shortly after I got home from work. Now we were finally having it out in my living room — and things were not going very well. I decided to turn the tables.

"And what about you and Ivy?" I said. "What kind of nonsense was that about a note? I don't believe any of it."

"I didn't either, at first." Frank was on my sofa focused on the cup of takeout coffee he had brought with him. He looked up at me.

"There was, in fact, a note. She turned it over to me and it's now being dusted for fingerprints."

"Really?" I stopped being angry. Now I was curious.

"Really. And the note was addressed to Greg."

"Did it come in the mail?"

"According to Ivy, the note showed up in their mailbox, in an envelope with no stamp or postmark, just Greg's name on the envelope."

"So someone hand delivered it."

"Looks that way. Ivy said she got home first and opened it by mistake."

"No mistake there," I said. "Just her insatiable curiosity."

"Well sure, but I could tell it hadn't been sealed. She said she wouldn't have opened it if it had been sealed."

"That's debatable. But anyway, what did it say?"

"The note was just three words. Ivy said she read it and was terrified. But when Greg came home and saw it, he downplayed the whole thing. She wanted him to go to the police but he refused. So she contacted me instead. We met at the Antler and she gave me the note."

"So what did the note say?"

"See for yourself. I made a copy."

Frank reached into a shirt pocket and pulled out a folded piece of paper. Overcome with curiosity, I sat next to him. He smoothed out the paper, revealing a message composed of letters cut out of magazines.

"Oh, this is classic," I said, struggling to make out the words. Some were print and some were script, some capitals and some lower case, the sizes varied. But when I put it all together it said; *You're next sucker.*

I stared at the words, trying to puzzle out a meaning. "*You're next.* What could that mean?"

Frank shrugged. "I don't know. Ivy doesn't either. And she doesn't want me to talk to Greg."

"Why not?"

"Because he told her to forget the whole thing. She doesn't want him to know she came to me."

"So there isn't much you can do."

"We'll see what we can get in the way of fingerprints."

The phone rang but I let the machine take it. It was Helen at the library scolding me because I hadn't returned the yearbook as promised. She begged me to get it back so she wouldn't get in trouble for letting me take out reference material. As the message ended, I glanced around my living room, trying to remember what I had done with the missing book. Or had I left it at work?

But then something clicked. I not only remembered the location of the Shagoni River High School yearbook, I was suddenly glad I hadn't returned it.

"Frank," I said, "I need to show you something."

So I located my briefcase and hauled out the yearbook. I sat next to Frank and leafed through it until I found the pages that featured snapshots of Vince Crawley and Greg Wetherell fishing and clowning and on a double date.

"This is Greg." I pointed to the photos. "And this is Vince. They seem to be spending a lot of time together."

Frank took the book and examined the pictures. "It looks like they were pretty good buddies in high school."

"Yes. Although he seemed to downplay their friendship — remember that night at Ivy's party when you asked him if he knew Vince?"

"I remember asking him. But I don't remember exactly what he said."

"Something to the effect that they both played basketball — but didn't run in the same crowd. Almost like he was trying to deny their connection."

"And now Vince is dead." Frank left the book open and placed it in front of us on the coffee table.

"Do you think that whoever killed Vince is coming after Greg?"

Frank bit his lower lip. "If that's the case, then why bother to warn him ahead of time?"

I had no answer for that. But at least Frank and I had forgotten about our quarrel.

Thursday was book club night. Jewell and I were planning to have supper at the Mexican restaurant in town and she suggested that we invite Fiona.

"I think it would do her good," Jewell said and I agreed.

When I arrived it was easy to spot the two women — Jewell with her soft blonde hair and Fiona with that mass of fiery curls. Both of them were sipping margaritas from frosted glasses which looked so good that I ordered one too.

After our food arrived, Fiona said, "I'm sorry I missed the last meeting."

"There's no need to apologize," said Jewell. "Under the circumstances, book club was probably the last thing on your mind."

"Anyway, thanks for inviting me tonight. I probably wouldn't have come otherwise."

"I just finished the book," I said. "Did you have time to read it, Fiona?"

"Not lately," she said as she turned her attention to the food. "But at some point I read all of the Father Blackwood mysteries. My mother buys every one of those books and passes them on to me."

"Oh," I said. "Because of the Irish connection?"

"The Irish connection and the Catholic connection."

"So were you raised in the church?" said Jewell.

"Oh sure, first communion and everything. But I pretty much gave up on the church after my first husband divorced me and then tried to annul our marriage."

"How about Vince?" I said.

"Same story, pretty much. By the time we met, he had lost interest in the church too."

"I guess it happens to a lot of people," said Jewell.

"But you know, it was kind of strange," said Fiona. "Or maybe it's not so strange. After he was diagnosed and knew that things were pretty bad, Vince talked to me once about wanting to see a priest."

"Did he ever do it?"

"I'm not sure. Apparently he had looked up the telephone number for Father

Radonis because I found it in our address book."

"Did he ever contact him?"

"I don't know if he made contact or not. Sometimes I got the feeling there was something that Vince wanted to get off his mind — but he would never discuss it with me."

We ate in silence until Jewell said, "How are you dealing with being alone?"

Fiona's reply was preceded by a bitter laugh. "I'm not exactly alone," she said. "Charlene is staying with me."

"I thought she just came for the funeral," said Jewell.

"That's what I thought too. But then Charlene said she was unemployed and wondered if she could stay around and offer moral support to her brother."

"So you said yes?"

"I couldn't think of any way to say no. The house belonged to Vince — it's the one she grew up in."

"How is that working out?"

"I guess as good as you could expect. I had to get on her about dirty dishes and late night TV but she does buy groceries. I think she buys them with food stamps but I'm not going to quibble about that."

"How long does she plan to stay?" said Jewell.

"No idea. I think she pretty much lives from day to day." Fiona shrugged. "In any case, she was a big help sorting through Vince's clothes and stuff. Charlene's own mother has disappeared — so I guess she's letting me be her mother figure for a while."

"Doesn't Charlene have any idea where her mother is?"

Fiona shook her head. "All we know is that Charlene's sister Rose went to California a while ago. Then the mother — that's Dixie — about a year ago, Dixie went out to visit Rose and just never came back. When Vince died, we couldn't reach either one of them. So I guess it's no wonder that Charlene is hanging onto Chip. He's all the family she's got."

"Does Charlene spend a lot of time with her brother?" said Jewell

"She does," said Fiona. "It's kind of funny because a lot of time she and Chip are with Woody Pucket. I call them the Gruesome Threesome. I don't think Woody is a very good influence, but right now Chip needs a friend."

"I heard that Chip was angry about his insurance premium," said Jewell.

"Oh sure. She told me all about that. So did he. But hey, he wanted the truck and I gave it to him. He's got to handle things himself now."

"Sounds like Chip is not very mature," I said.

"No, he's not. He's easily influenced. When the three of them are together, I see Woody getting Chip all riled up over something, I mean anything at all, and then Charlene tries to calm them both down."

"So maybe it is a good thing that she's staying," said Jewell.

"I think it probably is," said Fiona as she drained her glass. "Hey, do you think we have time for another margarita?"

CHAPTER TWENTY SEVEN

"I think you need more wax on your skis," Frank said as he paused on the trail and waited for me to catch up with him.

"I think you're going too fast," I replied, taking in great gulps of the cold air. "Besides, your legs are longer than mine."

Owing to a lapse of sanity I had allowed Frank to convince me that the best cure for my winter doldrums would be to get outside and enjoy the season. Or at least try to enjoy it. At the very least, pretend to enjoy the snow and cold.

So Frank had dug out his cross country skis and Jewell had let me try her daughter's set of skis, poles and shoes. A certain part of me had been hoping that the equipment would be the wrong size and I would be allowed to back out of the winter exercise. But I had no such luck. Everything fit perfectly and I had no excuse to spend another weekend indoors, complaining about the weather.

So there I was, bundled from toes to nose and already starting to sweat as I trekked along a trail through one of those splendid forests that had given Cedar County its name.

"Okay," I said when I caught up with Frank. "Let's put on more wax. And see if that helps." I was happy for any excuse to take a break.

Frank went a little farther until he found a spot that suited him, then stopped and used one of his poles to release the catch on his skis.

He kicked them off, picked up the skis and leaned then against the trunk of a giant maple.

I approached Frank and stood still, breathing hard and trying to figure out my next move. I had been on cross country skis a few times before — but that had been a long time ago and I was having trouble remembering the drill. Frank released the clamps that held the skis to my shoes.

"Just kick then off," he said.

So I did. "I'm exhausted," I said as I sat down in the snow and leaned against the tree. Frank pulled a cylinder of wax from his pocket and rubbed the wax on my skis.

"They should work better now."

"I hope so. I feel like I've just run a marathon."

"I know what you need." He stuck my skis into the snow so they were standing upright. Then he took off his mittens, tossed them on the ground by the tree and sat on them, leaning back against the trunk.

"Oh, you're smart," I said as I felt the moisture seeping through my pants. "Now I have a wet butt and you don't."

"It's not too late," he said.

So I pulled off my mittens and, in a series of awkward maneuvers, managed to reposition them under my derriere. Meanwhile Frank had reached into one of his commodious pockets and produced a Thermos of coffee. He twisted off the cap, which doubled as a cup, and filled it up for me.

"Careful," he said. "It should be hot."

I took a cautious sip from the metal cup and found the temperature to be just right. And so were the contents, strong and sweet.

"Truly the nectar of the gods," I said with a sigh. Then I reached into my own pocket, pulled out a pair of chocolate bars and handed him one.

"Isn't it great to be outside?"

I considered the question as I looked around. There was not another soul in sight, nor any sound or suggestion of human activity. The sun was shining on new snow, a squirrel was chittering in the tree above us and a pair of tiny birds flashed by.

I finally decided that the entire venture may have been worthwhile. "I'm glad you got me out here," I said. "It kind of puts things in perspective."

And this was true. We had given up our bickering about Steven's visit, about Frank's date with Ivy, and even the mysterious warning note someone had delivered to Greg. All of those issues seemed inconsequential compared to the quiet serenity of the forest.

For the moment, I was happy to be with Frank, sharing the bite of fresh cold air and the view of snow covered trees. Coffee and chocolate had never tasted so good. When Frank finished his chocolate bar he said, "When are Les and Daisy expected home?"

"Maybe tonight. At least I hope so. It feels a bit lonely without those lights next door."

"Remind me to go over and shovel the porch for them. Make their homecoming a little easier."

"Good idea. After a week in the Caribbean, they're bound to find the snow a bit of a shock." A shoestring of cloud drifted across the sun, which was approaching the tree line. "Shouldn't we be heading back?" I said, trying to calculate the amount of remaining daylight.

"No turning back. The trail is a loop. We just have to keep going and we'll end up where we started."

"I'll have to trust you on that." I finished my chocolate, put the wrapper in my pocket. "Are you planning to ask Daisy about what she saw that day by the lake?"

"I do want to talk with her. But I'll wait until Monday at least."

"That's considerate of you."

Frank knew what Daisy had seen — the man by Arrowhead Lake, dumping out the contents of a whiskey bottle. The detail seemed pretty inconsequential but we both knew that sometimes Daisy's observations turned out to be helpful. Now my thoughts turned back to the day I had found Vince Crawley's body.

"It's been five weeks," I said. "Do you have any actual suspects?"

Frank let out something between a groan and a sigh. "Fiona was my prime suspect — until we figured out why we couldn't find her that Sunday."

"Looks like she was canoodling with Todd Nagel."

"Right. Of course the two of them could be in it together, protecting one another."

"I suppose. But what do you think about the son Chip? He seems a bit wacky."

"I haven't ruled him out yet."

"And now Chip is spending a lot of time with Woody Pucket."

"Woody is a wild card too. But we don't have a shred of evidence against any of them. Or any kind of motive. Why kill a dying man?"

"That's a puzzle. But tell me about that prescription bottle your men found by the lake. The one with traces of chloral hydrate."

"There was only one corner of label left on it. But that corner had a partial phone number which turned out to be the Rite Aid drugstore in Muskegon."

"Does that tell you anything?"

"A little, maybe. I went to Rite Aid and talked to the chief pharmacist. Asked him to develop a list for me — everybody who had gotten chloral hydrate from them for the past two years."

"That could be a lot of people."

A snowflake drifted downward. And then another. More clouds were scudding in from the west.

"I think we'd better get going," he said.

I pulled myself upright and groaned. The rest had cooled me down and now my butt was wet. "I'm aching in muscles I didn't know I had."

"How about a massage when we get home?"

"You're on." I laid out my skis and Frank helped me get them on.

By the time we got moving, snow was falling in earnest. The clouds had coalesced into a solid band and daylight was fading. The trip didn't feel so idyllic anymore.

"You said we'd be back before dark."

"Dark's coming a little early. Didn't plan on this snowfall."

"Are you sure we're on the trail?"

"Let's save out breath for moving." Frank picked up the pace.

An edge of fear started pricking at me. The thought of spending a night in the cold held no romantic allure, even if I would be with Frank. It was dusk and I was scared. But I kept my thoughts to myself and pushed one foot after the other, following in the tracks that I couldn't always see clearly.

The silence was broken by an eerie wail. It might have been a loon or an owl, I didn't know — and I didn't care. I had no time for ornithology — I just wanted to get home. My legs and arms were aching, my chest felt tight and I was tempted to beg Frank to slow down. But I didn't. Instead, I tried to move faster. My heart was thumping and I felt light headed, with my feet throbbing and sweat trickling down my chest.

Frank was around a curve and out of sight when I hear him yell, "We made it."

Encouraged, I pushed hard around the bend. I felt like cheering when I saw the trailhead sign and, beyond that, our snow covered vehicle.

Frank was examining the sign. "I thought we were taking the shortest loop," he said. "Guess we took a longer trip than I planned."

"Remind me not to go on any more winter adventures with you."

"At least it turned out better than the ice fishing."

"Can't argue with that."

We packed everything into the Blazer, climbed in and turned on the heat. Now that it was over, I felt proud of myself for braving the elements. We headed down the two track and fell into a lively debate about where to go for supper.

We hit the main road just as the wind picked up. Churning snowfall made hypnotic patterns against the windshield — but I wasn't worried. During my time with Frank, I had developed complete confidence in his driving. Through rain, snow, sleet or tornado strength winds, Frank and his vehicle moved as one and they handled the elements flawlessly.

Tired from the exertion and lulled by the heat, I must have dozed off. I awoke with a start as I heard Frank yell, "Damn it!" The brakes slammed on, which sent me lurching forward against the seat belt.

Then came the sickening crash of metal against metal and an impact threw me against the door on my side, my head hitting hard on the window. Time stretched out as the Blazer went into a spin across the icy road, a spin that ended with a thud when we made solid contact with a snow bank.

I shook my head and struggled to get my bearings. A blinking yellow light was making strobe like patterns against my eyelids. Frank's hand was on my shoulder.

"You okay?"

I took a deep breath. "I think so. What happened?"

"Goddamn idiot went right through a stop sign and red blinker. I swerved when I saw them but they clipped us pretty good."

"Felt like we spun around."

"More than once. Right in the middle of the intersection. Lucky there was no traffic."

"Where's the other car?"

"Can't see it. Must have gone off the road and down the embankment." Frank already had his cell phone out and was calling nine-one-one. "Two car accident," he said and gave the location. "I'm going to go check on the other car." He reached under his seat and grabbed a flashlight. "You stay here and keep warm."

This was typical. Even if the guy who hit us was an idiot, Frank wasn't going to let him bleed to death. Frank swore softly while he struggled to get his door open. Then he got out and I saw him pause to check for damage to his vehicle before he walked across the road. Ignoring his instructions, I got out and followed him.

It wasn't hard to find the car that had sent us into the tailspin. The skid marks and broken guard rail formed a clear trail. I stood just behind Frank while he surveyed the rear end of a gray sedan that had its front end burrowed into the snow. He shone his flashlight through the back window but the headrests made it difficult to see how many people were inside.

Whoever it was, they were trapped in there. All four doors were blocked by the snow bank they had plowed into. And this wasn't ordinary snow. The road was lined with piles of ice, dirt and snow that had been accumulating all winter, refreezing into harder chunks each time the plows went by.

By this time Frank was aware of my presence. All he said was, "Go see if you can find a shovel in the back of the Blazer."

Then he started digging in the snow with his hands, determined to free the driver who could easily have killed us all.

CHAPTER TWENTY EIGHT

Back in the Blazer, I spent several minutes rummaging through tools and clothes until I found a short-handled shovel under the back seat. I delivered this to Frank who took it without a word and returned to his task of digging out the buried car. Using my hands, I did what I could on the other side of the vehicle. Fatigue and hunger were momentarily forgotten, as my body produced a mild spurt of adrenaline.

Within minutes the adrenaline was depleted and I was ready to collapse. But that was okay because a state police car arrived, followed by a sheriff's deputy, so I surrendered my task to some guys in uniform who had a lot more muscle than I did, and also had shovels. Then I stood by and awaited the outcome, a bit dazed by the blue and red lights flashing from the police cars.

The traffic on Arrowhead Drive was light and almost everybody slowed to a crawl as they passed by, until finally one car pulled over and stopped. A stocky bearded man in a green parka got out and approached me.

"Was anyone hurt?" he said. "I'm a doctor."

"We don't know yet," I said. "There's someone in that car and the guys are trying to dig them out."

"I wonder how long it will take."

"Anybody's guess." I nodded toward the car where the three men were doing battle with the snow. It looked as though they had freed up the rear doors, but still couldn't get them open.

I saw Frank knock on one of the car windows, trying to communicate with the occupants. The wail of a siren pierced the darkness.

"Must be an ambulance," said my companion.

The sound grew louder and, seconds later, the ambulance arrived with more flashing lights and maneuvered into position between the cop cars. Two EMT's hopped out.

When he saw the emergency personnel, my doctor friend said, "Looks like I won't be needed." I thought I detected a hint of relief in his tone.

"It was good of you to wait," I said.

"Truth is," he said, "I'm a doctor of veterinary medicine."

I stifled a laugh. "Oh. So if there were any injured animals in the car —-."

He chuckled. "I was helpful once at an accident. A lot of things are the same."

"I suppose that's true."

"But I wouldn't do anything beyond first aid."

"Tell me something," I said as he turned to leave. "Have you ever done CPR on a dog?"

"No, but I did give some oxygen to a schnauzer. After a fire."

After the Good Samaritan drove away, I realized that my feet were numb. I glanced at the Blazer and considered going back inside to keep warm. After all, that's what Frank had told me to do.

But while I was debating my next move, I saw that Frank had managed to open the driver's side door of the buried car. I saw him lean in to speak to the driver.

Then I saw the state cop pull open the passenger door and help a dark-haired woman as she struggled to emerge. As soon as the woman was able to stand upright she looked around and said, "What took you guys so long?"

That's when I realized that we had just rescued my friend Ivy Martin. Not surprisingly, the man who emerged from the driver side was Greg Wetherel. Within a few minutes the two of them met on the shoulder of the road where they shared a hug and surveyed their car, which still had the front wheels, bumper and hood buried in snow.

That's when Ivy looked around and recognized me. "Tracy," she said, "where did you come from?"

"That was Frank and me in the other car."

"Oh. My. Gosh. I can't believe you guys hit us. We were just on our way home from Boyne Mountain."

That explained why Ivy was decked out in baby blue ski jacket and pants, while Greg wore a North Face coat and both of them had ski lift tags on their zippers.

The state policeman seemed to be in charge of the scene. He wanted Greg and Ivy to be examined by the medical personnel, but they insisted it wasn't necessary. Frank stepped in and spoke to Greg in language a lawyer would understand, using terms like insurance claims, documentation and the possibility of post accident symptoms. So Greg acquiesced and the two of them got into the ambulance long enough to let the EMT's carry out their examinations.

Frank talked briefly with the state policeman, who placed a telephone call. When Ivy emerged from the ambulance, Frank said to me, "How about you and Ivy go get in the Blazer."

It was more of an order than a request. So I grabbed Ivy's hand and said, "Come on, let's go get warm."

Ivy let me lead her to the Blazer. We climbed inside and found the interior nice and warm. Frank was right behind us. He leaned in the passenger door and pulled some papers from the glove box.

"This will take a few minutes," he said. "Have to do the whole accident report business."

Ivy and I watched as Greg and Frank both got into the police car. Now that she was out of danger, Ivy started venting.

"I don't know why I ever let Greg talk me into this stupid trip. I told him I hate skiing. Not that I didn't do okay for a while. But I just got tired of it is all, so I went inside and spent the rest of the afternoon in the lodge. That was more fun anyway — I met two guys from Chicago and they bought me drinks. I mean, what could Greg say, he's the one who dragged me there against my will. And then on the way home, we nearly get killed. What happened anyway? Didn't you guys see us coming? Why didn't you stop?"

I tried to explain the situation as best I understood it — that the intersection had a yellow blinker for us, but a stop sign for them and they were the ones who were supposed to stop but didn't.

"I can't believe that. Greg is such a good driver."

"I'm not exactly sure of anything," I said, because I saw no point in arguing. I wondered if Greg had been drinking before he got behind the wheel, but decided that question was best left to the authorities.

She finally asked me why I was wearing the funny looking shoes and I told her that Frank and I had been skiing too, only ours didn't involve big hills and ski lifts.

"Oh look," she said, "here comes the tow truck."

The ambulance had departed, leaving room for the truck which carried another flashing light, this one orange. The truck stopped. Ivy and I watched as a cheerful looking young man, without gloves or hat, hopped out and began to drag chains which he managed to hook to the rear of the partially buried car.

Then Greg came along and conferred with the young man. There was some gesturing on Greg's part. Then the tow truck guy got down in the snow and added a second chain which he hooked farther underneath the car. This seemed to satisfy Greg.

Frank and one of the cops stationed themselves in the road to stop traffic while the driver jumped back inside his cab. The chains went tight, the truck made a lot of noise and issued a cloud of exhaust before it finally pulled the car free from its icy vault.

Now the three of them, Greg, Frank and the tow truck guy, stood and looked over the damage. They apparently decided that the car was not roadworthy because the driver pulled Greg's car up on tracks and prepared to haul it away.

"Oh shit," said Ivy. "I was hoping we could still drive it."

"Doesn't look that way," I said.

Frank came over and motioned for me to roll down my window. "You need to clear out the back seat," he said. "We're going to give these folks a ride home."

"Fine," I said, "but don't we have to get us out of the ditch first?"

"Sure, but Greg and I can handle that. You get in the driver's seat. Do you know how to find reverse?"

"Frank. I know how to drive this thing."

"Sure. Go for it."

Feeling less confident than I sounded, I got in the driver's seat and shifted into reverse. Greg and Frank got in front of the vehicle and each man leaned his weight against one of the fenders. After some tire spinning and rocking and Frank telling me how to crank the steering wheel, the tires finally found traction and we had the Blazer sitting on the shoulder.

Then I cleaned out the back seat for Greg and Ivy. The trip to Ivy's house took about twenty minutes and, during that time, there was a running conversation in the back seat.

"I can't figure out what went wrong," said Greg. "I know I hit the brakes. I'm sure of that. They just didn't work. Some asshole tampered with those brake lines. I'm sure of it."

"But honey," said Ivy. "We were fine all the way up."

"So it happened at the resort," he said. "The brake fluid probably started to leak out. We were on the freeway for the first thirty miles, didn't use the brakes much. At one point they did feel a little spongy but I didn't think too much about it. And then — wham. I don't like it — I don't like it. I hope those cops realize that I wasn't at fault. I don't need this on my record."

Now he was starting to sound like a lawyer. He was more concerned with his record than the fact that all of us could have been injured or killed. But Frank and I refrained from anything more than very brief comments. We didn't want to get either of them more agitated than they already were.

We reached Ivy's house and Greg stopped complaining long enough to thank us for rescuing them. We watched them disappear into Ivy's house and I heaved a sigh as we pulled away.

"What a relief," I said.

"I'll second that," said Frank. "But we're okay now and I'm hungry. What about some supper?"

We went to the Brown Bear and got hamburgers to go. We took them to my house where we opened two beers and relaxed on the couch.

"What do you think about the whole thing?" I said. "Do you think Greg made up that stuff about his brake lines being cut?"

"He seemed pretty intent on that theory. As soon as I got him out of the car, he started ranting about something being wrong with the brakes."

"Do you think that's what happened?"

"I don't know what to think. He seemed intent on finding some explanation other than incompetence on his part."

"I wonder if he'd been drinking."

"I didn't smell anything on him."

Then I sat bolt upright. "Hey, I just thought of something. Remember the note that Ivy showed you? What did it say?"

Frank thought for a second. "It was something like, *you're next sucker.*"

"So — do you think our killer is after Greg now — and someone did cut those brake lines?"

"I guess it's possible," he said as he finished his hamburger. "But who on earth could it be?"

"Someone who had a grudge against both of them."

"Maybe they both knew something — something detrimental to a third party."

"Right. So who's the third party?"

"I'll have to ask Greg about that." He took a swallow of beer before he continued. "You know, this reminds me of something my mother used say."

"What was that?"

"Three can keep a secret — if two of them are dead."

CHAPTER TWENTY NINE

"I guess we were lucky last night," I said to Frank. "Things could have turned out a lot worse."

"You're right about that. I've seen two bad accidents at that intersection and one of them was fatal."

It was Sunday morning and we were in bed having our first coffee of the day. Frank was up first so I had the pleasure of being awakened by that delightful aroma wafting in from the kitchen. Although I had slept well, the events of the previous day were still fresh in my mind.

"So what about Greg?" I said. "Do you think he'd been drinking?"

Frank shook his head. "The state cop did a breathalyzer and he came out clean."

"So maybe his brake lines were cut — the way he claimed?"

"Could be. I'm going to take a look at the car, first thing tomorrow. Then I'll have a talk with Greg."

So we left off speculating, got dressed and had a hearty meal of scrambled eggs and sausage which was late enough to be considered brunch. While we ate, we discussed our plans for the day, which were taking us in different directions.

"What is it you're going to do?" he said.

"I promised Jewell I would go to the Think Spring Fashion Show at the yacht club."

"So you ladies are thinking spring already?" He reached for the marmalade.

"I'll admit it's a challenge to get in the mood with so much snow on the ground. But it's a benefit for the Women's Shelter and it gives me a chance to be with Jewell. Did you get in touch with Arnie?"

"Yep, talked to him last night. I'm going to drive him to Grand Rapids and we'll spend the afternoon with his boys — take them skating or sledding or something."

"I think kids that age are into snowboarding."

"Then I guess I'll learn about snowboarding."

"It's good of you to play uncle."

"I'm trying to help. Arnie's sister said the last time they made plans, Arnie showed up drunk and his ex wouldn't let him take the boys."

"I don't blame her."

"I don't either," he said with a shrug.

"So now you're the social worker."

"Something like that. It's a family thing."

"Well, I hope things go better for them today. If you're back in time, you and Arnie can have supper here. I still have some venison stew in the freezer."

"Sounds good. Let's plan on it."

We finished eating, then Frank kissed me goodbye and was on his way. This left me with half an hour to figure out what to wear. I dug through my closet and found a white sweater with crocheted flowers on the sleeves. I pulled that on, added gray slacks and hoped the outfit would look sufficiently spring like for the occasion.

When I arrived, the dining room at the yacht club was nearly full. I said hello to a few people while I scanned the room for Jewell. Most of the women were wearing dresses that leaned heavily toward flowers and ruffles. Finally I saw Jewell waving to me from a table in the back so I returned the wave and started moving in her direction. Then I saw something that darkened my mood.

Jewell had Fiona with her again.

Selfish? Sure, I was being selfish, but Jewell was my best friend and I had anticipated some one-on-one time with her. Among other things, I wanted to discuss her upcoming trip to Arizona.

But now I was closing in on them — so I pasted on a smile and tried to think like a grown up. I didn't own Jewell. My best friend was a caring person who was being supportive of Fiona during a difficult time. I greeted them both as cheerfully as possible as I joined them at a round table graced with yellow daffodils. Fiona was already sitting next to Jewell so I took the empty chair on the other side of Fiona.

Fortunately, a bottle of champagne arrived just then, delivered by a young man who filled a glass for each of us. Then a girl brought out a generous plate of cheese and crackers followed by cookies and fruit. The food and drink distracted me from my ungenerous thoughts. I made small talk and munched a slice of pineapple until the program got underway.

As the amateur models strutted the runway, I sipped champagne and managed to relax enough to enjoy the show. Outside, another show was going on. The sun had broken through the clouds and the room was filled with dappled reflections from the melting surface of Arrowhead Lake.

About half way through the presentation, Fiona excused herself to the ladies' room so I slipped into her chair and fell into a whispered conversation with Jewell.

"It's nice to see clothes on real women," she said. "I can actually imagine buying something that I've seen here."

"And they're at local stores," I said. "Maybe you can find something for your trip out west."

"Maybe. But I'd rather buy something while I'm out there. But how about you, Tracy? Can you get time off to go with me?"

"Well, I did talk to Marge."

"And —?"

"I am due for vacation time. She said I should take it before June."

"So there you go —."

That's when Fiona returned. I offered to give back her seat, but she told me to stay where I was and she took over my chair.

Now the fashions switched from dresses to sportswear and tennis outfits. Then came the highlight which sent the audience into hysterics. Models appeared with little dogs in outfits that matched their own.

The dogs obviously didn't understand the runway concept so most of them had to be carried.

After that a high school girl sang *I love Paris,* accompanied by a piano player. Finally, a solidly built woman in a batik- print dress took the microphone. The woman said she was the director of the Women's Shelter and thanked us for our support. She explained a little about how our money was used — about the women who come to the shelter for help.

After the speech, Fiona leaned over and said, "It's a damn shame that men abuse their women to the point where they need to escape."

"Yes it is," said Jewell, "but as long as it happens, we need to help them."

"Well I gotta tell you," she said. "The minute any man raised his hand to me, he'd be out the door."

"Of course," said Jewell. "But you're a strong person. You're a nurse, you have friends and you have earning power."

"That's true," said Fiona. "But, you know, sometimes I wonder about Charlene — Vince's daughter? I think she had a boyfriend who knocked her around a little."

"Did she tell you that?"

"Not exactly. But I've gathered it's part of the reason she's staying with me instead of going back to Muskegon."

I thought about Charlene with her slumped shoulders and downcast expression and decided that quite possibly Fiona was right. While we were talking, the crowd had thinned out and the wait staff was beginning to clear the tables.

"Guess it's time to go," said Jewell.

We stood and began to move toward the exit, chatting with other stragglers. Just before we reached the door, Fiona paused and looked at me and Jewell.

"Would you like to come to my house for coffee?" she said. "I think I've got some chocolate doughnuts."

"I wish I could," said Jewell. "But I have to get ready for a meeting tomorrow." She glanced at me. "Why don't you go, Tracy?"

I thought for a moment and figured that Frank wouldn't be back for a couple of hours, so I accepted Fiona's invitation. We said goodbye to Jewell in the parking lot.

While driving to Fiona's house, I had a brilliant idea. I decided to ask Fiona if I could look at some of Vince's old photo albums. Maybe a third party would show up, someone from the past who had maintained a grudge against both Vince Crawley and Greg Wetherel.

But I never got to carry out my plan. We were barely in the door when Charlene met us, her face aglow with smiles.

"Fiona," she cried, "you won't believe who's here!"

I heard Fiona take a deep breath before she said, "So now what?"

"Rose is here," said Charlene. "My sister Rose has come home."

"And guess where home is?" Fiona whispered to me. "My place, of course."I squeezed Fiona's arm. Then Rose came out of the kitchen.

Charlene introduced her estranged sister. I looked at the two young women, searching for the family resemblance. It was there of course, same height, same facial shape. But, compared to her sister, Rose looked like the result of one of those magazine makeovers.

Instead of straight brown hair, hers was highlighted, cut short and teased to an illusion of fullness. Rose wore make up that subtly altered the contours of her long face. She was also slender but on her it was a plus. A red leather belt was slung across her hips at the point where a striped sweater met a pair of black jeans.

Rose gave Fiona an awkward hug. "I just heard about Dad," she said. "I came back as soon as I heard." She explained that a friend had seen her father's obituary and sent it to her. "I would have called before I came, but I didn't know anybody's number."

Tears were shed, tissues came out and noses were blown while Fiona and I took off our coats. Charlene and Rose dithered about the kitchen, finally served up coffee and the four of us sat down in the living room. The two girls did most of the talking and I kept glancing from one to the other, still baffled at how sisters could look so different from one another.

Then Rose directed a question at Fiona. "Would it be okay if I stayed here a few days?"

Before Fiona could reply, Charlene broke in. "She can stay in my room. It's got a double bed."

Fiona was sitting next to me on the sofa. I glanced at her, remembering how I had resisted allowing another person into my home. But she handled the situation graciously.

"Sure you can stay," she said to Rose. "After all, it's your dad's house."

"Oh thanks," said Rose. "I won't be here very long."

"Maybe you girls could sort through some of your father's stuff in the basement," said Fiona. "He's got boxes down there that haven't been opened in years."

I'm not sure how long the four of us were in that living room but I know it was well over an hour. A couple of times I started to leave, but Fiona urged me to stay, so I got the feeling that my presence was providing her with moral support. When I finally did get up and retrieve my coat, she followed me out to the foyer.

"Thanks for being here," she said. "And I'm sorry there weren't any doughnuts."

"No problem. But do you think you can handle this?" I nodded toward the living room.

"Not much choice," she said with a shrug. "At least I have a job so I can get away."

"You're always welcome to come and stay with me."

"I'll keep that in mind," she said. We both laughed and I gave her a hug.

It was almost dark when I got home and the first thing I did was call Jewell. We were still talking when Frank and Arnie arrived. So I rang off and went to the kitchen where Frank was already heating up the venison stew. After supper, Arnie said thanks and good night and then he was out the door. Seconds later we heard the roar of his pick- up truck.

"Did things go okay?" I said.

"The boys had a good time."

"No bar stops?"

"Not even on the way home."

"So you are a good influence."

"I truly am."

When I told Frank about my afternoon, he was interested to hear that Vince's daughter Rose was in town.

"Did she say where her mother is?"

"We didn't talk about that."

"I'd like to talk with her," he said. "Could you call her and see if she'll meet with me?"

"Sure. I can do that."

So I called Fiona's house and spoke to Rose. I explained who Frank was and why he wanted to talk with her. She was agreeable. So I let Frank talk to her and they set up a date to meet at Jennie's coffee shop the following day.

"Thanks for doing that," he said when he was finished.

"I'm glad to help. And now I have something else to tell you."

"What's that?"

"I finally made a decision. I've decided to go to Arizona with Jewell."

He was quiet for the few seconds it took him to absorb the information. "Well good," he said. "I mean, I'll miss you — but everyone deserves a vacation. Ever been out west before?"

"Never."

"I spent some time in Nevada. It's pretty nice." He pulled me close. "Maybe I should worry. Maybe you'll find a handsome cowboy."

"Or Indian."

"Well, that too."

"Don't worry," I said, kissing him lightly on the cheek. "This trip is a matter of research. We're going to track down my missing ex-step-daughter."

"You mean Brooke?"

"That's who I mean. The elusive, non-communicating, parent-frustrating Brooke Quinn."

CHAPTER THIRTY

Five days later, Jewell and I were on our way.

Jewell always knew exactly what to do, since she had visited her brother in Phoenix many times. So I just followed her lead, racing through the Detroit airport to make our connection and finally settling in for the long flight to Phoenix.

I probably held my breath during take off but, once that was over, the two of us fell into our usual pattern of effortless conversation. Jewell told me about her older brother Mike, who lived in Phoenix with his wife Joni. The couple had raised three children who were all out of the house now, so they were happy to have Derek staying with them.

"I was sorry when they moved so far away," she said. "But things have worked out rather nicely. Mike and Joni come to Michigan in the summer, then Paul and I usually visit them in the winter. But with Paul tied up, I'm glad you decided to come with me."

"I'm glad too," I said. "It feels great to get out of town and away from my job. But you know — every once in a while I think about Fiona. I wonder how she's managing with the two girls living in her house."

"I stopped by her place a couple of days ago and met Rose. Fiona seemed to be doing okay."

"Rose comes as quite a surprise, doesn't she?"

"Rose certainly is different from her sister. But I didn't get to talk with her very much. Did you?"

"No, but Frank met with Rose and they talked for a long time — I think it was a couple of hours."

"You never told me what he found out. Is it something you're not supposed to talk about?"

I shook my head. "No. It's just that — it's such a long story and we've both been busy. I wanted to wait until we had time for the whole thing."

"I think we have time now. Four hours to Phoenix — so let's hear it."

I was trying to figure out where to begin when the stewardess came by with beverages. I asked for a soda and Jewell got coffee. By the time we had our drinks in hand, I was ready.

"Okay," I said. "Here's what Frank found out when he met with Rose at the sandwich shop. The strangest part of the story has to do with Vince's first wife, Dixie. Rose explained why her mother wasn't at the funeral — why no one has heard from her for nearly a year."

"I heard that Dixie had gone out to California to visit Rose."

"She did. And here's what happened, as best we know." I took a sip of my Coke. "Rose was living in San Francisco. She shared a flat with two roommates and worked a couple of jobs to make ends meet. The three of them got along okay. They didn't have any real problems — until her mother came to visit."

"Was this unexpected?"

"Rose knew that her mother was coming. It was no big deal at first. All of the flat mates had visitors from time to time. So the mother, Dixie, arrives in town. Rose takes her around and mom really likes San Francisco. She kind of moves in and doesn't leave. For a while it's okay because she acts like a housemother, does most of the dishes and occasional laundry. But eventually things go sour."

"Like how?"

"After a month, the other girls said if Rose's mom is going to stay, the rent should be split four ways and Dixie should pay her share. Dixie agrees and supposedly is looking for a job but doesn't find any work. Instead she finds a tattooed boyfriend who is a known dealer and now Dixie seems to have money for rent. It doesn't take long for the girls to figure out that Dixie is involved in the guy's business — doing a few deliveries, holding stuff in her room."

Another stewardess came by and gave us pretzels. I opened the package but then pushed them aside. "The flat-mates said Dixie had to either dump the boyfriend or move out. They didn't want a dealer living with them, and that's what Dixie was at this point."

"So what happened?"

"Dixie left the flat and moved in with her druggie boyfriend. After that, Rose still saw her — they'd meet for lunch about once a week, and she could see that her mom was going downhill. Dixie lost weight, always wore the same clothes but, worst of all, she couldn't seem to remember what the hell she was doing most of the time."

"Sounds like an addict."

"That's what she was. Rose said her mom took to wearing long sleeved shirts but one day Rose saw the needle marks on her mother's arms. She confronted her mother, tried to reason with her, but —." I stopped, searching for words.

"There's no reasoning with an addict."

"Right. This went on for a couple of months until the guy found another girlfriend and kicked Dixie out. She was homeless for a while, probably selling herself for a fix. Rose said she didn't see her mom and didn't even want to think about that period. Finally Rose tracked her mother down and got her into a shelter. After a couple of weeks, Dixie said she was ready to kick the heroin and wanted help. Of course, every public facility had a waiting list a mile long — but Rose found a private one that would take her mom, provided they could come up with twenty thousand dollars."

Jewell whistled softly. "That's a lot of money."

"Yes. And this is where it gets kind of interesting."

"Did somebody rob a bank?"

"No. They got the money from Vince."

Jewell's eyes widened. "From Vince? Her ex-husband?"

"That's what Rose said. And I don't think Fiona ever knew about it. Apparently he kept a separate business account."

"Gee whiz. The last best thing he did before he died."

"Looks that way. So Dixie's in rehab now. But she doesn't even know that Vince is dead because she's not allowed any contact with the outside world — not even her daughter Rose."

"That's pretty draconian. On the other hand, I've heard about the reasoning behind such measures. So where is Dixie?"

"This is a little bizarre. She's in Prescott, Arizona."

Jewell paused with a pretzel midway to her mouth. "Why Prescott?"

"I don't know. Rose said that drug rehab is fairly big business out there. Maybe because the place is somewhat isolated."

Jewell took a bite of pretzel. "Are you going to look for Dixie?"

"Frank told me it was okay to try. But the first thing I want to do is find Brooke."

"Now we have a second missing person. Maybe Prescott is some kind of black hole that swallows people up."

"I guess we're going to find out, aren't we?"

When we touched down in Phoenix, I stared in awe at the sun baked tarmac radiating visible heat waves. Minutes later I saw suntanned airport workers in shorts come out to unload our luggage. Clearly we weren't in Michigan any more.

After that we endured the long shuffle as passengers stood, stretched and brought down luggage from the overhead compartments. I followed Jewell off the plane, struggling to hold my winter coat on one arm and both my purse and carry-on with the other. All the while I wondered what I had done with my baggage claim check.

Finally we were through the bottle neck and in the terminal where throngs of people were talking on their cell phones as they walked down the concourse. All of them looked confident and purposeful. I did not feel either confident or purposeful. I was tired and sweating and beginning to wonder why I had left home.

Jewell noticed my flagging spirits and slowed down to walk beside me. "There's always a bit of a culture shock at this point," she said. "Climate shock anyway. But just wait until you see the escalator."

Minutes later we were on the down escalator, where I tried to keep a grip on the moving rail without losing my coat or baggage. The surfaces that slid by us on either side were the color of sandstone and the texture of weathered rocks.

"It's supposed to look like the Grand Canyon," Jewell said. "Or at least some kind of canyon. They've got plenty of them out here."

I kept my eyes on my feet as I stepped off the escalator. When I looked up, I saw a lanky young man striding toward us. It was Jewell's son Derek, his face split with a welcoming grin. Immediately his long arms were around Jewell and then around me.

"Welcome to Arizona," he said. "It's great to see you both."

"Thanks, Derek," I said as I looked him over. The hair on his arms was golden and his skin was bronzed to a tone that no one ever achieves in Michigan. "This place must agree with you."

"Gotta love the heat," he said. "And then everything is okay. Let's get your luggage."

I needn't have worried about finding my claim check. All I had to do was point to my suitcase when it came around on the carousel and Derek grabbed it for me. Same for Jewell. Derek led us out of the terminal into the parking area and that's when the heat hit me like a wave of something solid. Even as it neared the horizon, the sun still packed a wallop. I felt a little bit woozy.

"Sorry I don't have any AC," he said as we climbed into his Toyota. "But other than that, it's a good little car."

Derek passed me a water bottle and I took a long drink. Then I just gawked out the window as we moved through Phoenix which looked like block after block of cement baking in the sun, intersected by slow moving lines of vehicles and punctuated by signs advertising retirement condos. The only green thing I spotted was an occasional palm tree.

"Tracy, how you doing back there?" said Derek.

"I'm still breathing. Is it always this hot?"

He laughed. "Actually this is pretty mild. But you'll feel a lot better tomorrow."

"I will? Why?"

"Because I'm taking you and mom up to the mountains."

"It's cooler there, right?"

"Much cooler. Prescott is where Phoenix people go to escape the heat. Prescott is the Mile High City."

CHAPTER THIRTY ONE

"Here's to Arizona." Jewell and I raised our glasses for a toast.

"And to our visitors," said Derek.

There were five of us seated around the dining room table in the home of Jewell's brother Mike and his wife Joni. I was still a bit dazed by the altered climate but our hosts were welcoming and the house was air conditioned.

And the meal set before us looked both exotic and enticing.

The main dish was a whitefish called tilapia served with wild rice, artichokes and a salad loaded with avocados and strawberries. All this was served with white wine and for dessert, a layered pudding called tiramisu. My conversation was limited to assuring everybody that I had enjoyed the flight (a little lie) and the food was wonderful (true). After that I was content to enjoy the food while the others caught up on family news.

I was feeling both fatigued and exhilarated. I tried to calculate how my internal clock was being affected by the time change. If it was nine o'clock in Phoenix, was it midnight in Michigan? Or was it the other way around? Was I justified in feeling exhausted or was I just being a wimp?

In any case, I started yawning and shortly afterward Joni told me I was welcome to go to bed if that's what I felt like doing. So that's what I did. The guest room had twin beds so I never even knew when

Jewell joined me. I slept a deep and dreamless sleep after my eventful day.

I awoke to the sound of Jewell in the shower. When she came out, she told me there was no big rush but we would be leaving for Prescott after breakfast. The plan was for Derek to borrow his parents' car and the three of us would drive to Prescott, that fabled city in the mountains. Feeling renewed and excited, I hopped out of bed and took my turn in the shower.

The breakfast table was waiting with a plate of fresh fruit. Jewell poured me a cup of coffee and told me the beans had been ground only an hour before. Joni whipped out plates of tortillas wrapped around spicy scrambled eggs. Derek ate two of everything.

Derek, Jewell and I were under way by eleven and I was relieved to find that our transport was fully equipped with air conditioning.

"I am so grateful to your brother for letting us use his car," I said to Jewell.

"Mike and I were raised in Minnesota," she said, "so he understands what it's like to leave the north and land here in the heat of the desert. Plus we are in a much safer car."

"There's nothing wrong with my little Toyota," said Derek.

"I didn't mean to insult your vehicle," she said with a laugh.

It took us over half an hour to escape the cement confines of the city. Then the scenery underwent a sudden alteration and we were surrounded by desert. My gaze swept across a flat landscape of sand and stones. Saguaro cactus with their curious arms stood like sentinels guarding the occasional motel or house trailer.

The terrain shifted when we left the north-bound freeway and angled westward. We began to climb, gently at first — but then I felt the car change gears as the road grew steeper and our ascent more labored. We were definitely in the mountains now. I saw steep rock faces rising close to the road with cactus that seemed to grow right out of the stone.

As we continued to ascend, the road made sharp turns and each one revealed a new face of rugged cliff. The land fell away on one side and the guard rails did not look very reassuring. I said a little prayer and tried to enjoy the view.

Eventually Derek pulled off the road at a scenic turnout and we got out to stretch our legs. The view was breathtaking. Rocky gorges snaked around below us with cars that looked like bugs crawling along the highway. Derek said we were about half way to Prescott.

"Let's trade seats now," Jewell said to me as we headed back to the car. "You should be up front so you can see more."

"I'm pretty happy in the back," I said. "I'm not sure I want to see any more."

"Oh, come on," said Derek. "There's some really cool road signs up ahead."

"You deserve a good view," said Jewell.

With some trepidation I took the seat next to Derek. I tried not to think about the fact that I was trusting my life to a twenty-one year old kid. But Derek appeared both competent and comfortable, even as we met eighteen-wheelers on the down grade and jockeyed for position with lumbering motor homes heading upward.

"Look at that," said Derek as he pointed out a road sign that said Big Bug Gulch.

"I wonder what that's all about?"

"No idea," he said. "Make up your own story, I guess."

"Maybe some wagon train camped there and had bug trouble," said Jewell.

We continued to entertain ourselves with speculation as we passed signs directing us to Dead Horse Drive, Rattlesnake Canyon, Bitter Spring Arroyo and, best of all, Bloody Gulch.

"I guess this really is the wild west," I said. "Or at least it used to be."

"I'm really glad we're making this trip," said Jewell. "Until now, I figured all of Arizona was pretty much like Phoenix."

Eventually the road leveled out and signs of civilization appeared. Civilization took the form of gas stations, motels, a string of tract homes and a movie theatre.

"Is this Prescott?" I said.

"Not yet," said Derek. "This is Prescott Valley — I guess you could call it a suburb. But Prescott — well, you'll see. It's really old and it's got a ton of history. Brooke said it started out as a mining town and then it was the capital of the Arizona Territory."

"Speaking of Brooke," I said, "I sure hope she is okay."

"Me too," said Jewell.

"Do you think we'll be able to find her?"

"No problem," said Derek with that unshakable optimism of the young. "I promise we won't leave until we do."

Now we were passing through grassland scattered with sprawling ranch style houses, some of them sitting up on bluffs. Then came more motels, a shopping mall on one side of us and a hilltop casino on the other. A populated basin stretched out before us and, just beyond that, an oddly shaped lump sitting on the horizon.

"What on earth is that?" I said.

"That's Thumb Butte," said Derek. "It's a landmark. If you ever need to get oriented, look at Thumb Butte and you'll be facing west."

Next we passed restaurants, stores and office buildings. Some of them could have been in any city, anywhere, while others were trying for a southwest style, with pale stucco and graceful arched doorways.

"Looks like we've arrived," said Jewell. "What's the plan?"

"Last I knew," said Derek, "Brooke was living on Whipple Street — which is not far from here. That would be a good place to start."

"Do you think we'll find anybody at home this time of day?" said Jewell.

"It's hard to tell," he said. "Everybody just comes and goes, keeps irregular hours."

"So let's check it out," I said, feeling like some kind of fictional detective. Had I really traveled to this place in the Arizona mountains to track down my ex-step-daughter? And was I doing this for Steven?

No. I was doing it for myself. Besides, I was with Jewell and I was having fun.

Derek made a right turn that took us down a street of one-story homes with small front yards. I saw signs that advertised hair salons, massage, or pet grooming and an intriguing one that offered palm reading.

"Hey," I said. "I just noticed what's different about this town."

"What's that?" said Jewell.

"There's trees up here. Honest to goodness trees." We passed a small park where willow trees bent over a tiny stream.

"You're right," said Jewell. "What kind are they, Derek?"

"Most of them are cottonwood. And I think there's some eucalyptus. And a lot of pines too. The only thing they don't have here is grass. Most people do their landscaping with rocks. Okay, I'm turning on to Whipple now. It's somewhere in the eight hundred block so watch the house numbers for me. The house we want is on the right and it's kind of hard to miss. It's painted purple."

Minutes later Derek slowed to a stop in front of a sprawling wooden house that was definitely showing its age. The window frames were askew and weather damage on the boards showed right through the recent coat of paint.

"Well, look at that," I said. "Must be some artistic types living here."

The object that had my attention was a tin man of sorts, made from rusty tools welded together — one hand was a metal claw and the other was a trowel raised in a salute. It stood beside a leafless tree hung with tiny pieces of broken glass, bits of bone and tattered ribbons. Other vegetation was limited to tufts of brown grass and a circle of prickly looking bushes. But a tall pine tree loomed over the house, lending shade.

"So this is it?" I said.

"This is it," said Derek. "Brooke was living here with three other people."

"I don't see any cars," I said.

"Nobody even owns a car," he said with a laugh. "This is biking distance from the college. Or people just walk. That's why it's a student rental."

Jewell shrugged and said, "Okay, let's see what we can find out."

I opened the car door, prepared for a blast of heat. But the expected heat wave did not materialize. Even with the sun high in a clear sky, Prescott didn't feel like an oven. What it felt like was pretty darn comfortable. And there was an indefinable tangy smell in the air.

"Hey, I like the weather here," I said.

"Figured you would," said Derek.

Jewell and I followed him along a crumbling sidewalk to the back of the house. A plastic bucket filled with empty beer cans and wine bottles had tipped on its side, disgorging half the contents. The walkway led us to a door that was flanked by a weathered gnome and a one-eared rabbit.

Derek knocked but there was no answer. He opened the door and yelled "Anybody home?"

Still no answer. A calico cat appeared in the doorway, looked at us with golden eyes and took advantage of the situation to slip outside.

"Doesn't look very promising," said Jewell.

"I'm starting to wonder if this trip is a wild goose chase," I said.

"Not to worry," said Derek. "We'll come back later. And I know exactly what we all need."

"What's that?"

"We need lunch — and I know a great little place nearby."

Shortly afterward the three of us were scanning menus at a tiny restaurant that featured Asian/Hawaiian specialties. Jewell chose a chicken-pineapple salad and I ordered the same. Derek had a ham sandwich.

With food in my belly I felt more optimistic and ready to renew the search. We went back to the place that Jewell had christened the purple hippie house and spotted a pair of mountain bikes leaning against the big pine tree. This time Derek's knock aroused someone inside.

The girl who came to the door had a towel wrapped around her head. She peered at us curiously.

"Hey Sunshine," he said. "How are you?"

"Good," she said, as she opened the door and came outside. Sunshine wore a tank top and khaki shorts with cargo pockets. "Hey, you were here before — with Brooke, weren't you?"

"That's right," he said. "And now we're trying to find her. Have you seen her?"

"Sure. I mean, I see her at school — but she doesn't live here any more."

"I know that — but do you know where she lives now?"

"Sure — I went out there once. She's got a sweet little place. It's an old log cabin and it's just outside of town."

"We're trying to find her," he said. "Can you give us directions?"

"Oh god, I couldn't tell you how to get there. Have you tried to call her?"

"Yes, but we never get any answer."

A tall guy with no shirt appeared in the doorway. "They're looking for Brooke," Sunshine said to him. "Do you know anything?"

"Hey, I just saw her at the coffee house," he said. "I think she was on her way to the farmers' market. She's got herself a neat little motor scooter."

"Is that the farmers' market by the student center?" said Derek.

"Yep. If you hurry you might be able to catch her."

"Okay thanks, thanks a lot." Derek turned to Jewell and me. "Let's get going."

Jewell and I added our thanks, then turned and headed for the car. Derek jumped into the driver's seat and told us to hurry up. I barely had my door closed when the car started to move.

"For heaven's sake," said Jewell. "Take it easy."

"No time to waste," he said as we peeled out of the driveway.

CHAPTER THIRTY TWO

The chase was on.

I knew that Jewell wanted to tell Derek to slow down but she held her tongue as he rolled through a few stop signs and ran a yellow light in his effort to find Brooke before she disappeared from our radar.

This was starting to feel like a scene from a cheap action movie. All I could do was pray that our car chase would not be climaxed by a close encounter with law enforcement or another car or, worst of all, a pedestrian.

The whole thing lasted only a few minutes. Then I heard Derek say, "Hey that's her." As he said this, he simultaneously hit the brakes and honked the horn.

The object of his attention was a young woman in a brown serape who was clutching a straw bag full of leafy greens as she made her way into a dusty parking lot.

"Are you sure that's her?" I said.

"Sure. I've seen her wearing that cape thing."

"You're going to scare her to death," said Jewell. "She doesn't know this car and she doesn't have any idea who you are."

"Yes mom, I know," he said. "But we can't let her get away." He swung the car into the parking lot and stopped, blocking the exit.

Derek jumped out of the car and sprinted toward the girl with the bag of greens. She paused as he drew near and then squealed with delight when she recognized him. .

So it was Brooke after all. Jewell and I got out of the car and followed Derek. As we approached, I recognized the young woman who had lived with me for the previous summer. In some ways she looked the same, still tall and slender, with that splash of freckles on her cheeks — but her style had changed. The long auburn hair was contained in a single braid which was tied with a strip of leather.

"What are you doing up here?" she said to Derek.

"Came to see you," he said. "And you have visitors."

By this time she saw the two of us which led to increased squeals of delight. "Oh my god," she said. "It's your mom — and Tracy."

She handed her bag to Derek, hugged Jewell and then me.

"I can't believe you guys are in Prescott. What a treat." Her face clouded. "Is this bad news? I mean — is anything wrong?"

"No, nothing's wrong," I said. "It's just that your dad is — well he's kind of wondering about you."

"Oh him," she said. "Since when has my dad ever worried about me?"

"Maybe since he started paying your tuition." I was trying very hard not to sound judgmental.

Brooke was happy enough that she took no offense. "Well, I guess it does make sense."

"Sunshine said you've got new digs," said Derek

"Yes, it's true. I got a great deal house-sitting — actually it's a cabin and a pair of cats. I'm just heading home. Come on out and see where I live."

"Sure, we'd love to."

"Just follow me," she said. "It's about four miles."

"Okay," said Derek. "We'll follow you. Want me to take the groceries?"

"Oh sure." She handed them over.

Brooke mounted her scooter, fired it up and headed out of the lot. We followed in the car as she led us out of town and turned onto a dirt road. Eventually she passed a mailbox and then turned down a long driveway. Following her, we drove past a fenced pasture where a couple of horses barely raised their heads to look at us.

When a log cabin came into view Derek said, "That must be it. What a neat place to live."

"Nothing like Phoenix," said Jewell.

"Nothing at all," I agreed.

We pulled into the yard and found Brooke parking her scooter next to a woodshed that faced the back door of her log house. The building was bordered on two sides by sprawling trees that looked a little out of place in the rocky landscape.

"What a lovely spot," said Jewell as we climbed out of the car.

And it was. We were just high enough to have a view of the town below and the ring of mountains beyond.

"This is so cool," Derek said to Brooke as she came to stand beside us.

"The cabin's over a hundred years old," she said. "Every one who lived here kept planting more stuff. There's apple and pear trees, nuts and berry bushes. It's been in the same family since nineteen- thirty. The lady who owns it says none of her relatives wants it any more, but she can't bear to sell it. Anyway she's on a trip to Europe, so I'm here and all I have to do is take care of her cats and stuff."

As if on cue, a black long-haired cat peered at us from behind a wood pile.

"That's Elmer," she said. "And Moses is around somewhere. Come on inside."

We followed her into the cabin and found ourselves in a low ceilinged room that apparently served as kitchen, dining and living room. The space might have felt oppressive except for a large, south facing window that offered a view of the entire valley.

In the center of the space was a pot bellied stove with a chimney that rose to the ceiling.

"Is that your only heat?" said Jewell.

"That's it," said Brooke. "I usually build a fire about now because it gets chilly at night. But I do have an electric stove to cook on. Can I make you guys some tea?"

CHAPTER THIRTY THREE

Brooke made a pot of peppermint tea and served it to us in a variety of chipped ceramic mugs. As we drank the tea, she filled us in on the details of her life in the cabin. She showed us the addition to the original structure which gave her a bedroom and a bathroom.

"I've got all the modern conveniences," she said. "The toilet, sink and shower all work. The only thing I don't have right now — is a water heater. The original one busted and it never got replaced. So I heat water on the stove to wash dishes."

"Does that mean you take cold showers?" I said with a shiver.

"I tried that once, but only once. Right now — well, I just grab a shower at Whipple Street — or once in a while at school. One time I warmed enough water to fill the copper tub for a bath — but that was an awful lot of work. As soon as the weather gets better I'll be able to use the solar shower out back."

When we were all seated in her living room area, I decided it was time to get to the heart of the matter.

"Look," I said, "nobody has had any word from you. No e-mail, telephone or even a post card. What's up with that?"

"Oh, I'm sorry. I didn't mean to worry anyone." She seemed genuinely surprised. "Is that why you're here?"

"Yeah," said Derek with a grin. "We all came up here just to make sure you were still alive."

"Oh, I'm sorry," she said again. "But my cell phone got water damaged and I couldn't afford another one. And there is no land line, never has been."

"But what about your e-mail?" said Derek. "I must have sent you half a dozen at least, before I gave up."

"I apologize for that. I don't have any kind of internet connection out here so I gave up on keeping up with e-mail."

"But there must be computers at the school library," said Derek.

"There are, of course. And I guess I should have been checking my e-mail at the library but I'm always in a hurry when I go there and I never even think about it until maybe after I get home. I've been working fifteen or twenty hours a week so it makes things kind of tight."

Brooke spread her arms toward the view of the town below. "I've just been living out here in never-never land. In a way, it's kind of nice."

"I can see where it might be," I said. "But you know, we've all been a little concerned about you."

"I'm really sorry about worrying everybody. This whole thing happened so fast that it kind of swallowed me up. I got the chance to move here, someone offered to sell me the scooter and suddenly, here I am."

"I have to admit you've got a pretty neat set-up here." I was thinking about my lackluster days in a college dormitory. "You're going to school and having a little adventure at the same time."

"I've never lived like this before," she said. "In fact, it's the first time I've ever lived alone."

Then Jewell said, "That was a mailbox I saw at the end of the driveway, wasn't it?"

"Oh yes," Brooke said with a laugh. "The post office knows where to deliver my bills."

"Then how about giving us your mailing address," said Jewell.

"Oh sure." Brooke grabbed a scrap of paper, wrote down her address and handed it to me.

"Okay," I said as I slipped the paper into my pocket. "We're making progress. But now comes the big question."

"The big question?"

"What shall we do about your dear old dad?"

"Oh him," she said. "Guess I'll have to write him a letter. Do you have his address?"

"I can give it to you," I said. "But — I'm afraid you may lose it before you get around to writing."

"I've got a better idea," said Jewell. "Let's call your dad — we can use my cell phone." Brooke was frowning but Jewell ignored her and continued. "That way you can talk to him yourself. Do you have his number, Tracy?"

"I think so. He gave me his business card and I stuck it in my wallet before we left Michigan."

Brooke was starting to look like a trapped animal. Her expression made it clear that she would be happy if I couldn't find Steven's phone number. But I did. I produced the business card and Jewell pulled her cell phone out of her purse.

"Do I have to do it right now?" Brooke bit her lip.

"You might as well get it over with," I said.

Brooke sent a pleading glance in Derek's direction.

"Better just do it," he said.

"I think your dad deserves a call," said Jewell. "But you don't have to do it in front of us. We can go outside or something."

"You don't have to leave," Brooke said with a sigh. "It's really not such a big deal."

Jewell passed me her phone and I punched in the numbers. After four rings, I heard Steven answer. "Hey," I said, "I've got someone here who wants to talk with you. Hold on a second." I directed an encouraging smile at Brooke as I handed her the phone.

"Is it him?" she said softly.

"It's him," I whispered.

No doubt Brooke had been hoping we would reach Steven's voice mail. But she had no such luck. Her father was on the line. *I'll just go outside* — she mouthed the words at us as she walked toward the back door.

"Guess we kind of put pressure on her," I said.

"I think she can handle it," said Jewell.

"I just hope they don't talk too long," I said, "considering it's your phone time she's using."

"Not to worry," said Jewell. "This is important. In fact, this is pretty much the whole reason you were willing to come out here with me."

As it turned out, Brooke's conversation with her father took less than ten minutes. Jewell and I used the time to wash up our cups and play with the cats. Derek started a fire in the woodstove.

When Brooke came back inside, Jewell and I were sitting in a pair of rocking chairs, admiring the view.

"Well, that's done," Brooke said as she handed the phone back to Jewell.

"How did it go?" said Derek.

"Not too bad, actually." Her face mirrored relief. "In fact — I'm glad you guys made me do it."

"Did the two of you get things settled?" I said.

"We did. I gave him my mailing address and promised to send him a letter on Monday — with a copy of my grades from last semester. That ought to keep him quiet.

My grades were pretty darn good."

"Hey, mission accomplished," said Derek. "So now — how about we all have supper in town?"

"Supper in town sounds good," said Brooke, "but then —." She glanced from Derek to me and Jewell. "You guys — you're not going to leave tonight, are you?"

Derek shrugged.

"I mean you came all this way to see me, so you might as well stay over. I've got to work in the morning but I'll be done by noon. And then we can go on a picnic or something."

"We could take them up to Jerome," said Derek.

"Yes, that would be perfect. We can show them Angie's place." She looked at me and Jewell. "So how about it, ladies? There's a futon in the living room and I've got an extra mattress and a couple of sleeping bags."

I considered the invitation. Jewell and I had both packed overnight stuff because we didn't know how long it might take us to find Brooke. And I definitely needed more time in Prescott because my business was only half finished.

"Please don't be offended," Jewell said to Brooke, "but Tracy and I would like to stay in a motel — with a real bed and shower."

"Oh, I'm not offended," said Brooke. "I just want you to stay."

"I can take mom and Tracy to a motel," said Derek. "But I'd love to camp out here in the cabin."

"Okay then," Brooke said as she picked up Elmer, the fuzzy gray cat, and scratched him behind his ears. "Have they been downtown yet? To Whiskey Row and all that?"

"Nope," Derek said with a shake of his head. "We came here to find you and that's all we've done so far."

"Then we should take them downtown and have dinner on Whiskey Row."

"Good idea," said Derek. "Let's take them to Coyote Joe's."

"You're going to love it," they said, almost in unison.

Derek drove us downtown. We began with a stroll around the century-old courthouse. It was a magnificent stone building, bordered by a green lawn and tall elm trees, plus a number of statues involving horses and cowboys. By the time we finished, the sun had gone down and the weather was changing from perfect to chilly. I zipped up my jacket and wished for an extra sweater.

We crossed the street to the infamous Whiskey Row. Brooke said the street got its name in the early days when miners and cowpokes stumbled from one saloon to the next. Now it was prime commercial real estate with more art galleries than bars.

Our guides led us past a wooden Indian into Coyote Joe's Bar and Restaurant. We fell into single file as we made our way through a crowded room with booths on one side and a bar on the other. Pretty soon we were heading out the back door and I asked Brooke where we were going.

"We're going to eat outside," she said.

"Isn't it awfully cold for that?"

"It'll be great," she promised.

I suspected that Brooke's idea of comfort was a lot different from mine. But minutes later all was well. We were seated at a table next to a crackling fire contained in a screened fire place. The surrounding walls sheltered us from the wind, but overhead there was nothing but sky, black as ink and spackled with stars.

"I love the smell of that smoke," I said, taking a deep breath.

"That's because they're burning mesquite," said Brooke.

"Whatever it is, I like it."

Jewell and I ordered fish tacos, Derek got a steak and Brooke, who had recently become a vegetarian, had a grilled plate with lots of Portobella mushrooms. We ate and talked and laughed.

The crowd around us was mostly college students, dressed in blue jeans and sweatshirts — and vests — and jackets — and scarves — and knit hats. I was beginning to understand how a population without cars dealt with the fickle weather of a mountain town.

After dinner we walked a few doors down to a place called the Brass Rail. The interior had a lot of dark wood paneling and a long bar with a shiny brass rail at foot level. Off to the side was a gray - haired man pounding out familiar tunes on a honky- tonk piano. A lacy garter graced the sleeve of his striped shirt.

"I guess the only thing missing is the spittoons," I said.

"And thank goodness for that," said Jewell.

We all had margaritas and then Brooke suggested we go to another place where we could hear a live band. But Jewell and I begged off, pleading exhaustion. So the kids took Jewell and me to the Mohawk Motel and stayed until we got checked in.

Derek promised to be back in the morning. "I'll pick you up and take you to breakfast," he said.

"Fine," said Jewell. "Just don't make it too early."

The motel was nothing fancy but clean enough, the two beds topped with chenille bedspreads. It had been such a long day that I figured I would be out the minute I hit the pillow and closed my eyes.

But it didn't work that way. Instead of drifting into the relaxed state that precedes sleep, my brain decided to shift into overdrive.

I had come to Arizona with two distinct goals.

Now that we had found Brooke one of those goals was accomplished.

But I had promised Frank that I would try to locate Vince Crawley's first wife, Dixie. According to what Rose had told him, Dixie was living somewhere here in Prescott. But even her own daughter didn't know exactly where and was not allowed to communicate with her.

What on earth had made me think I was going to locate this missing woman — who may or may not have information about her deceased husband? This was definitely a long shot.

I really wanted to talk to Jewell about it — but she was fast asleep.

CHAPTER THIRTY FOUR

The next morning I did talk to Jewell about finding Dixie Crawley, who was supposed to be in a drug rehab facility somewhere in town. We kicked around some ideas and looked in the yellow pages of the phone book, which did list a couple of such places. But when we called the numbers, all we got was a machine which directed us to leave a number or to call back on Monday.

"I guess we're not to accomplish much on a Sunday," she said.

"I'm afraid you're right."

"So let's just relax and enjoy the day."

I took a shower and, while I was dressing, gave some thought to how I wanted to spend my remaining time in Arizona. Jewell was just coming out of the bathroom, her hair wrapped in a towel.

"Jewell," I said, "I know Derek is planning to drive back to Phoenix tonight."

"That's right. He needs to be back for work tomorrow."

"And you need to spend the time with your family. But that leaves me with three days and I'd like to spend the time here in Prescott. I think I'll just stay with Brooke."

"And endure the cold showers?"

"I can rough it. Maybe we'll fill up the boiler for a bath."

"Be sure to get a picture," she said with a chuckle.

"But then I have to get myself back to Phoenix. Do you know if there is any bus service?"

"Not exactly a bus," she said, "but there is a shuttle that goes right to the airport in Phoenix."

"Hey, that would be perfect. I could just meet you at the airport on Thursday."

Derek arrived and waited patiently while we finished our ablutions. Then he suggested a couple of options for breakfast, and we decided to go to the coffee shop where Brooke was working.

The Good Grains Coffee and Bagel Shop had a bike rack out front which held several bicycles and also a couple of well behaved dogs. We entered a sunny room about half full of people, some talking, but more absorbed in their laptops. A wealth of newspapers was scattered around the empty tables.

"My word, this place smells good," Jewell said as we chose a table.

"They roast their own coffee here," said Derek. "Roast it and grind it and brew it. Can't get much fresher than that."

Brooke, who was busy behind the counter, finally saw us and waved. Service was at the counter so Derek told us to sit tight and he would wait on us. First he brought us coffee and later, plates of scrambled eggs and croissants with melted cheese inside.

We took our time with breakfast, enjoying the sunshine and reading newspapers. I learned that Arizona had water issues, football loyalties and immigration problems. I saw dogs out front snap to attention when their owners appeared, usually bearing a treat for their canine companions.

Finally Brooke's shift was finished. She took off her apron and joined us, hugging Jewell and me as though she hadn't seen us in years.

"We have big plans for today," she said. "We're going to visit my friend Angie who lives in Jerome — in a genuine miner's cabin."

"It's right on the other side of Mingus Mountain," said Derek.

"I'm not sure I'm ready for any more mountains," I said.

"It's just a little one," he said. "You'll love it."

Half an hour later, we were at Brooke's place. The sun was climbing, the temperature rising, and we were getting ready for a trip over another mountain.

"How about water bottles?" said Derek

"I've got two of them," said Brooke. "Plus apples for munchies. I figured we could have lunch over there."

"Sure," he said, "we'll take them to the Haunted Hamburger."

"This is starting to sound a little scary," I said.

Derek repeated his mantra. "Don't worry — you'll love it."

As it turned out, Derek's idea of crossing a little mountain gave me plenty of white knuckled moments, even though I wasn't at the wheel. The narrow road snaked its way upward in a series of hairpin curves and switchbacks. I saw steep cliffs rising on one side of me and nothing at all on the other side where the terrain fell off into deep gorges. I was glad to be in the back seat with Brooke. Jewell had the honor of the front seat and I didn't envy her such a close-up view of eternity.

Eventually we crested the mountain and started down, passing a sign that told us we were entering the city of Jerome. The town literally clung to the side of the mountain so the main street continued the pattern of curves and switchbacks. The street was lined with buildings, some brick and some wood, and some of them boarded up. Brooke explained that Jerome had been a boom town until the copper mines closed in the fifties, when it became something of a ghost town.

But then, she said, Jerome had been discovered. A motley crew of writers, painters, hippies and other visionaries had reinvented the place as something of an artists' colony. So now it was a weekend destination and, this being Sunday, the place was busy with day trippers.

It took a while for Derek to find a parking place, but he finally squeezed in between a camper and a space that held four motorcycles. We got out and started walking uphill on the sidewalk, dodging foot traffic and keeping an eye on the cars that crept by us only a few feet away. We explored some galleries and I almost bought a gnarled piece of wood that had been carved into a distorted face. When I saw the price, my better judgment prevailed.

Eventually, Jewell and I said we were hungry.

"Then it's time for the Haunted Hamburger," said Brooke.

"And where is that?"

"Up there." Derek pointed to a street almost directly above us. It looked like about a half mile walk.

"We can take the stairs," said Brooke.

So we did. The stairs clearly had been chiseled into the mountainside as a shortcut across town. We managed the multiple staircases with only one rest stop and finally were seated at an outdoor table that gave us a stupendous view. We overlooked a valley that seemed to go on for miles and miles.

The hamburgers were good, decorated with stuff like avocados and cilantro, mushrooms and leeks. While we ate, Derek pointed out the old insane asylum (still higher above us) which had been converted into a hotel. Apparently every structure in town had been converted from its original use.

"How about this building?" I said. "What was this?"

"It was a house —." Derek actually blushed. "It was a house of —."

"It was a brothel," said Brooke.

"Now, that is a convenient word," I said. "Isn't it great to have a college education?"

Brooke said that after lunch we were going to visit her friend Angie.

"Angie has a degree in agronomy from Prescott College and now she has her dream job. She's managing a vinyard."

"This doesn't look much like grape country," I said.

"It definitely isn't," said Brooke. "They had to dig huge holes and haul in topsoil for every vine. But it's working. There's plenty of sun on the south side of the mountain."

We took the staircase downward, reclaimed the car and drove a short distance to Angie's house where parking was once again a challenge, since there were very few horizontal surfaces other than the road.

Angie's house was attached to the side of a mountain and we approached it by crossing a little wooden foot bridge. But once we were inside, the two room structure felt pretty secure and Angie presented us with toast and apricot jam.

"This really was a miner's cabin," said Angie, who had short spiked hair and a nose ring. "Now the cabin belongs to the guys who own the vinyard. They're part of a heavy metal band called Wrench."

"This whole project must be very expensive."

"It cost more than you could ever imagine," she said. "But the band makes a lot of money and the lead singer decided that he wanted a vinyard on top of Mingus Mountain. It took a couple years just to get the grapes planted. A bunch of guys from Prescott used to come here every day to work on the digging. One of them told me they needed someone to live here and look after the place. So I got my dream job."

Angie brought out a bottle of wine and we sampled some Mingus White. But then we had to leave. Derek had a long drive ahead of him since he would be going all the way back to Phoenix. On the return trip I asked Brooke if it would be okay for me to stay with her for a few days.

"Sure, I'd love that," she said. "It'll be just like last summer when I stayed with you."

"Except this time it's your house. You get to make the rules."

"Oh yeah, I'll be tough on you."

When we reached Prescott, Derek unloaded me and my belongings at Brooke's place. After brief goodbyes, he and Jewell were on their way to Phoenix.

So there I was, hanging out in a log cabin in the high desert country of Arizona. It felt weird but it also felt pretty good. I was beginning to understand why Brooke had embraced this new life so readily and enjoyed it so much.

We made supper together and, while we were cooking, I explained to Brooke that I had two reasons for staying in Prescott. I wanted to spend time with her, but I also had a job to do. I told her I was looking for a woman and, if I could find her, she might be able to help in a murder investigation.

"This sounds exciting," she said. "Tell me about it."

We filled our plates and, while we ate, I gave her a condensed version of the events surrounding the death of Vince Crawley back in Shagoni River. I told her I wanted to find Dixie Crawley, the dead man's former wife, who was supposed to be in a drug rehab facility in Prescott.

When I finished, Brooke said something that raised my spirits immeasurably.

"I think I might be able to help you with that," she said.

CHAPTER THIRTY FIVE

"Do you really think you can help me find Dixie Crawley?"

"I can't promise anything," said Brooke, "but I have an idea."

"I hope it's a good one. I've got exactly three more days here in Prescott."

"That's not much time."

"I know. I'm beginning to wonder what I was thinking — that I would run into her on a street corner?"

Brooke and I were at her cabin, finishing up a late dinner of vegetable stir fry and something called tabouleh. I had filled her in on the mystery surrounding Vince Crawley's death, ending with the fact that his first wife Dixie was supposed to be in Prescott and I was hoping to find her.

"But even if you found her," she said, "what would Dixie be able to tell you about him? It sounds like they haven't seen each other in years."

"I know. But they were together for a long time. Frank is thinking maybe she knows something — something from his past that would explain why he was killed. I know it's a long shot — but we're giving it a try because I'm here and because we really don't have anything else to go on."

"You said the guy had cancer?"

"Yes, pancreatic cancer. It's a killer."

"So he was probably going to die anyway."

"No probably about it. Vince Crawley had only a few months to live."

"So maybe —." Brooke puckered her brow in concentration. "Maybe he knew something that nobody else knew — some kind of secret."

"Possibly. A secret that he now has carried to the grave, as they say. But anyway — what do you think you could do to help me?"

Brooke brought out a jar of applesauce and spooned it into bowls. "My idea was to talk to one of the teachers at school — I had a class with him last semester. He mentioned that he used to work as a drug counselor."

"Here in Prescott?"

"I think so. See, he taught sociology and there was a section on drug abuse. When we covered that, he mentioned that quite a few people living in Prescott had originally come here to kick their habit."

"Must be they liked the town and decided to stay."

"That's part of it. But also because there are support groups. It would be hard for them to go home and not to go back to their old druggie friends."

"You seem to know a lot about it."

"A little. I wound up writing a report about it for class."

"Great. So what is this guy's name — this teacher?"

"Mister Pearson. Claude or Chad or something like that."

"Well, at least it's a place to start. This applesauce is good, by the way."

"I made it myself. Got the apples at the farm market."

I finished eating and began to stack my dishes. "So this teacher of yours. When can we get in touch with him?"

"I'll see what I can do tomorrow. I've got classes most of the day, but I'll stop by his office and try to make an appointment for you."

After dinner we sat in her living room and watched as lights flickered on in the town below us. It was a nice change from television and left plenty of room for conversation. I told Brooke about Steven showing up at my house.

"How did that go?" she said. "For the two of you, I mean?"

"Not too bad — after I got over the shock of seeing him. But Steven was really worked up about you. He thought you must have run away or been kidnapped or something."

She giggled. "Dad does tend to be a little dramatic. But anyway, we've chilled him out for now. And I'll try to write him once in a while."

"Don't just try, Brooke. Do it. You are his only child and he does care about you." *Why on earth was I defending the man?*

"Okay, promise."

"But anyway — how was it for you — coming way out here to a new school?"

"It was scary at first. But I knew all along it was the right move. I feel like it's the best thing I've ever done for myself."

"Better school?"

"Much better — for me at least. But that's just part of it. Everything is different here because we're not isolated on a campus. I mean, look at this wonderful place I'm living. And I love the town because there's such a big variety of people." She paused for a moment. "Back home, everyone was so — well — so Midwestern."

"Midwestern. Is that a bad thing?"

"Not bad, but limiting. Out here, there's more room to be different. We had a big Mardi Gras party and half the guys dressed as women. There's a class called Gender Studies that I want to take next fall. Guys are okay with long hair or no hair. Girls too. I'm thinking I might shave my head."

"Oh no." The words slipped out and I realized that I had always identified Brooke with her mass of long wavy hair.

"See, that's what I mean. People have one idea of me and maybe I've outgrown it. Maybe I want to be someone different. Maybe get a tattoo."

I wondered how her father would react to a daughter with a shaved head and a tattoo, but decided that would not be my problem. "Go ahead and be different," I said. "But give me a little warning if I have to see you without hair."

She asked me how things were going with Frank. I told her that we had run into a few bumps but so far had always managed to work things out.

Brooke confided that she had been seeing a boy named Kyle who was a student in outdoor education but also played guitar in a punk band. I wanted to tell to be wary of guys who played in bands — but I realized that such advice would fall on deaf ears.

"And what about Derek?" I said. That sort of slipped out, too.

"Derek and me? We'll always be good friends."

And that seemed to settle the issue. At least for her.

In the morning we had a quick breakfast and then I had to face the ordeal of riding behind Brooke on her motor scooter. I wasn't eager for the adventure but it was pretty much the only way I was going to get into town. So I dressed myself as she had advised — layering jacket over sweater over shirt. The morning was clear and chilly as Brooke mounted the Vespa and I climbed on behind her. Then we jammed her backpack full of books and other essentials in between us and I grabbed her around the waist.

Brooke turned the key and the motor coughed to life. She put it in gear and I hung on tight as we lurched forward. First we bounced down the dirt road which jarred my teeth and spine. Then we turned onto a paved road and traveled faster, with traffic zooming by us on both sides at perilously close proximity.

But Brooke knew her machine and we reached the campus parking lot unscathed. She parked the scooter and locked it while I was still climbing off. Then she grabbed her back pack, told me to meet her in the cafeteria for lunch and made a run for class.

So I was on my own for the morning and wondered what to do with my time. The campus was small, by any standards, just a few buildings around an open courtyard with a garden in back that sloped away to a little creek. I did some exploring outside, sat on the grass and soaked up the sunshine before I retreated to the library.

The library had high ceilings and exposed beams with natural light flooding in through windows and skylights. There was a wall full of magazines, many that I had never seen before. So I spent a couple of hours reading about Tai chi, wild food, organic farming, water conservation and how to make mud bricks.

I found the cafeteria, which had windows overlooking the gardens, and Brooke met me there as promised. We both ate huge salads which offered a variety of greens, generous slices of avocado, tomato and red pepper, plus hard boiled eggs and three kinds of cheese.

The food was great but the news was not encouraging. Brooke told me she had not been able to find Claude Pearson.

"But I went to his office and the schedule on his door said he has office hours today from four until five. So just plan to be there. Maybe I can still see him this afternoon." She told me how to find his office, which was near the library.

"Okay," I said, "I'll be there. But I just thought of something else."

I told her about the foray Jewell and I had made into the yellow pages while we were at the motel and that I wanted to try some phone calls. Brooke told me where to get change, pointed out the payphone and then she was off to more classes.

I got a handful of quarters and made three telephone calls, to places called The Rest of Your life, Sunshine House and New Hope Center. Two of the calls reached recorded voices that invited me to leave a call back number. On my third try I reached a live person. The woman who answered told me that unless I was a doctor, a counselor, or a prospective patient, she had no authority to speak to me.

I thought fast and decided to be a prospective patient. I told her I had a serious problem and was looking for help. She told me where I could pick up an application form and that I should mail it in and someone would contact me.

So much for that clever ruse.I still had time to kill so I decided to take a walk. Brooke had provided me with a map and assured me that I was within walking distance of downtown. So I headed off campus. The sun was high and hot and I understood why Brooke had advised me to dress in layers. I took off my jacket and tied it around my waist.

Eventually I found a bookstore and a coffee shop, then a place called Angel Lights. Intrigued, I made my way inside the angel store.

The place smelled heavily of patchouli. A serious looking young man behind the counter told me I was just in time to hear a visiting author. I figured why not. So he directed me to a door in the back of the store. I made my way through a beaded curtain to a room where a dozen people, mostly women, were sitting in a circle. I joined them.

The speaker was a raven- haired woman of indeterminate years, wearing a gauzy blue dress with a lot of turquoise jewelry. She told us that she regularly communicated with angels, who send us signs if only we know how to recognize them. When she finished her presentation, she offered to do individual life readings for anyone who wanted to pay fifty dollars.

I was tempted but, fortunately, had no such cash on me.

So, no angelology for me. But at least the visit had killed some time. I was back on campus by 3:30. I planted myself outside Claude Pearson's office, just to be first in line in case there was a rush.

There wasn't any rush. In fact there was no activity at all in the hallway and I began to wonder if Pearson would decide to skip his office hours and go home for the day. Probably he didn't like Mondays any more than the rest of us.

But I needn't have worried. About twenty minutes later, a tall man came walking down the hallway, moving with a long-limbed, easy gait. As he approached I saw a bronzed face topped by a thatch of dark, gray-flecked hair.

I moved from my slouch against the wall and stood straighter

The man nodded in my direction as he unlocked the office door. He smiled and said, "You must be Brooke's friend."

"That's me."

"Come on in."

I followed him into his office. His large wooden desk was scattered with oddly shaped stones that may have been serving as paperweights.

"I'm Claude Pearson," he said, extending a large hand

"Tracy Quinn," I said, noting calluses during the handshake.

"Have a seat." He gestured toward a leather covered chair.

I slid into the chair and he sat behind his desk. Afternoon light flooded in from the window behind him, making a halo of his hair.

Not a bad looking man, all told. Too bad I only had two more days in town.

"What can I do for you?" he said, while he shuffled through some papers on his desk. Claude Pearson seemed a bit distracted. He probably wanted to finish up and go home.So I got right to the point.

"I'm hoping you can help me find a woman here in town," I said. "Her ex- husband is dead and it looks like he was murdered."

Pearson stopped shuffling papers. "Someone was murdered?"

"Yes, this happened in Michigan. That's where I've come from."

"I don't understand where I come into this."

"Vince Crawley is the dead man and I'm trying to find his ex- wife, Dixie. The daughter said her mom got into heroin while they were both in San Francisco. And now Dixie is here in a rehab facility. Brooke said you know a little about — about that kind of stuff." My voice trailed off. I wondered if I was making any sense at all.

Claude Pearson regarded me through narrowed eyes. He rubbed his chin and said, "So, what are you — a detective?"

"No I'm not. Just a friend of a detective. And since I was flying out to Arizona with my friend — she has family in Phoenix — and we came up to Prescott because of Brooke — because we hadn't seen her for a while. Anyway since I was coming out here to see Brooke I told my friend — the detective, that is — that I would try to find out where Dixie was and see if I could possibly talk to her and — ."

Claude Pearson was regarding me with an inscrutable expression. I stopped talking and tried to see myself through his eyes. What I saw was a slightly deranged woman babbling about a murder in Michigan and doing her best to involve him in her delusions. I wondered if he was getting ready to call security and have me escorted off campus.

He was quiet for a moment. He put his elbows on the desk, steepled his fingers and regarded me carefully.

"I can probably find out if she's in one of the facilities in town," he said. "But it's unlikely that you'll be able to talk to her."

"Why not?"

"There are some things you have to understand."

CHAPTER THIRTY SIX

"Okay," I said to Claude Pearson. "Tell me what I need to know."

He continued to regard me, his expression unreadable. Finally he said, "Brooke was correct in assuming that I know something about drug rehab facilities, because I've worked in more than one of them."

My pulse quickened. The reporter in me was ready to pull out a notebook and start scribbling. But I didn't want anything to threaten the flow of information. So I just sat still and made it clear to Mr. Pearson that he had my full attention.

"Changing addictive behavior patterns isn't easy." Pearson leaned back in his chair and clasped his hands behind his head, which made me think he was assuming his teaching mode. "Over the years," he said, "certain measures have been developed that are effective in changing these behaviors. But these measure often impress the lay person as pretty severe — bordering on the draconian."

Cripe, what was he talking about? Electric shock? I nodded and did my best to follow his line of thought.

"In most cases, the only thing that works is a live-in facility with twenty-four hour supervision. And during the first few weeks the addict, the patient, or the client, if you will — as a rule, the person being treated is not allowed any contact with the outside world. No visits, no letters, no phone calls, no e-mail, from anyone."

"Not even family?"

He shook his head. "Sometimes family is part of the problem."

"I guess that would explain why no one was able to notify her of Vince's death."

"Yes, it would. Especially if she's still in the first two months of the program. After that, the restrictions are eased, but only gradually. I'm sorry, but that's the way it is."

"Okay," I said. "But could you — could you at least find out if she is here in town?"

"I can do that," he said with a glance at his watch. "I'll get on it tomorrow morning."

"That would be great. I, ah, I don't want to take up any more of your time. Can we talk tomorrow?"

"Sure. I have a two hour break so we could meet for lunch. But I'd rather do it off campus."

"Sure. Anywhere."

"Do you know the coffee shop over on River Street?"

"Yes. I saw it today."

"They have sandwiches. Meet me there at twelve-thirty."

This time I did grab my notebook and wrote down the appointment. Lunch with Pearson. The Daily Grind. 222 River St.

"He wants to meet me off campus," I said to Brooke that evening. "I wonder why."

"It makes sense," she said. "He probably wouldn't want to give out sensitive information in the school cafeteria. He might be bending some rules for you."

"Oh sure. I hadn't thought of that."

"Plus, maybe he doesn't want to set off any rumors. Mr. Pearson is divorced —or maybe the divorce is still in process. Anyway, his private life is a pretty hot topic with some of the girls."

"He is nice looking," I said. "I wonder what his story is."

"Want me to find out?"

"Thanks, but I think I have enough on my plate already."

The next morning Brooke had to work at the bagel shop. So I rode in with her, dawdled over coffee and a bagel while I read every available newspaper and wondered what it would be like to work for one of them. Then I set out on a walk designed to end on River Street. The sun was not shining. In fact the sky was overcast and the gutters ran with little streams from an early morning rain, but I reminded myself that Michigan was probably under several feet of snow. I spent an hour browsing through a book store and a consignment shop.

I reached the Daily Grind, and found Pearson already there, seated at a table in the back. He was wearing a string tie with a silver clip which gave him a gentleman rancher look. I joined him and ordered a grilled cheese sandwich. We made small talk until our food arrived and then, after the waitress was gone, he pulled a pamphlet from his pocket.

"I found your Dixie Crawley," he said as he pushed the paper across the table to me. It had a picture of a large Victorian looking house. "She's at this place — over by the city library. It's called Harbor House."

"That's great," I said. "Will I be able to see her?"

"It's not that simple. Remember what I told you about restricted access?"

"Well sure, but — it's not like I'm an old druggie friend of hers — or a dealer — or anything like that."

"Frankly," he said, "and no offense intended, but we don't really know who you are."

"This seems preposterous. That I would come all this way out here — and they won't even let me talk to her."

"I told you that things seem draconian — to anyone who is not involved in the field."

I took a deep breath and let my anger drain out. "Isn't there anything that we — or you — can do?"

Claude Pearson regarded me with a faint smile. "I don't want to get your hopes up — but it's not over yet. I'm going to talk to the director this afternoon — and I'll find out if Dixie is getting near the end of her isolation period."

"So there's a chance?"

"There is a chance you'll be able to meet with her. But you may need to talk in the presence of a third party."

"Well sure," I said. "Whatever it takes."

"I'll know something tomorrow."

"I certainly hope so. Because tomorrow's my last day in Prescott."

"Stop by my office at noon."

I probably wasn't very good company for Brooke that evening. No matter what we were doing, part of my mind was consumed with thoughts about meeting Dixie Crawley. I tried to figure out what I would say — wondered how I would feel if the whole thing fell through.

I had told Brooke everything that was going on and we went to bed early so I would be rested for the day ahead. But then anticipation just kept me awake. When I did sleep, I woke frequently, wondering if the futon was a device made specifically for night time torture.

By 11:30 the next morning, I was waiting outside Pearson's office. He showed up as promised but his expression betrayed nothing as he unlocked the door."Come on in," he said.

I followed him in.

He dropped his briefcase on the desk and then turned to face me. "I've got good news," he said, with a flash of smile. "I pulled a few strings and Dixie's counselor has agreed to let you meet with her this afternoon."

"That's great!" I wanted to give him a big hug but restrained myself. "What time?"

"Three o'clock. The address is on that flyer I gave you. Do you still have it?"

"Of course. Right here."

"Don't be late. Ask for Margaret Langley. She's in charge of the whole operation so, whatever you do, don't aggravate her."

"I'll be good."

He glanced at his watch and said he had a noon meeting. I thanked him effusively and said goodbye.

241

I was starting to leave when he said something that surprised me. "I have to admit that this thing has piqued my interest. Will you let me know how it all comes out?"

"Sure. I'd be glad to."

"Here's my e-mail." He smiled as he handed me his business card. We shook hands again.

Though I was thinking really hard about meeting Dixie Crawley I couldn't help noticing for the umpteenth time that Claude Pearson really did have a killer smile.

CHAPTER THIRTY SEVEN

There is no such thing as public transportation in Prescott, so I set out on foot for my appointment at the drug house. On my way across town, I stopped and grabbed a sandwich for lunch. Then I walked uphill past the library and turned south on the street that was supposed to take me to the New Hope facility.

I was in a residential section with lots of big, old well-kept homes on both sides of the street. The house numbers were not always obvious but I recognized my destination from the photo on the pamphlet. It was a three-story house, painted dark green with lots of yellow trim. The building sat on a hill so the yard sloped downward toward the street until it met a stone wall which bordered the sidewalk.

I walked up steps onto a broad porch with a swing on one end and flower boxes on the railings. The petunias were pink and white. The place looked like any other house on the block, no different from a private home.

Until I reached the front door and saw a sign by the doorbell.

The sign said, "RESIDENTS ONLY. No solicitations. No visitors."

This gave me pause, but only for a moment. After all, Pearson had assured me that I had an appointment. So I rang the door bell and waited for at least a minute before I rang again. I was debating a third try when I saw some movement inside.

The door opened slowly, revealing a short woman with ash-colored hair who peered at me through wire rimmed spectacles. She could have been anywhere from forty to sixty and wore a faded yellow shirt which I searched in vain for a name tag. A pair of black polyester slacks stretched around her ample thighs.

"I'm Tracy Quinn," I said. "I have an appointment at three — to see Dixie Crawley." The woman continued her owlish stare but did not reply.

Oops. Too direct maybe. "Actually I need to see Margaret Langley. Claude Pearson called about me."

She finally nodded and said, "Okay, that's me. I'm the director. Come on in, I guess."

I followed Ms. Langley inside to a dark living room that boasted a small TV in one corner, the focal point for the rest of the furniture which included two sofas and a half dozen chairs. The furniture was mismatched and worn, suggesting that it had been donated by people who were moving on with their lives.

"Just follow me," the woman said without any change of expression.

She led me down a hallway covered with linoleum and into a small room with a counter and a sink, coffee maker and a tin cupboard. There was one tall window with no curtains. In the center of the room was a Formica table with chrome legs, surrounded by wooden chairs.

"Sit down," she directed. So I sat.

She sat on another chair and continued to scowl while she looked me over. Finally she spoke.

"Dixie Crawley has been with us two months," she said, "and seems to be making progress. But, of course, it's easy to avoid drugs when they aren't available. I'm here to make sure that you are not supplying her with anything."

I held out my empty hands. She nodded toward my fanny pack, an accoutrement that Brooke had provided for me when I started riding her scooter. I unbuckled it and pushed it toward her.

"Keep it if you want to," I said.

She put the pack on the counter behind her. "We're also concerned," she said, "about any news that might upset our client. I understand that her former husband has died."

"That's true," I said. "In fact, that's why I'm here."

"Well, I already told her about that, and she seemed to handle it okay. So just wait here and I'll bring her out. But if you do or say anything that upsets her, I'll have to terminate the interview."

"I understand."

"Just wait here."

She left the room and was gone for several minutes. Rubbing my hands together, I discovered that my palms were sweating. I found a paper cup and got a drink of water. When Margaret Langley returned, she was followed by a thin woman dressed in sweatpants and a faded tee shirt, whom she introduced as Dixie Crawley. I tried for a reassuring smile, shook her hand and stared in spite of my best efforts not to.

I'm not sure what I had expected Dixie to look like. I had seen photos, of course, but they had been taken years ago. The woman facing me had pasty skin with blotches on her neck and arms. Her listless hair was straight and bi-color — dark for the first two inches and beyond that, a bad bleach job. Her lips were chapped and her fingernails were bitten to the quick.

I managed to deliver the opening line I had been rehearsing. "Hello Dixie," I said. "I've seen both of your daughters. And your son too."

"How are they?" Her voice was hoarse and it seemed an effort for her to speak.

"They're all fine. The girls are living together at the moment." I saw no reason to mention that they were living with Fiona.

"I suppose they're in Michigan because Vince died."

"That's pretty much the case. Charlene was already there, and Rose came back when she got word about it."

"How about Chip?"

"He's still around too. He's got a trailer out by Crystal Valley."

"Well that's good. Chip was kind of a loner and I worried about him."

"Well look," I said. "The reason I'm here is —." I paused, glanced at our chaperone and tried to think of a delicate way to phrase my next statement.

But I couldn't see any easy way to do this, so I waded right in.

"The reason I'm here is because somebody killed Vince. I wondered if you can tell me anything that might help us figure out who it was — who would want to kill Vince."

"I've been thinking about this," she said, "and I guess there is something I should tell you." She bit her lower lip and looked around. "Is it okay if I smoke?"

We both looked at Margaret Langley. The director nodded and produced an ashtray. I nodded too, ready to accept any amount of second-hand smoke if it would loosen Dixie's tongue. Dixie produced a smashed up pack of Marlboros, extracted one and leaned forward.

Langley produced a lighter and lit the cigarette with a quick expert motion.

Dixie inhaled deeply and held the smoke for a long moment before she reluctantly let it go.

"Okay," she said, focusing on the burning tip of her cigarette, "Here's what happened. It was back when Vince and I were first married —."

Once she got started, Dixie Crawley talked for nearly an hour with a minimum of prompting. When she finished, I asked a couple more questions which she answered. Then our time was up. We shook hands and I promised to tell her children that I had seen her and she was doing okay.

The last I saw of Dixie Crawley, she was following Margaret Langley down the shadowy hallway.

But our time together had been productive — very productive. I knew immediately that the information Dixie had provided was making my journey to Arizona well worth the time, money and effort I had expended.

That should have made me very happy.

But I wasn't happy at all. In fact, I felt a whole lot like I wanted to throw up.

CHAPTER THIRTY EIGHT

The next morning I rode the shuttle bus from Prescott to the Phoenix airport. Slightly disoriented, I made my way through the multiple gates and desks which relieved me of my luggage and rewarded me with a boarding pass.

When I reached the waiting area for my flight, I was delighted to find Jewell already there. We shared a hug and I slid into the seat next to her, struggling to stifle an uncontrollable yawn.

"Looks like you're going to need some coffee," she said.

"Early morning. I was up before daylight to catch the shuttle."

"So how was that?"

"Not bad. Worst part was the ride with Brooke on that little scooter. I thought I was going to freeze to death. But the bus was nice and warm so I caught a nap before I watched the sun come up over the desert."

"Did you ever find Dixie Crawley?"

"I found her," I said. "And we talked for nearly an hour."

"Good job. Did you learn anything?"

"Yes I did, but — ." I left off talking so we could hear the announcement coming over the public address system. It was the call for us to board our flight. "I'd better wait and tell you about it later." We located our boarding passes, grabbed our carry-on baggage and joined the line of passengers.

As soon as we were in our seats on the plane, Jewell returned to the subject at hand. "I can't believe you actually found Dixie. How did you manage that?"

"Believe me, I never could have done it without Brooke." I told her about Claude Pearson and how he had found Dixie and then cleared the way for me to visit her at the drug treatment house.

"I had to walk across town and deal with the dragon lady director, but I finally got to talk with Dixie. And what I found out — well, I'm not sure — but I'm afraid it's going to be a bit of a bombshell."

"Can you tell me about it?" Jewell laid aside the glossy magazine she had brought with her.

"I thought maybe I should tell Frank first," I said. "But I can't keep this to myself any longer. It's already starting to drive me crazy."

"My lips are sealed," she said as the plane lifted off the runway. "And once again — we've got a fairly long flight ahead of us."

"Okay then. Here's what she told me." I had scratched down some notes shortly after my conversation with Dixie, but I had no need to refer to them. The whole story was burnt into my brain.

"First of all, Jewell, I need to tell you about a party that Ivy had at her house — when Greg Wetherel moved in with her."

"I knew he had moved in," she said. "I didn't know there was a party."

"Right. And I was there with Frank. This was only a week or two after Vince died. Late in the evening Frank asked Greg if he had ever known Vince Crawley."

"Guess Frank is always on the job."

"Right. But here's the interesting thing. When Frank asked him about Vince, Greg acknowledge that they had been in high school together. He said they both played basketball but didn't run with the same crowd."

"This must have been in the seventies."

"Right. But now, according to Dixie, either Greg was lying or he has a very bad memory."

"So she told a different story?"

"Dixie said that Greg and Vince were very close. The friendship continued after they graduated, even though Greg went to college and Vince did a couple of years in the army. After he got out, Vince and Dixie got married and started their family."

"But Greg stayed single?"

"Apparently, Greg dated different girls but always came back to one called Amy. Their friends figured they were unofficially engaged."

"Did he and Amy ever get married?"

"No. Because she died."

"She died? But how?"

"Well that's the story. It was the summer of '77. Vince had just got out of the service and Greg had finished his third year of college — so they decided to celebrate. The two couples rented a cottage out at Silver Lake for the weekend. They had a lot of friends over for a cook-out. There was a boat, water skis, and of course a lot of alcohol. Everyone was in high spirits."

I stopped talking as a steward came by offering beverages. I followed Jewell's suggestion and got some coffee. Jewell had a soft drink.

"Let's see. Where was I?"

"The party at the lake."

"Right. So, on the last night, after everyone else had left, the four of them decided to go skinny dipping. They were fooling around, splashing and ducking each other, the usual horseplay." I lowered my voice a bit. "Dixie said that she and Vince wandered off by themselves, wanting to see what it was like to have sex in the water."

"Sounds like fun. How did that work out?"

"I guess they never found out — because all of a sudden Greg started yelling that he couldn't find Amy."

"So that killed the mood."

"Definitely. Everything changed. The three of them started looking for Amy and calling her name. At first they thought she was just fooling around and hiding from them. Greg went to the car and got a flashlight, but there was still no sign of her. The whole thing got really scary. They argued and debated until finally Vince called the police who came with cars and searchlights. Nothing."

"Nothing?"

"Not until morning. That's when they found Amy's body. She was face down in the water. Under the neighbors' dock."

"Now that is weird."

"Very weird. There was an investigation, of course. Greg said that he and Amy had been arguing because she wanted to get married but he insisted on waiting until he graduated. He said she swam away, probably expecting him to follow — but instead he went ashore and got another beer. And then he couldn't find her."

"Was there an autopsy?"

"Of course. The conclusion was death by drowning."

"Did they consider suicide?"

"That was considered. But in the end, the death was ruled accidental."

Jewell sipped her soda and glanced out the window. "Of course, everyone was partly responsible — considering they had all been drinking."

"Yes. But here's the interesting part. The post mortem also revealed that Amy was pregnant."

"Aha. So she had reason to pressure Greg for marriage."

"Right. But in the end there were only three people at the scene. Dixie and Vince were preoccupied so they didn't really know if Greg's account was accurate or not. They were relieved when the investigation was over. Still —."

We paused and looked up as the steward handed each of us a freshly baked chocolate chip cookie. The cookies occupied us for a few minutes. I, of course, got chocolate on my fingers.

"So the case was closed?" said Jewell.

"Case was closed."

"Was that the end of the whole business?"

"Yes and no," I said, remembering the grim look on Dixie's face as she revisited the incident. "Dixie said that she and Vince talked about it many times afterward. They both knew it was possible that

Greg had deliberately drowned Amy. And Dixie came to believe that he had."

"Did she do anything about it?"

"No. The sticking point was that Vince was determined to protect his friend. So they went along with Greg's version of events and didn't voice their suspicions. Eventually Greg finished law school and started moving in a different circle of friends. Dixie said that she and Vince got busy raising their kids and she tried to forget the whole thing.

"But the incident was always stuck there in the back of her mind. It stayed there through all the years of their marriage. She said maybe that was why Vince drank too much though he would never admit any connection. So that was one more reason for her wanting to leave Vince — his presence always reminded her of the secret they were keeping."

"I wonder if that secret contributed to her drug abuse," said Jewell.

"Could be. She said that after a while Vince refused to talk about that night — but she knew that he couldn't have forgotten it either."

"Do you think Dixie was telling you the truth?"

"I'm not an expert on this kind of thing," I said. "But can you think of any reason why she would lie — after all this time?"

"No. I really can't."

We both looked out the window but there was nothing to see except clouds. Jewell turned back to me and said, "When Vince was diagnosed — when he knew he had only a little while to live —do you think he might have wanted to clear his conscience about Amy's death?"

"Believe me, the thought has crossed my mind. But I'm trying hard not to think about the implications of all this. I'm just going to tell Frank everything and let him decide what to do about it."

CHAPTER THIRTY NINE

It was nine p.m. Michigan time when Jewell and I arrived in Grand Rapids where Paul was waiting for us. I was disappointed that Frank wasn't with him. Paul explained that Frank was tied up at work but had promised to be at my house when I got home.

The roads were clear and we made it back to town in less than two hours. When I saw light spilling from the windows of my house, I knew that Frank had kept his promise. He met me on the porch and wrapped me in a bear hug. Paul and Jewell came inside and we invited them to stay for coffee.

"I'd love to," said Jewell, "but I need to go home and get ready for tomorrow."

"Working on the weekend?" said Frank.

"It's called a retreat for hospital administrators."

"Sounds terrible."

"It is," she agreed, "but at least I got a vacation first. Tracy and I had a great time in Arizona."

"I'll bet you did. While Paul and I were stuck here in Michigan."

Jewell laughed as they told us goodnight and disappeared into the darkness. As soon as they were gone, Frank and I engaged in a prolonged kiss.

"Welcome home," he said. "I really missed you."

"That's good," I said, catching my breath. "But remember, you go away for days at a time. Don't you miss me then?"

"That's different."

"I guess the person left behind always feels more lonely," I said.

"I understand you found Brooke."

"I did. Not only Brooke, but Dixie Crawley too."

"Good job. Did she have anything to tell you?"

"A whole lot."

"That's great," he said as he let me go. "Why don't you just sit down? I brought a bottle of wine. I'll pop it open and you can tell me everything."

So I sat down and had the pleasure of being waited on in my own home. Frank fiddled around in the kitchen and returned with two glasses of wine plus a plate of cheese and crackers. We cuddled up together on the sofa.

"Okay," he said. "Let's hear everything about your trip."

So I told him how Derek had led us to Brooke. And how Brooke had put me in touch with Claude Pearson, who then tracked down Dixie Crawley and arranged for us to meet.

"And what did you learn from Vince Crawley's first wife?"

"Before I tell you about Dixie," I said, "we need to back up a minute and talk about Greg Wetherell."

"Ivy's boyfriend?" he said. I nodded. "So what does he have to do with it?"

I took a deep breath and tried to arrange my thoughts. "Remember that night at Ivy's house when you asked him about Vince Crawley?"

"You mean the night of her party?"

"Right. And Greg told you that he hardly knew Vince back in high school — they weren't close friends or anything."

"I remember."

"Well, that was a lie. Greg and Vince were really tight — during high school and for several years after."

Frank put down his glass now, giving me his full attention. He listened quietly, asking the occasional question, while I relayed everything Dixie had told me, ending with the night that Greg's girlfriend Amy had drowned while the four of them were frolicking in Silver Lake.

"This definitely raises some questions," he said.

"I agree. What questions would you start with?"

"I wonder what Vince Crawley might have been thinking toward the end of his life."

"Jewell said maybe things were weighing on his mind — and he wanted to clear his conscience before he died."

"That's what I'm thinking too. But more important, there's a good chance that Greg Wetherel knew about Vince's diagnosis — and was afraid his old friend might talk to the police. That would definitely put Greg on the hot seat."

"Would the authorities reopen a case that old?"

"There's no statute of limitation on murder. But even if the case didn't come to trial, it would create a huge shadow on Greg's reputation."

"So do you think that Greg might have be the one —?"

"I think there's a good chance that Greg put the chloral hydrate in Vince's whiskey."

"Right." Frank had finally given voice to the suspicion I had carried ever since my talk with Dixie. It was a thought I had been trying to ignore — quite possibly out of loyalty to Ivy. "So what now?" I said.

"I need to pay Greg a visit and ask him some questions." Frank looked at me appraisingly. "I think it might work best if you come with me. Make it look like a social call on him and Ivy."

"Well sure, if you'd really like me to go along." I started to feel a little excited. "When shall we do it?"

"I'm thinking tomorrow morning. Not too early. Just early enough to surprise them."

CHAPTER FORTY

The roads were icy the next morning when Frank and I drove to Ivy Martin's place. We parked and looked around. There were a lot of car tracks in the snow but only Ivy's car was parked out front, covered with a frozen white crust.

We approached the house and Frank knocked on the door. Nothing happened so he knocked again. He was about to make a third try when the door opened. There stood Ivy, wrapped in a blue robe with her hair in disarray and her face lacking the usual cosmetic enhancement.

Ivy peered at us and shook her head, as though to clear away some cobwebs. "Frank and Tracy. What brings you out so early?"

"We were in the neighborhood and thought we'd stop by." Frank offered the lie with a straight face. "Got any coffee?"

"Well sure — I mean — I can warm some up. Excuse my —." She coughed, cleared her throat. "We had a rather late night — karaoke at the Antler and then some friends over for —-. But anyway, come on in." She stepped back and motioned us inside.

"Who's there?" Greg's voice came floating down the hallway.

"It's Tracy and Frank," she said. "We're going to have some coffee — ."

Greg's response was undecipherable. As we followed Ivy through the living room, I heard a toilet flush.

The state of the kitchen left no doubt that her story about the previous night was true. A half bottle of Jack Daniels was on the counter next to a number of glasses and an empty vodka bottle. She swept these aside and turned on the coffee maker which still held half a pot of coffee.

"This coffee is actually pretty fresh. I made it about four this morning before we sent our guests out onto the road." She directed the comment at Frank as though to assure him that she and Greg had been responsible hosts. Maybe she thought we were bringing news of an early morning car crash.

Frank and I sat down at the kitchen table. Within minutes Greg joined us. He was unshaven, red-eyed and clearly less than happy about the early morning incursion. Ivy put four cups on the table and filled them. Greg took his cup, found the whiskey bottle and poured in a generous shot.

"Irish coffee," he mumbled

"Hair of the dog," Frank said sympathetically.

The silence that followed was awkward and I was unable to conjure any small talk. Frank didn't even try. He just drank his coffee and stared at our reluctant host.

It was Greg who finally spoke up. "So what can we do for you folks?"

"I wanted to talk to you," said Frank.

"Me? About what?"

"About Vince Crawley."

"Vince." Greg rubbed his bristly chin. "But why? I hardly knew him."

"So you say. But there's somebody who remembers differently."

"Really? And who would that be?"

"That would be Vince's first wife, Dixie."

I heard Greg's sharp intake of breath. "And what did Dixie have to say?" He glanced from Frank to Ivy and then his eyes began to dart nervously about the room.

Frank looked straight at Greg while he answered. "Dixie told us that she and Vince were with you when Amy drowned in Silver Lake."

"That bitch!" Greg spoke with such vehemence that Ivy jerked away from him.

Frank didn't flinch. "So you see," he said, "we need to know where you were on January twenty-third."

"Why in hell do you want to know that?" said Greg.

"Because January twenty-third is the day that someone sedated Vince Crawley so he would freeze to death in his ice shanty."

Ivy spoke, her voice unnaturally high. "What makes you think Greg had anything to do with that?"

Frank ignored her, not taking his eyes off Greg. "It was a Saturday. Can you tell me your whereabouts that day?"

"Good lord, that nearly two months ago. How am I supposed to remember something like that?"

"Well, that was before you moved in." Ivy was trying to be helpful. "Probably when your father was sick. Maybe you were with him at the hospital."

"This whole thing is ridiculous," said Greg. "But just to get you off my back, I can likely figure this out for you. I usually keep a journal."

"Really?" Ivy looked surprised. "I never knew you kept a journal."

"Well, I haven't since I moved in. Everything here is such a mess."

"Greg, I'm trying. I'm really trying to —."

"Never mind. I'll go find the journal. It should be somewhere in the bedroom." Greg stood and started down the hallway that led to their bedroom. "Just hold your horses," he said. "I'll be right back."

Minutes later Greg called from the bedroom. "Ivy, come in here. Where did you put my filing box — I swear, I can't find a damn thing."

Ivy rolled her eyes and whispered, "He's such a baby sometimes." But she stood and went down the hallway to the bedroom.

Frank and I exchanged looks but kept quiet.

The silence was broken by a chilling scream from Ivy. The scream was followed by garbled words that sounded like, "Greg — don't, please!"

Frank stood up so fast he tipped over his chair.

Seconds later the two of them appeared, moving toward us down the hall. Ivy was in front with her head cocked oddly to one side. When they reached the doorway I saw the reason for Ivy's awkward posture. Greg had a fistful of her hair in his left hand and was using it to propel her in front of him.

Then I saw the glint of light against metal and realized that Greg's right hand held a pistol. And the business end of the gun was pressed tightly against the side of Ivy's head. His voice came out in a snarl.

"You two get out of here — before I blow her brains out."

CHAPTER FORTY ONE

"Get out of here before I kill her."

The twisted expression on Greg's face left no doubt that his threat was serious. He kept his grip on Ivy's hair and waved the gun at me and Frank before he returned it to rest against her temple.

"Please — please do what he says." Ivy choked out the words.

I'm ashamed to report my next thoughts.

Unbidden, some part of my brain started a tally of all the unpleasant things Ivy had done — the times she left me stuck with the tab for her lunch; how she used an excuse to make a date with Frank; but, worst of all, her seduction of Jewell's husband. Maybe, just maybe, the world would be a better place without this woman's aggravating presence —-.

"I'll count to ten," said Greg. "If you're not gone, the bitch gets it."

Reason returned. I stood on wobbly legs.

"Let's go," said Frank as he grabbed my arm and pulled me around the table.

Frank positioned himself behind me as we moved across the living room toward the front door. As soon as we were close enough, Frank jerked the door open and pushed me through.

He closed the door behind us and said, "Walk fast, but don't run. Go straight to the Blazer and get in."

My heart drummed in my ears as I moved toward his vehicle and prayed that the door I was aiming for was unlocked. It was. I slid inside, slammed the door and felt my breath release.

Almost immediately Frank was beside me. "You okay?"

Not trusting my chattering teeth, I nodded. Frank leaned across me, opened the glove box and pulled out a leather holster containing a pistol. The unexpected sight of the gun restored my power of speech.

"Geez, Frank, I didn't know you carried that around."

"I don't usually. But I brought it today because I wasn't sure what to expect."

He touched my hand. "I'm sorry I got you involved. I really thought he would come quietly to avoid a scene."

"Guess we were wrong about that."

"Dead wrong."

"Now what?"

Frank didn't answer because he had his telephone out and was punching in a number. Seconds later he said, "Benny, this is Frank. I've got a hostage situation and I need back up —- everything you can give me." He gave the sheriff the address. "Yes, the SWAT team. The guy's in the house with his girlfriend and a gun. — No, he's not faking. I think he's already killed two people. —- I'm parked in the driveway — the house is pretty far off the road and there's a lot of trees — just come in behind me, quiet, no sirens or flashers. We'll take it from there."

Frank ended the call and proceeded to fasten the gun onto his belt. While he did this, he interrogated me.

"What do you know about doors to the house? Where are the outside entrances?"

"The kitchen has a door that opens onto a deck in the back."

"Any side doors? On the side we can't see?"

"I don't think so. I think that end is just bedrooms."

Frank started the engine and shifted into reverse. He backed up and gave the wheel a twist. When he stopped, the Blazer was parked at an angle that blocked the driveway and provided a view of both front and back doors.

"What do you know about their cars?"

"That's Ivy's car in the drive way."

"What about Greg's car?"

"I don't think it's back from the shop yet."

"Could it be in the garage?"

"Near as I can recall, Ivy's garage is full of Greg's extra furniture."

"What do you know about the neighbors?"

"See that brick house over there in the trees?" I pointed to our left. "I think that's a family with a couple of kids."

"Let's hope they're not playing in the woods. What else?"

"We passed a couple of cabins just before we turned in here. But I think they're empty. Just summer cabins."

"The woods behind her house. How far back do you think — ?" Frank stopped talking when the Cedar County Sheriff's car pulled up behind us.

"I need to talk with these guys," he said. "You stay here. Keep an eye on both doors. And the windows too."

"And what if I see Greg trying to leave?"

"Lay on the horn."

Frank got out of the Blazer, leaving the engine running. As an afterthought he turned back and said, "You can drive a stick shift, can't you?"

"Of course. But what —?"

"Never mind. Just watch the house."

Frank got out and I stayed in the Blazer keeping watch. But I positioned the rear view mirror so I could see what was going on behind me.

I saw a uniformed man emerge from the car behind us. It was Sheriff Benny Dupree, a big guy whose prominent ears were red from the cold. He was immediately joined by another man whom I recognized as my old friend, Sergeant Curt Laman.

Both men were in uniform with an unnatural bulk under their jackets suggesting the presence of bullet-proof vests. Suddenly I wished that Frank was wearing one of those vests. I wouldn't have minded having one myself.

As instructed, I kept my eyes on the house while Frank conferred with the two men. But I also slid over to the driver's side and opened the window a couple of inches, in order to eavesdrop on their conversation.

I couldn't hear everything they said but it was clear that Frank was filling them in on the situation inside the house. Another squad car must have arrived because I saw two more deputies approach. One had snowy white hair and the other was about forty, with a neat blonde moustache. They joined the group and Frank repeated his summary of the situation. There were expressions of disbelief when Frank revealed that the man holding his girlfriend hostage was our village lawyer, Greg Wetherel.

One of the deputies left and returned with a road map. He unfolded the map and all of them pored over it for a few minutes. Frank pointed through the trees at the brick house. The older deputy left and, minutes later, I heard a car backing out toward the road.

Then Sheriff Dupree sent the other two men off on foot, moving in opposite directions through the pine and birch trees. I figured those two had been assigned to keep watch on the house from the sides that we couldn't see.

Finally Frank leaned down and spoke to me through the open window. "See anything?"

"Just your guys sneaking off into the woods. Do you think Greg would —?"

"I don't think Greg would set out on foot, but we can't rule anything out."

By now, I had recovered enough for my reporter mode to kick in. I searched my pockets for the pencil and little spiral notebook that I always carry with me. Because I realized that I was sitting on a front-page story for the next edition of the *Shagoni River News*.

    HEADLINE
    crazed lover holds girlfriend at gunpoint or maybe
    village lawyer flips out over accusation
— the possibilities were endless.

Frank and the sheriff went into conference again. They were a little farther away this time, so I wasn't picking up very well but I kept hearing the words like *state police* and *mediation* and *mediator.*

Minutes later, Frank came over and asked me if I knew Ivy's phone number.

"Sure."

"Is it a land line or cell?"

"Land line."

"Okay, let's have it please."

And that, of course, is when my mind went blank. "Just a minute," I said. "Let me see if I've got it in my wallet." I shuffled old grocery coupons and frequent shopper cards until I finally remembered her phone number, which, lord knows, I had called plenty of times.

I gave him the number.

After that Frank was standing close enough that I heard most of what transpired. He had his cell phone out and was starting to punch in Ivy's number when the sheriff said, "We've got company. Why don't you hold off a minute?"

Sheriff Dupree left and returned with another man. The newcomer looked to be about sixty with steely gray eyes that peered from under bristling eyebrows. He wore a tan overcoat and a Greek fisherman's cap.

The sheriff introduced the newcomer. "This is Lawton Underwood," he said. "He's had experience with hostage situations. Maybe he should make the call."

Frank hesitated a moment, but then agreed. "Good idea, actually. Greg isn't too fond of me right now. Hearing my voice might set him off."

So Lawton Underwood used his own cell phone to call Ivy's house. I heard the phone ring about five times before her answering machine came on. I knew the exact message he was hearing. "This is Ivy Martin with the Manistee Chronicle. So sorry I missed your call. Just leave your number and I promise I'll get right back to you."

The man with the eyebrows spoke to Ivy's machine, using a conversational tone. "This is Lawton Underwood with the state police," he said. "We don't want anyone to get hurt. So please just come out of the house — with your hands where we can see them. Greg, if you aren't ready to come out, just let the woman go. None of this is her fault. Here's a number you can call if you want to talk with us." Underwood left a number I assumed to be his own cell phone.

Everyone was quiet while we waited for some kind of response. I tried to distract myself by composing lead sentences for the news story, but the problem was that I had no idea how the whole thing was going to end.

I had a vision of Ivy lying in a pool of blood as her life ebbed away. I had a lot of visions. None of them were good.

CHAPTER FORTY TWO

The pale winter sun passed its zenith while we kept vigil outside Ivy's house — Sheriff Dupree, Lawton Underwood, Frank and me. Frank got in and moved the Blazer to make room for a large unmarked van that he referred to as the Command Bus. Now the big van was in the line of fire if anything should happen.

There were a lot of questions I wanted to ask. But Frank was on duty and I was trying to keep a low profile so nobody would send me away. So I just sat there, scribbled in my notebook and waited. It was pretty much all I could do.

Another guy arrived, this one in a blue uniform which identified him as a state policeman. Though I couldn't see them all, I figured the place must be littered with police cars, deputies and cops. I heard the state cop tell the sheriff that all of the residents within a mile had been apprised of the situation and told to stay indoors.

Frank sat with me for a few minutes. I hid my notebook and asked if there was anything he could tell me. He said that calls to Ivy's phone were getting no reply, not even the answering machine. He said that Underwood was setting up a speaker so he could talk to them from the command bus. And the men in the field had not seen any kind of action — neither inside the house nor anywhere near it.

So maybe Ivy and Greg were both dead? New headline — *Murder Suicide?* But wouldn't we have heard gunshots??

Eventually I couldn't sit still any longer so I got out to stretch. Underwood was out of the bus and saw me for the first time. I saw him lean over and speak to Frank. Frank motioned me over.

"This is Tracy Quinn," he said to Underwood and the state policeman who had been helping with the sound system. "She's a close friend of Ivy, the woman inside. She's agreed to stay here in case she might be helpful when — when we resolve this situation."

Sheriff Dupree knew who I was. But he had the good grace not to mention that I also happened to be Frank's girlfriend. And Frank was astute enough not to mention that I was a reporter for the local paper.

"Best keep her in the vehicle," the sheriff said to Frank. Frank gave me a look so I did a few more stretches and moved toward the passenger door.

Just then attention was diverted by the arrival of an ambulance. It stopped near the end of the driveway, its white bulk barely visible through the trees. Minutes later two EMT's appeared, a stocky blond guy and a woman with a little grey in her hair.

I listened as Sheriff Dupree briefed them on the situation. Then he sent them back to their ambulance, with instructions to stand by and not come any closer until he sent for them.

The next thing I saw was the sheriff helping Underwood position a black box on a tripod outside the command bus. The box proved to be an amplifier because, minutes later, I heard Underwood's voice coming through the device.

"Greg Wetherel. We don't want to hurt you and we don't want to hurt the girl. But you can't get away. The place is surrounded. If you're not ready to come out, send the girl out first. Give us a call and we can discuss this like reasonable people. But there's no need for anyone to get hurt."

By this time I had crawled back inside the Blazer. But I kept the window down so I could hear what was going on.

Underwood came out of the bus and said to the sheriff, "Let's wait a few minutes and try the telephone again."

So that's what he did.But this time the phone line was dead. The house might have been empty for all we knew.

Another hour crept by. My stomach alternated between hunger and nausea. My mental state alternated between anxiety and boredom. But my bladder sent a consistent message about the coffee I had consumed. I did my best to ignore it.

Shadows lengthened as the sun continued its arc toward the horizon. It was almost dusk when a young deputy arrived with sandwiches and drinks. Frank took a couple of sandwiches, came over and opened the door on my side.

"This guy isn't staying," he said with a nod toward the latest arrival. "You could leave with him, if you want to."

"Do you think I should?"

"I don't want you to get hurt."

"I don't want you to get hurt either."

"But this is my job," he said.

"Are you sending me away?"

"No, it's up to you."

"Then I'm staying," I said. "After all, Ivy's in there. I can't just desert her."

This was a real sacrifice on my part because it meant that I finally had to tell Frank that I needed to take a potty break. Then, of course, he had to share this information with all of the officials on the scene. It also meant that I had to wander in the woods for a bit, until I found a bush which offered suitable screening.

But I wasn't about to leave. Because I had realized by then that, whatever her faults, Ivy was my friend and she needed me.

I was shivering by the time I accomplished my mission in the great outdoors and climbed back inside the Blazer. Underwood was on the speaker again, using a calm persuasive tone. Frank had saved a sandwich for me. I ate half of it and gave him the rest. The sun was gone and darkness was imminent when I saw a yellow glow blink on inside the house.

I heaved a sigh of relief. At least someone was alive in there.

Frank trained the spotlight from his vehicle on the front door of the house, along with his headlights. Underwood did the same with lights from the bus. Then the waiting resumed. I was close to dozing off when I saw something that brought me instantly awake.

Frank had moved up to the front of the Blazer. He had his pistol out, gripped in both hands and aimed at the front of the house.

Then I saw why.

The door was slowly opening.

CHAPTER FORTY THREE

At first, all I could see was a white handkerchief.

Then I saw a hand waving the handkerchief, followed by a bare arm. Finally a slight figure appeared, dressed in jeans and a tee shirt.

It was Ivy and she appeared to be alone. Among all the other thoughts racing through my mind, I had to admit that the handkerchief was a nice dramatic touch. She stood on the stoop and peered in our direction, like a deer caught in the headlights.

"Cover me," Frank said to the sheriff. Frank holstered his gun and began to walk toward Ivy — which scared me to death.

I saw no reason why Greg couldn't be lurking behind one of the windows ready shoot the man I loved. Damn. If Frank died because of Ivy I would never forgive her — never.

But Frank kept walking and nobody shot at him. Ivy started walking toward him.

When they met, Frank put a protective arm around her and turned back toward the convoy. Seconds later Ivy and Frank met the sheriff and they pulled her into the safe area behind the vehicles. I was waiting for her there.

Ivy shivered as I wrapped my arms around her. Her shoulders shook silently for a moment and then she started crying. "I was so scared," she sobbed. "I was just so scared." Fortunately she had her own handkerchief.

"It's okay." I held her and smoothed her messy hair. "You're all right now, Ivy. Everything's okay."

"Is Greg still in there?" said Frank.

She nodded emphatically.

"Then we're going in," he said. "Where do you think we'll find him?"

"In the kitchen."

"You sure?"

"Yep. In a chair — with his head on the table."

"Passed out?"

"Out cold." I put a sweatshirt around Ivy and she seemed to regain some measure of composure. "Greg told me to make him some coffee so I did. But I used decaf and when he wasn't looking I threw in a handful of Benadryl — those allergy tablets that make me so sleepy."

"So Greg drank the coffee and fell asleep?" I said.

"Right there in the kitchen. Of course, he'd finished the bottle of whiskey so that helped too."

"He could wake up at any time," Frank said to the sheriff. "Maybe we'd better try talking to him again."

"He won't wake up," said Ivy.

"How can you be sure —?"

She answered with a slightly hysterical laugh. "Because I gave him a serious whack on the head — with his own iron skillet."

CHAPTER FOURTY FOUR

Frank put Ivy and me inside the Blazer and told us to stay put. Then he went into a huddle with Sheriff Dupree, Laman and the state policeman. The first thing they did was turn off all of the lights they had trained on the house.

When my eyes adjusted to the darkness I saw the four of them, looking for all the world like some old western movie, walking toward the house with their guns drawn.

They reached the front door and one by one disappeared inside. I held my breath until I saw the kitchen lights come one. But there was no sound of gunfire — or anything else.

The next thing I saw was the two EMT's on their way to the house, hauling a folded up stretcher. They emerged about ten minutes later, surrounded by lawmen and pushing the stretcher which now held a body. When the procession got closer, I saw that the unconscious body on the stretcher featured a handcuff which held one wrist to the frame. It was Greg Wetherel, of course.

As they wheeled him by, Ivy let out a sob. "What a creep," she said. "And all this time I thought he loved me."

So I did my best to commiserate with Ivy about the volatility of men and the inherent disappointment of relationships. She put it more succinctly. "All men are pigs," she said. "I'm through with men. Forever."

Cars began to disperse. Lawton Underwood left the scene. The sheriff and Laman stayed but moved their car to allow us to leave.

Frank drove Ivy and me to the hospital and I stayed with her while she was checked out. No Doctor Blue Eyes for her. The ER doctor was a brown-skinned woman with a kindly manner. She asked Ivy a lot of questions, poked and prodded, listened to her chest and peered into her eyes. Then she ordered some x-rays and, after examining them, concluded that Ivy had suffered no physical damage.

Ivy's mental state, however, was a different matter. Her emotional trauma was obvious to anyone within earshot as she alternated between crying jags and torrential rants about what she would like to do to Greg Wetherel.

The doctor said that Ivy was suffering from nervous shock and should not be left alone. She wrote out two prescriptions — one for anxiety and one for sleep. By this time Sergeant Laman had arrived. He took Ivy aside for an interview while Frank and I went to a pharmacy and had the prescriptions filled. When we got back, Laman was through with Ivy but said she couldn't go home because her house was a crime scene.

So what now? Ivy couldn't go home and couldn't be left alone. I didn't relish the thought of babysitting her at my place and having to monitor her drug use. Besides, I wanted to be alone with Frank.

Fortunately, someone in charge had called Ivy's sister in Muskegon, who arrived just in time to save the day. The sister, whose name was Glinda, seemed a little high strung. But Glinda said she would take Ivy home with her and keep her as long as necessary. I thanked her profusely.

Frank took me home but said he couldn't spend the night. He had reports to file and, besides, we both had to work in the morning.

Then it was Monday morning and work. Jake and I were collaborating on the Big Story when Sergeant Curt Laman interrupted us to record my version of the events of the previous day. By afternoon I was dodging calls from other newspapers and also dealing with multiple calls from Ivy. I put her off until after work and then she bent my ear for two hours. I certainly didn't envy her sister.

I hung on at work until late Tuesday when the paper went to press. Then I told Marge I was taking a personal day or a sick day or whatever she wanted to call it, but I wouldn't be in to work and I wouldn't be home if she called. Frank did the same and we retreated to his cabin in the woods.

The mini-vacation felt like heaven. Frank and I spent most of the morning in bed, then had brunch and took a long walk in the woods. The sun was out, pushing the temperature close to fifty degrees. We saw buds on some of the trees and he cut a bunch of pussy willows for me to take home.

It was after dark when Frank drove me back into town. Jewell had been wanting to see us so we accepted her invitation to stop by for dessert. Paul was there and the four of us sat at the kitchen table while she served up slices of chocolate cake.

"How was it having Greg Wetherel as a patient?" I asked Jewell.

"He pretty much behaved himself. But then, he didn't have a whole lot of choice. There were deputies outside his room around the clock."

"Is he still there?" said Paul.

"He was transferred to jail yesterday," said Frank.

"He really didn't want to leave," said Jewell. "But all he had was a minor concussion — and a hangover. Normally, we would have discharged him after twenty-four hours. But the doctors kept him longer as a precaution because he is, after all, a lawyer."

Frank laughed. "Greg now has a lawyer of his own who is trying to get him out on bail."

"What exactly will he be charged with?" said Paul.

"We'll start with felonious assault and kidnapping," said Frank, "which are damn serious. And I'm afraid you and I are the star witnesses, Tracy. Then of course there's the murder of Vince Crawley."

"What about the girlfriend who drowned?" I said.

"It might be tough to make that one stick," said Frank. "It all happened over twenty years ago and Dixie Crawley, the only living witness, is a former drug addict. They may have to let that one go."

"But who was after Greg?" I said. "Who wrote that threatening note and then cut the brake lines on his car?"

"Nobody."

"Nobody?"

"Greg did that himself," said Frank. "He figured that if he could make himself look like a victim, no one would suspect that he was the killer."

"Almost worked."

"Almost. And yesterday I went and talked to Daisy Fritzell again — or maybe she's Daisy Tattersall now. But remember what she said about a man pouring out half a bottle of whiskey by the lake?"

"I remember. Do you think the man was Greg?"

"I'm sure of it," said Frank. "Remember, she said the guy had little paper tags on his jacket?"

"Yes, that seemed like an odd detail."

"Greg was wearing his ski jacket. And those tags were ski lift passes."

"So bring me up to date," said Paul. "What do you figure went on in the ice shanty?"

"Here's the way it looks," said Frank. "Greg knew that Vince drank Jim Beam. So he brought his own bottle, poured out half of it, then added the chloral hydrate."

"Where did he get the chloral hydrate?" said Jewell.

"It was his mother's prescription — left over after she died. Remember I did check with the pharmacy — but she had a different last name from Greg so we didn't get any hits there. Anyway, he put the doped up bottle in his coat pocket and went out to spend some time with Vince. When the time was right, he switched bottles on him."

"So he killed Vince," I said, "because he thought his old friend was getting ready to spill the beans about that night at Silver Lake?"

"Right."

"But do you think Vince was really going to do it?" said Jewell. "Was he going to accuse Greg of drowning his girlfriend?"

"That's something we may never know," said Frank. "Father Radonis said Vince made an appointment to meet with him — but he never kept the appointment." Frank helped himself to a second piece of cake. "But Greg didn't want to take any chances about Vince clearing his conscience before he died. "

"So, thanks to Greg, Vince didn't live long enough to die of cancer," said Paul.

"Nope," said Frank. "Vince just drank some whiskey and went to sleep."

"Fiona told me that Vince hated hospitals," said Jewell. "And he didn't want to die in one."

"As it turned out, he didn't," said Frank. "So in the end maybe Greg did his old friend a favor."

EPILOGUE

Funny how things like this create spin off romances.

Word is out that Charlene Crawley has moved in with Woody Pucket. Go figure.

And then, of course, there is Ivy. It took about two weeks for her to recover from the ordeal and then she was back to work. A week after that, she was looking for social life again.

She called me on a Friday and invited me to meet her at the Belly Up. Since Frank was out of town, I said yes. Instead of being late, Ivy was waiting when I arrived. She actually bought me a beer before she got around to the business at hand.

She asked me if I would give her the e-mail address for Steven, my ex-husband.

"I thought he was kind of cute," she said. "You don't mind, do you?"

No, I didn't mind. Not one bit. I gave her the information she wanted, and wondered briefly if I should warn her about Steven's record with women.

But I didn't.

"Lots of luck," I said. Thinking that maybe those two deserved each other.

THE END

Would you like to see your manuscript become a book?

CPSIA information can be obtained at www.ICGtesting.com
Printed in the USA
BVOW071640090112

280145BV00002B/22/P